Praise for the Colorado Wine Mysteries

"*Killer Chardonnay* offers a wonderful blend of suspense and humor. You'll raise your glass to Parker Valentine, the charming sleuth at the center of this twisty and satisfying mystery. A most delightful debut!"

—Cynthia Kuhn, Agatha Award–winning author of the Lila Maclean Academic Mysteries

"Parker Valentine . . . will steal your heart and pair it with a smooth mystery in this sparkling debut. A wine rack full of suspects won't stop the determined sleuth and vintner from bottling up a killer and saving her dream. *Killer Chardonnay* has legs!"

—Leslie Budewitz, Agatha Award–winning author of the Spice Shop Mysteries

"*Killer Chardonnay* is an engaging mystery filled with wine knowledge, romance, and a gutsy protagonist. Kate Lansing is a delightful new voice in the mystery genre, and I can't wait to read the next one in this series."

—Nadine Nettmann, author of the Anthony, Agatha, Lefty, and Mary Higgins Clark award–nominated Sommelier Mysteries

"Lansing's brisk style and her heroine's efficient approach make her debut a treat." —*Kirkus Reviews*

"Lansing does an exceptional job of planting red herrings and keeping readers on their toes." —Fresh Fiction

Titles by Kate Lansing

Till Death Do Us Port

Kate Lansing

BERKLEY PRIME CRIME
New York

BERKLEY PRIME CRIME
Published by Berkley
An imprint of Penguin Random House LLC
penguinrandomhouse.com

Copyright © 2023 by Kate Lansing
Penguin Random House supports copyright. Copyright fuels creativity, encourages
diverse voices, promotes free speech, and creates a vibrant culture. Thank you for buying
an authorized edition of this book and for complying with copyright laws by not
reproducing, scanning, or distributing any part of it in any form without permission.
You are supporting writers and allowing Penguin Random House to continue to
publish books for every reader.

BERKLEY and the BERKLEY & B colophon are registered trademarks and
BERKLEY PRIME CRIME is a trademark of Penguin Random House LLC.

ISBN: 9780593546277

First Edition: March 2023

Printed in the United States of America
1 3 5 7 9 10 8 6 4 2

Book design by Alison Cnockaert

This is a work of fiction. Names, characters, places, and incidents either are the product
of the author's imagination or are used fictitiously, and any resemblance to actual persons,
living or dead, business establishments, events, or locales is entirely coincidental.

PUBLISHER'S NOTE: The recipes contained in this book are to be followed exactly as
written. The publisher is not responsible for your specific health or allergy needs that may
require medical supervision. The publisher is not responsible for any adverse reactions to
the recipes contained in this book.

To my family, near and far

Chapter One

There are as many types of goodbyes as there are varietals of grapes. There are the bittersweet goodbyes full of hugs and promises to see each other soon. The final goodbyes no one is ever ready for. The relieved goodbyes from guests who overstayed their welcome. And then there are the ambiguous goodbyes.

Where there are too many words left to be spoken, none of which can do the parting justice. Or give any indication as to the future. Where the best way to communicate is through actions, which for me, ironically, also involve lips.

Gripping the collar of Reid's shirt, I pull him in for another kiss. Memorizing the taste of him, the feel of his glorious mouth pressed against mine, the way he trails his fingers down my back and tugs me closer.

He breaks away and bestows a featherlight kiss on my forehead, tucking a strand of hair behind my ear. "I can stay," he says. "Push my meeting back, get a later flight, go to this shindig with you."

"The invitation clearly said black tie," I quip with a not-so-subtle survey of my boyfriend's attire. The blue collared shirt, khakis, and boots might be more zhuzhed than his usual T-shirt and jeans, but they're a far cry from what's expected at my cousin's wedding.

Reid isn't dismayed in the least. "Come on, Parks," he whispers, his nickname for me rolling off his tongue as if I'd always been Parks instead of Parker. "Let me be your plus-one. We'll bring down the house."

While this isn't the first time he's offered, it's the most tempted I've been to accept. I take a shuddering breath and steel myself. As much as I want to postpone the inevitable, I can't.

This goodbye is a pit stop for Reid, his final destination being the airport, where he'll jet his way to the Bay Area to scout locations for a new restaurant, his esteemed establishment on Pearl Street in such high demand that investors approached him and he couldn't do anything but expand.

Because food is Reid's passion. Taking his culinary concoctions transcontinental is a dream come true. And I'm not one to stand in the way of someone achieving their dream. Especially not someone I love. Given all that, and the fact that he'll be living on the West Coast if—nay, *when*—he finds the perfect place, hiring a kitchen staff and developing a menu, I'd better reacquaint myself with flying solo. Why not start now?

"First off," I start, "the house needs to remain standing today and there are enough cracks already." I cast a dubious glance at the venue chosen by my cousin.

Sure, the Longview Lodge is a historic building, composed of natural stone and wood paneling, a mixture of rustic and comfort that was no doubt a sight to behold in its heyday. Which has long since passed. The decades haven't been kind to the quaint motel, the landscaping wild and general upkeep fallen into disrepair, the bulk of its clientele being students at the neighboring university. Of course, all of this would be perfectly fine if it weren't for the construction.

Between the jackhammer raging in the background and the forgotten tools and stacks of plywood, there's something to be desired in the romance department. Particularly given the possibilities in Boulder and the surrounding mountainscape.

But perhaps this was the only place available; June is wedding season, after all. Only, I thought that was why my cousin Emma hired a wedding planner. Or rather, why her pushy stepmother encouraged (read: *forced*) her to hire one.

I continue, running a hand through Reid's hair, sandy with undertones of port, relishing the contact, "Second, as dashing as you are, pretty sure the spotlight is supposed to be on the bride."

Reid catches my hand and twirls me, mischief sparking in his green eyes. "Hate to break it to you, but in that dress, all eyes are gonna be on you."

"What, this old thing?" I ask coyly, even though we both know I'm wearing one of my favorite numbers for the occasion. A little black dress with a fitted top embossed with an elegant vine texture that flares into a knee-length skirt. And let's not forget the silk-lined pockets; a dress isn't a dress without pockets, IMHO. "Besides, you've never met Emma. She's a looker, and so sweet birds literally eat out of the palm of her hand like some sort of real-life Disney princess."

"I would get to meet her if I stayed," Reid points out.

"I'm protecting you, I promise." That, at least, is the truth. My family is not for the fainthearted. I take a step back, out of the gravitational field that is Reid, already missing his warmth, even as the temperature climbs upward to eighty degrees. "Now, you're going to miss your flight, and that poor Uber driver is about to blow a gasket."

We both look to where the smart Audi is idling in the roundabout, and the driver within craning his neck every few seconds to shoot us an impatient glare.

"Eh, I'm sure he's seen worse," Reid says.

"Even so, I can't have my rider rating dinged."

Any self-respecting girlfriend would have driven their guy to the airport under such circumstances, only, pitiful as it might sound, driving and me don't mix. And while I have plans to correct that, there was nothing else for it this morning. Hence, rideshare.

A high-pitched wail rises from inside the motel, so loud it carries through the sliding glass doors that lead to the lobby and competes with the rumble of a nearby forklift.

Reid and I turn in unison toward the guttural noise. All I can make out is our reflection in the glass, two star-crossed lovers desperate to extend the moment. But another shriek reaches our ears, this one transitioning into a sob.

"I should really go make sure everything is okay," I say, eyebrows furrowed in concern.

I plant a swift peck on Reid's lips and retrieve the case full of wine and palate-cleansing crackers waiting at my feet. This may seem like an odd wedding gift, but Emma specifically requested my label for the celebratory libations, and I was pleased as punch to acquiesce. The wedding industry is lucrative. If I could wedge even my pinky toe in that figurative door, it could be huge for my business. Huge as in, well, I don't know exactly what yet. But I'll worry about that if I succeed.

With my heels clicking against the cement in time to clinking bottles, I start toward the entrance to the motel. But suddenly, I stop. Who knows when I'll see Reid again? I set the case on the ground and jog back to him, throwing my arms around his neck for one last kiss.

"You just can't get enough of me, huh?" Reid asks, the dimples making their grand appearance.

"Never," I say, my voice growing hoarse.

He traces a small circle on my bare shoulder with his thumb. "Same here, Parks." Another sob sounds, this one closer to a howl. Reid gestures toward the motel. "Go, do your thing. I'll text when I land."

I nod and smooth the front of my dress, the picture of decorum once more, or as close as I can get. Then I hightail it into the lobby and the family drama inevitably waiting for me.

Sometimes a bottle of wine is the celebration. With the tell-tale pop of a cork, any hardships of the day fade into the background, the senses engaged by layered aromas, silky textures, and lush flavors, the clinking of glasses elevating the experience. This is even more true when the hallowed beverage is your own craftsmanship. Although, as delectable as my wines may be, I hoped there would be a worthier event to laud at my cousin's wedding.

You know, like the bride and the groom tying the knot. The *I do*s and culminating kiss. The first dance, and toasts with friends and family. The cake.

Instead, this soiree is one mishap away from a full-on catastrophe.

The crying that Reid and I heard outside hailed from a distraught bridesmaid, who is currently center stage in the lobby.

Josie strikes a pitiful image. Her round face is blotchy and streaked with tears, glistening smudges of mascara rimming her eyes. Her shoulders heave, causing the tulle of her floor-length gown to rustle. A dainty bouquet of peonies is loosely clutched in one hand. Wrenched sobs choke out of her throat.

No one seems to know how to handle the weepy attendant. Not the receptionist behind the desk, not the disheveled groomsman slouched on the couch, not me.

I approach Josie hesitantly. "Hey, are you all right?"

She just shakes her head and lets out an even louder sob.

"Can I get you something—someone?" I ask with more than a hint of desperation.

"I—I can't . . ." Josie blubbers, overcome with a fresh wave of emotion.

Luckily, at that moment, my older cousin, Carolyn, sister of the bride and maid of honor, charges onto the scene.

She has a fistful of her dress in one hand and in the other, what appears to be a black ribbon. Her honey-brown hair has been curled and spritzed with something that makes it sparkle, and her makeup wouldn't be out of place in a beauty pageant, rouge cheeks and shimmery eye shadow that matches her teal dress.

"Josie," she snaps. "Pull yourself together. Today isn't about you. It's about Emma."

These words, while harsh, apparently do what my soothing could not. Maybe the reminder of her childhood friend was all Josie needed.

Josie hiccups and gives one more doleful sniff before

wiping at her eyes. "You're right." She lifts her chin, nary a wobble in sight. "I'm sorry."

"Go pull yourself together," Carolyn orders, and then swivels on the groomsman sprawled on the couch, looking worse for the wear with bags beneath his eyes and the unmistakable stench of booze emanating from him. "Jack, get up and get yourself a cup of coffee." She turns on me next and I recoil at the fire in her eyes. "And you, follow me."

I collect my case of wine and jog after Carolyn, barely able to keep up. "You look—"

Carolyn interrupts me with a wave of her hand. "I beg of you, do *not* finish that statement."

My lips twitch, but I dare not laugh. Truth be told, I've never been as close with Carolyn. Maybe because she's four years my senior, or maybe because we're so similar: type As to the core.

We dart down a hallway and into a vast ballroom, signs of construction present even here with tarps and crudely covered workspaces stashed in alcoves. Rows of folding chairs with tulle bows attached face the opposite side of the space, a threadbare rug cutting a path down the middle, where an embossed wooden altar stands. Stained glass overhead casts a kaleidoscope of colors over banquet tables lined with steaming chafing dishes and a luscious buttercream centerpiece, scents of roast chicken and sugar blending with sawdust.

Carolyn slows to a stop in front of a kitty carrier, a steady stream of meows coming from within. "You're good with cats, right?"

"Uh, yeah," I answer hesitantly.

"Perfect, you're on ring-bearer duty," she says, gesturing between me and the creature with yellow eyes peeking through the mesh bag. "Clyde, this is Parker. Parker, this is Clyde."

"But what about my wines?" I ask, plunking the hefty box on the floor for emphasis. "I'm supposed to be setting up. Can't the wedding planner help with this?"

"You would think," Carolyn says, sarcasm dripping from her voice like wine legs down the sides of a crystal bowl. She hands me the ribbon, which is actually a bow tie, and a small velvet box. "Loop the ribbon through the rings, fashion it into a collar, and bring him to the staging area. Good luck."

Before I can muster another argument, her phone pings and, after reading the screen, Carolyn curses under her breath and starts back toward the lobby.

Wrenching my eyes from her retreating figure, I swallow my misgivings. As long as Emma was happy, I was determined to be happy for her and help make this day memorable.

"Guess it's just you and me, buddy." No stranger to kitties, I cautiously remove the ring bearer from his carrier and pull him into my lap. "That's right," I coo. "Easy does it."

All stealth, I stroke Clyde's soft orange, black, and white fur. He leans into my palm, seemingly agreeable. That is, until I attempt to wrap the ribbon around his neck and fasten the rings in place. That's when his claws come out. He squirms in my arms, paws awkwardly flailing, until I finally release him with a sigh, the cursed bow tie spilling onto the floor. Clyde might be an adorable calico cat, but rule follower? Not so much.

Clyde turns his smug, squashed face toward me and tumbles onto his side, emitting a satisfied purr. Because when has a cat ever done what it's told?

"Punk," I grumble, sitting back on my heels and obligingly scratching behind his ears. "Promise you won't say anything, but I don't blame you."

My great-aunt Harriet, owner of said furry charge, sidles up. She's in a lavender getup with a matching hat sporting a protruding feather so tall I make note not to sit directly behind her.

"Parker, where is that boyfriend of yours I keep hearing about?" Harriet asks.

"Out of town," I explain vaguely.

Leave it to extended family to know exactly which question I'm not keen to answer, my goodbye with Reid weighing on my heart. Especially since I'm still wrestling with how I feel about his new venture.

I mean, couldn't Harriet have asked how my winery, Vino Valentine, was faring? (Very well.) Or about my recent climbing exploit in Rocky Mountain National Park? (Thrilling.) Or how my mom, dad, and brother were doing? (I could only imagine they were being put through similar interrogations.)

"The best way to get a man thinking about marriage is to bring him to a wedding," Harriet says, peering at me over frames with such thick lenses they could pass for magnifying glasses.

I stifle a laugh, realizing she's not joking. "I'm not—" I start, blinking rapidly. "I mean, we're not quite ready for that step."

Harriet scrutinizes me from head to toe in a judgy way, clicking her tongue. "Don't wait too long, dear."

Perplexed, I glance down at my little black dress to make sure the skirt isn't tucked into my underwear or something equally embarrassing. Wardrobe intact, I shrug off Harriet and her poorly veiled insinuations with a tug on my beaded necklace, a dainty silver chain dotted with tiny bunches of grapes. The necklace was a gift from my late aunt Laura, who, to be honest, would've gotten a kick out of all this. I wish she were here, for more reasons than to remind us there's always joy to be found, even amid chaos.

Clyde draws my attention back to him with a mew, batting at the dangling end of the bow tie with an outstretched paw, and I smile.

"Any tips?" I ask Harriet hopefully.

"My little Cly-Cly is going to be so dapper prancing down the aisle." She pats *Cly-Cly* on the head before hobbling off, leaving me to actually get her beloved pet to the aisle.

"Are you going to behave now?" I ask sternly.

Clyde blinks as if to say yes.

"Good."

I act quickly, snagging the ribbon and securing it and the rings in place. Task accomplished, I scoop Clyde into my arms and make my way through the double doors and into the space that will serve as the staging area. Where was the rest of the wedding party? By the clock on the wall, the ceremony would be starting soon and my wines were still definitively corked. Not even close to ready to impress the attendees—let alone the wedding planner.

The steady shuffling and chatter of guests traipsing through the entrance incites me to action.

With my arms full of Clyde, I dash down a dim hallway in search of anyone who can assume the role of cat herder. This hotel was obviously built in an era predating open-space floor plans, which the owners are clearly trying to rectify with current renovations. Everything is closed off—either by original walls or sheets of plastic. I pass restrooms and a door marked EMPLOYEES ONLY that looks like some sort of utility closet. The hallway splits, one direction being a shortcut to the ballroom and the other leading to the service entrance.

I start down the latter but the sound of raised voices sends a shot of adrenaline through my system and I backtrack to where the hallway forks, ducking around the corner.

I immediately recognize the shrill-yet-decisive tone of the wedding planner. "You call this food," she scoffs. "It doesn't taste like anything, which is more than can be said for the texture. It's so tough I can barely chew it." There's the distinct sound of spitting.

Curiosity gets the better of me and I risk a peek, Clyde seeming just as intrigued as I am.

The corridor is narrow, barely wide enough for two people to walk astride, and there's a door at the end that leads to the loading dock. In the middle is Prynne Pearsall, the ringleader of this circus. She's in an ivory pantsuit with ruby pumps the same shade as her perfectly manicured nails. She stands off against the caterer, whom she's apparently cornered en route from her van with another course.

The caterer is a stocky woman with a slightly berated demeanor—or perhaps that's just the effect of Prynne. A hairnet fastens her errant locks in place and she holds a tray of canapés balanced on an open palm. The offending hors d'oeuvres look like tiny slices of baguette topped with some sort of soft cheese and vegetable mixture, a difficult dish to screw up.

She's clearly the head honcho of her business, the two servers in her employment falling in line behind her, dutifully carrying their assigned load of supplies while pretending not to listen.

"This was what the bride and groom agreed upon at their tasting," the caterer replies evenly. She's in a simple black blouse with an apron that sports the words IRIS CATERING on the chest. "I can provide something else, although the options are limited."

"Don't bother," Prynne says with a disgusted sniff. "No doubt whatever you procure will be just as . . . disappointing."

"Really, me and my sous chef tasted everything, the flavors are fine." She casts a desperate glance at one of the servers, who must double as her sous chef, but the young woman fumbles with a stack of napkins, her ears turning pink as she feigns ignorance.

The caterer rolls her eyes, exasperated with more than the wedding planner.

"Exactly," Prynne responds coolly. "They're *fine*. Not exemplary, which is what's expected on the happiest day of your life."

For half a beat, I consider interrupting. My cousin is the last person to care about such things. Growing up, Emma was that kid who felt deeply; the accidental squashing of an insect or injured bird actually affected her. Which is probably why she became a vet technician—now she gets to help creatures, big and small. But I hold my tongue, not wanting to put a target on my back before my wines are even showcased. Which will happen only if I can, you know, unpack them.

I expect Prynne to realize she has more important places to be, battles to be had, like shepherding the wedding party down the aisle so Emma can marry the man of her dreams. Unfortunately, she's not ready to pull an Elsa and let it go.

Prynne stalks toward the caterer, wielding her smartphone as if it were a weapon, which I suppose for her, it is. "You're done in this industry."

"You two," the caterer barks at her servers, "get moving."

The two uniforms usher past their boss and Prynne and my sad excuse for a hiding place, not even acknowledging my—or my feline ward's—wayward presence. Shameless rubberneck that I am, I continue peering around the corner.

"We've put too much work into this." The caterer shakes with palpable anger, her carefully constructed canapés disassembling on the tray. The silence that follows balloons, taut with tension, until she responds, so quiet I almost miss it: "I'll take you down with me."

Hair rises at the nape of my neck at the seriousness in her tone and I force myself to swallow.

"Ha," Prynne barks. "You're fired. Leave now and take these strips of rubber you're trying to pass for food with you. The guests would rather have nothing than your drivel."

My jaw drops. Because it has to be some sort of universal truth that wherever booze is served, food should be readily available. Trust me, as a winery owner I know all too well the drama that can unfold without sustenance to soak up alcohol. And my palate-cleansing crackers won't go far with this crowd.

But hey, this is Boulder we're talking about, not some remote campsite—we can order delivery! Or Grubhub! And maybe this means the rest of the ceremony will go off without a hitch.

When will I learn not to tempt fate?

While I'm making auxiliary meal plans, I miss Prynne whirl and start toward me. She turns the corner at a speed I didn't think was possible in heels and crashes into me—and Clyde.

The best that can be said is we stay on our feet. I rub my sternum, which somehow made contact with her bony elbow. And Clyde hisses and scrambles to get free, his hind legs digging into my ribs. I barely manage to hang on to him, calmly shushing him so he doesn't escape, or worse, wriggle out of his bow tie.

Prynne looks at me as if I were beneath her, and, okay, *technically* I am in a physical sense, my chin having bumped into her shoulder, which is surprisingly sharp. But still, we're equals. Equals where one of us wants to supremely awe the other.

I shift Clyde to my other side and play this the only way that could lead to a business relationship instead of a tongue lashing. "They need mirrors in these hallways, am I right?"

"Excuse me," she says icily, and I yield, giving her the go-ahead. *Guess she won't be helping with the ring bearer.*

Prynne storms past, a tornado of purpose, glamor, and spite.

I make my way back to the ballroom, where I pawn Clyde off on a reluctant Carolyn. "One ring bearer reporting for duty. Any chance you can take over?"

"Okay, but I expect a full—and I mean full-to-the-brim—glass of wine later," she says as I pass her the cat.

Can't blame her. Something tells me this bunch will be jonesing for a drink.

Clyde gives a dismal mew and clings to my forearm. Apparently, I made an impression despite our rocky start.

With no time to waste, I hop to.

On a banquet table covered with a cream linen cloth, I arrange bottles of wine from lighter- to heavier-bodied so that the Vino Valentine label faces outward, showcasing intertwining grapevines punctuated by rays of sunshine.

There are six carefully selected varietals for the occasion. The nomenclature of my offerings pays homage to the

locale, which the locals find entertaining, tourists appreciate, and makes me smile.

The Mount Sanitas White and Chautauqua Chardonnay
chill in marble holders to keep them a crisp fifty degrees
Fahrenheit while the Pearl Street Pinot and Campy Cab are
uncorked and in the process of aerating. And last but not
least are my dessert wines, the Ski Lodge Cherry and the
newest addition to my menu, the Pikes Peak Port-Style, a
ruby port that's all kinds of luscious.

It was a risk I took during my first harvest, siphoning
some of my precious grapes and vat space to make a vintage that might never see the light of day. Because the thing
about port is, it takes time. This one has aged for two years
and remains on the young side. When I first made it—an
art that involved adding brandy to halt fermentation at op-
timal sugar concentration—I had the faintest hope that Vino
Valentine would last long enough for me to serve it. Yet,
here I am.

Is it a gamble serving it today rather than sticking with
my tried-and-true varietals? Absolutely. But perhaps it will
impress Prynne, if that's even possible. Besides, I saw the
way Emma's face lit up when she tried a sip during her tasting, comparing it to caramel with a kick, and couldn't help
but include it. Weddings are all about decadence, after all.

And port has this way of warming you from the inside
out, long after the initial buzz. Not dissimilar from those
fuzzy feelings inspired by true love.

The jackhammer rattles, shaking me from my reverie,
sparkling crystal glasses clinking together ominously. Jaw
clenched, I put more space between the rows of stemware.

The rest of the tables are nearly barren, in the process of
being painstakingly cleared by the caterer. I watched as the

head caterer instructed her servers, one burly college-aged student and the skittish twentysomething who doubles as her sous chef, to start the teardown. Saw the tears of frustration in the woman's eyes at their silent surrender. After all their work preparing dishes, transporting them to the hotel, *and* lugging them inside, they have to pack up and vamoose.

The caterer approaches the three-tiered wedding cake solo, head bowed.

"I'll be sorry to see that go," I say with an encouraging smile. We in the service industry have to stick together. "I've been dying for a slice."

She merely grunts in response.

Chewing on my bottom lip, I offer, "Need an extra hand?"

"No, thanks," she replies glumly, barely looking at me. Her phone rings and she seizes the excuse to put off her task, answering with a forced cheery, "Hello, Iris Catering, this is Iris speaking." She listens to the other line and then leaves the ballroom, talking through pricing options with a potential client.

Maybe she'll forget the cake is here. Maybe one of her helpers will accidentally cut into it and a piece will miraculously fall onto a plate. Maybe I can sneak a nibble.

No, that's preposterous.

My mom bustles to my side. She's in a constellation-print tunic with wide slacks, her frizzy silver hair as wild as ever, and her polka-dot cat-eye glasses perched on her nose. To be honest, I kinda love that she somehow always manages to look like a scientist, just like how I admire the layer of chalk that follows my dad from his office on campus, where he prefers to teach tech via the old-school medium. They are who they are, unapologetically.

"You should put the Pearl Street Pinot up front." She

would always find something to nitpick, but, as I continually remind myself, she means well.

I raise one eyebrow at her. "Just because it's your favorite doesn't mean it gets preferential treatment." To think, a little over a year ago, my mother preferred creating spritzers out of my wines by dousing them with sparkling water and now she's basically an aficionado.

"For a good reason," she argues. "It's your best seller."

"You know what's going up front?" I ask. "Crackers. Unless the wedding planner has a backup caterer on speed dial, they're gonna be the only food available on the premises." I fill three baskets with palate-cleansing wafers and set them prominently between each varietal. Honestly, I grabbed them purely out of habit, but now I'm glad I did.

"That's a recipe for disaster . . ." my mom mumbles. "I'd better make sure Michael knows. The Cooper clan does *not* handle hangry well." Michael is my uncle, her younger brother, and father of the bride. She searches the vicinity with purpose and then hurries off, intercepting Michael on his way to the staging area.

I stash the case and spare bottles under the table so they're camouflaged and then stand back to survey my display, brushing my hands together with satisfaction.

"Where have you been hiding?" my brother asks, popping up at my side.

Liam and I both have raven hair and blue-gray eyes, and I used to think that was where our similarities ended. But recently he's proven we also share the same stubborn determination to follow our passions and hustle to make them a reality. That's wine for me and photography for him, which we were both tapped to help with today.

Liam focuses on me through the lens of his Canon Rebel T7i camera, which is draped around his neck.

I strike a pose through a series of shots before crinkling my nose at him. "I've been hiding in plain sight." *Except when Clyde and I were eavesdropping in the service hallway.* "Mostly."

He swivels, twisting his lanky frame this way and that as he continues capturing candid moments in the name of documentation. "Harriet cornered me for a solid twenty minutes."

"Did you get the wedding spiel?"

"About not waiting too long, yeah." He visibly shudders as he studies the screen of his camera.

"Given you're dating my best friend, who is one of my favorite humans, I think you're overreacting."

"You're one to talk," Liam says. "We haven't been seeing each other as long as you and Reid."

I give an exaggerated wince, wanting to go there less with Liam than I did with Harriet. Because Reid was Liam's friend long before he became my *anything.* "Truce?"

He nods. "Truce."

The officiant, an elderly man with a subdued composure and dressed in all black, makes his way to the altar, hands clasped in front of him.

"That's my cue," Liam says.

"Mine, too."

Liam gets into position on the outside of the aisle while I dart into the row of seats my parents and best friend, Sage, secured for us. Even though she's known my folks since we roomed together as freshman at CU, Sage is clearly shy and awkward in her new role as their son's girlfriend. Which is fairly adorable.

"Then I rolled a fourteen and we completed the campaign," she prattles, regaling my parents with her latest D&D quest.

Sage is a self-proclaimed nerd, obsessed with all things epic and fantastical. Given her wardrobe typically revolves around cosplay, she's toned her style down with a pretty floral sundress, while still honoring fandom with sparkly Wonder Woman earrings.

"Huzzah!" Sheer relief floods her face when I sit down next to her. "I heard you were enlisted as cat whisperer. How'd it go with the ring bearer?"

I brush a stray cat hair off my lap. "A battle of wills, but Clyde will be making his debut any minute now."

"Ah well, it's a burden he never should have had to bear."

I side-eye Sage. "Wait, is that from *Lord of the Rings*?"

"Why, yes. Yes, it is." With a wink, she tosses her strawberry-blond hair over her shoulder. "Paraphrased, of course."

A symphony of strings sounds over the loudspeakers to the tune of Pachelbel's Canon and, with a collective shifting in our seats, every head turns toward the back of the ballroom where the double doors stand open.

I expect to see Prynne flitting in the background, directing the party down the aisle like a helpful gnat. Instead, a panic-stricken Carolyn, still clutching a squirming Clyde in her arms, is assessing everyone with wide eyes.

I have no idea where Prynne is, or what it means that she isn't back there doing her job. Those questions leave my mind as the procession begins.

Chapter Two

At the DNA level, almost all varietals of wine are related. No matter how different they may taste or how far the grapes are scattered across the globe. Chenin blanc and Trousseau are siblings, pinot noir is a parent to chardonnay, cabernet sauvignon is the love child of cabernet franc and sauvignon blanc, and so on.

Grapes have a gnarled, intertwining family tree that rivals the most complex soap opera. And, apparently, the wedding procession.

First, to my shock, comes the stepmother of the bride.

It was a big scandal when it all went down. The revelation that my uncle had an affair with a woman named Chastity from work, who happens to be a little older than me and roughly the same age as Carolyn. We found out in the cringiest way possible—a Facebook post. It was meant to be a private message, but somehow ended up as a status update. Which Michael inadvertently got tagged in. Nuff said.

They surprised us all by staying together through the uproar and divorce, and moreover by getting hitched themselves. The dust has mostly settled, although we're still a far cry from applauding the new couple.

Following Chastity is the mother of the bride, Grace, regal in a silk navy midi dress with her silvering hair au naturel around her shoulders. Chin held high, she more glides than walks down the aisle. Grace reacted to the affair with, well, grace. Instead of mourning the loss of the life she'd always known, she embraced her newfound freedom, returning to school and getting her teaching license. That being said, it doesn't escape my notice that her jaw clenches as she takes her place on the other side of Chastity, an empty chair creating a buffer between them.

Next comes the groom, a man I've met only a couple of times, but immediately warmed to. Nash is tall with brown skin and a full head of dark, wavy hair and a radiant smile. And he's as smart as he is handsome. He and his business partner are researching a technology to capture carbon in the atmosphere. Which means he's literally working to make the world a better place.

Yeah, my cousin did all right.

On the middle step of the altar, Nash bobs his head toward his mother and grandmother, in the front row kitty-corner to me. Nash's family may be small, but they're tight—and quiet, easily overshadowed by the Cooper-Valentine tribe. But they don't seem to mind, supporting their son and grandson as he prepares to start his own family. Nash fidgets with the sleeves of his dapper suit jacket, eagerly watching the back of the ballroom with the rest of us.

The bridesmaid and groomsman march down the aisle and, in an impressive show of pettiness, shoot metaphorical daggers at each other. The hungover groomsman, Jack, a longtime friend of the groom, practically drags Josie, who, despite Carolyn's best efforts, still sports remnants of her tantrum, red blotches on her neck and dark smudges of makeup at the corners of her eyes. She tries to smile brightly—to be supportive of her friend—and would have pulled it off, too, if not for a sharp yank from Jack. Josie misses a step and visibly digs her fingers into Jack's forearm until he yelps in pain. He wrenches away from her and they take the last few paces apart.

I shiver at the iciness that passes between them, and beside me, Sage mouths *Wow* at their open hostility.

The maid of honor and best man are a welcome palate cleanser. Carolyn has since shed Clyde and is instead paired with Xavier Hudd, Nash's business partner. There's a sheen on Carolyn's brow and she's showing more teeth than usual, and Xavier's glasses are slightly askew. They're both on edge, whether from frayed nerves or dealing with one issue after another, I can't tell.

Once they reach the front, Xavier and Nash fist-bump and Carolyn gathers her tulle to stand next to a brooding Josie.

My stomach drops when I realize whose turn it is: the ring bearer.

Legs splayed and tail twitching with skepticism, Clyde is given a gentle nudge by disembodied hands. He trots a few steps and I find myself holding my breath. The cute-meter is off the charts, and it's almost as if Clyde is aware of the attention he's garnering. And of what exactly we want him to do. Therein lies the rub; once a cat catches a whiff of expectations, they'll do the complete opposite.

Halfway down the aisle, Clyde freezes and proceeds to roll onto the floor, stretching his torso to its full, rather impressive length. He's more accordion than cat.

Bubbles of laughter escape the attendees, but no one makes a move to remotivate the distracted ring bearer. Whose idea was it to have an animal attendant, anyway? It couldn't have stemmed from Emma. As a vet technician, she would have seen this coming. Not to mention, she would have chosen one of her beloved dogs over Harriet's cat.

With an aggrieved sigh, I make a beeline for the unsuspecting Clyde, hurriedly deliver him into Carolyn's waiting arms, and, giving an awkward wave at the officiant, return to my seat.

"You are the Sam to Clyde's Frodo," Sage whispers.

"Sidekick to a frisky feline, could be worse."

Sage tilts her head in acknowledgment.

There's a pregnant pause like the seconds between lightning and thunder, their passing heightening our anticipation.

An extra loud rumble from a jackhammer shatters the moment. My shoulders tense, moving closer to my ears, which ring from the noise. Something about the unpredictability and, oddly, inevitability of construction puts me on edge. The fact that there will be more ruckus, just no telling when. Don't they realize someone's life is about to change forever? Probably not. I mean, lives are constantly in flux, with or without our knowing.

Emma and her father stride out to a chorus of oohs and

aahs, my voice included, extra loud to try and drone out the clamor from outside.

Emma is a vision. A vision in billows of blinding white.

Swaths of fabric cascade to the floor, her sleeves puff up to her chin, and a sweetheart neckline is encrusted with clear sparkly gems.

Her golden-brown hair is held half up by an elegant tiara attached to a veil that drapes down her back. Her cheeks are rosy and there's a dusting of freckles across her tanned face. Happy tears swim in her eyes and she exudes a glow— a joy that's contagious.

All the memories of us playing together as children flood back to me—of us baking banana bread and playing card games and catching ladybugs—and for a moment, I can hardly believe it's her wedding day. She's an adult! And she's getting married!

As Emma moves closer, it becomes apparent she's unsteady on her feet. She wobbles slightly and gets a firmer grip on her dad, who is keeping her upright.

The problem is her dress—and likely the impractical heels underneath, although those are hidden from view. The train is no doubt heavy and cumbersome, and the bodice so tight around her frame it inhibits her movements.

I send Emma positive vibes as she passes.

I'm a big believer in vibes; that our thoughts have power when unleashed on the universe. Or maybe I've lived in Boulder too long.

With patient plodding and perseverance, Emma and Michael reach their destination. Michael exhales from exertion, sandwiched between Emma and Nash, still supporting his daughter, although not seeming to mind one bit.

The officiant clears his throat and in a distinct voice,

states, "We are gathered here to celebrate the union between Emma Cooper and Nash Bregar." He pauses for
dramatic effect. "Who gives this woman to be married to
this man?"

"Her mother and I do," Michael says huskily. He places
a kiss on Emma's cheek before retreating to the chair between Chastity and Grace, the two virtues by which my
uncle seems ironically the most drawn despite exhibiting
neither.

"If anyone can show just cause why they may not be
lawfully wed, speak now or forever hold your peace."

A scream tears through the ballroom and a loud crash
comes from the hallway.

Liam is first into the hallway, his long legs and position as
photographer giving him an edge. The rest of us are hot on
his heels, though.

If there's one thing that can be said for my family, it's
that we're curious. I'm not sure how this will impact our
continued survival, whether this trait will help or hinder us
in the long run, but here we are, all attracted to a scream
and a crash.

I jostle through the doorway and shrink at what I see.

Prynne lies splayed on the ground, eyes fixed glassily on
the ceiling. A strip of teal tulle is wrapped around her neck
and there's a deep gash on her forehead, burgundy blood
dripping onto her ivory suit.

Facts infiltrate my brain, even as panic thrums in my
chest and acid churns in my gut. Muddy footprints mark
the carpet, leading to the service entrance. A pungent cologne hangs in the air, artificial pine and spice. The petal of
a peony rests near Prynne's calves. And caught on a splin-

tered edge of the baseboard is a long silvery-blond strand of hair.

Towering over Prynne is the caterer, her hands over her mouth. The three-tiered lemon poppyseed masterpiece is toppled at her feet, the buttercream smooshed into the floor, the bride-and-groom topper buried in a layer of dislodged sponge.

I take a second to mourn that cake.

I know, there are obviously more pressing matters at hand—a person in dire need of assistance, or worse—but still the sight of that demolished cake sends a pang of regret through my body.

The frantic mumblings of the caterer careen me back to present. "Oh no. Oh God. Oh no." She rocks forward and backward, her eyes flitting over the crowd, landing on no one in particular.

Gasps of shock rise from my fellow oglers like bubbles in a glass of champagne. There's a standard reaction to morbidity, jaws slackening, stillness except for a faint tell, a hand brought to a cheek or perhaps a beloved accessory, and an inability to look away while our brains grapple with the unfathomable.

We imbibe the horror before us. My fingers grip the beaded grape chain around my neck so hard my knuckles turn white, Great-Aunt Harriet fans herself, my mom stares wide-eyed as she reaches blindly for my dad's hand. The only stark movement comes from Carolyn, who struggles to keep an increasingly agitated Clyde in check.

"Someone needs to call the police," I hear myself say, as if from a distance. "And an ambulance." Although, as I kneel beside Prynne, even before touching her cool skin, I can tell it's too late. She's gone.

"On it," Liam says. He gestures with his phone, which is

pressed against his ear, his face uncharacteristically pale. He turns away as he speaks into the receiver. "Yes, there's been an accident."

That last word rattles through my mind. There's a wrongness to it, a sour note like an over-tannic red that hasn't had enough time to breathe, but my mind can't—won't—process fast enough.

I force myself to study Prynne. There are no signs of shock on her face; in fact, she appears more relaxed than I ever saw her in life, eyes closed and lips parted. And her cheeks have a peachy tinge, even with the tulle wrapped around her neck, which is . . . unexpected. The only sign of trauma is the gouge at her temple, blood matting her hair and a bruise forming.

"The authorities are on their way," Liam says, his cell still pressed to his ear. "Everyone needs to stand back."

I nod numbly, pushing myself to my feet and backing up until I'm flat against the wall to give Prynne more space. Not that she's aware. But it isn't for her—not her comfort, at least. It's for the imminent investigation. Blood pounds in my ears and my mouth goes dry as harsh truths trickle into my mind.

I cast my gaze about. Through the shifting crowd and attempts at eye contact, my attention catches on a sliver of sunshine basking the adjacent wall in a stream of dusty yellow light. It's coming from the service-entrance door, which is a crack open. Narrowing my eyes, I peer closer.

There's a rock propped in the doorframe. Not just any rock, a stout one, roughly the size of a football, a jagged corner coated with a shiny red substance. Blood.

Sweat beads on my upper lip, from cloying heat sneaking in with the sunshine and claustrophobia. Feeling woozy,

I let my head loll back, my throat bobbing. I will the grainy texture of the stone wall, the sounds of construction outside, to ground me and keep me from passing out.

If there was any doubt before, it's gone now. This was no accident; this was murder.

Chapter Three

Everyone is gathered in the ballroom. Gathered like a bushel of grapes awaiting the crusher de-stemmer and wine press, ready to have every paltry detail rattled and squeezed out of us.

Liam is in the proverbial stainless-steel vise now. My brother stands with his shoulders hunched and hands thrust into his slacks pockets, trying to appear as nonthreatening as possible as he chats with a uniformed officer who diligently takes notes.

Sage sits beside me, watching them with undisguised interest. She rubs her bare arms, goose bumps visible among freckles, an enthusiastic air-conditioning vent positioned directly above us. "So, this is what it's like, huh?" she asks under her breath.

"What?" I ask, matching her whisper.

"To have a front-row seat to a homicide investigation."

My chair is nudged by the man sitting behind me as a pit opens in my stomach. I ignore both and go for noncommittal. "You'd know better than I would."

Sage is a public defender, and a brilliant one at that. Trust me when I say she has *plenty* of insights into the criminal justice system, occasionally sharing some of the more farfetched cases that cross her desk, from accidental car thefts to modern-day duels.

"By the time I get assigned, all the evidence has been sealed and delivered." She tilts her head to the side, the ruby of her Wonder Woman earrings catching the light. "To be honest, it's pretty uneventful."

"Says the person who watched all of *Star Wars* in one night."

"Come now, only episodes four, five, and six. I have standards."

I lick my lips, which dip into a frown. "Let's hope it stays uneventful, for all our sakes."

My brother waves Sage over while the officer responds to something on his radio. My friend bounces to her feet and is across the room in the time it takes me to find and pluck another orange cat hair from my dress.

With the absence of my friend, a chill settles around me that has nothing to do with the frigid air blasting overhead.

My parents huddle together near my uncle and Chastity and the rest of the wedding party, who each seem to embody a different stage of grief. There's the morose bridesmaid, defeated Carolyn, calm Grace, dazed best man, and grim-faced groomsman. And, resembling a giant puff ball, Emma flits between them all, offering soothing remarks and a gentle pat on the back.

It's just so *her*, offering comfort when she should be on the receiving end.

Her fiancé is never more than an arm's length away, alternating checking on his subdued mother and elderly grandmother while making sure his bride-to-be is taking care of herself along with everyone else.

In short, everyone has someone, except me. I wish Reid were here; I already miss him. His steady presence, unflinching in the face of adversity. His scent, a combination of his body wash and whatever herb he's been handling. His warmth and touch.

But his absence was my own doing and, dammit, I'm a strong, independent woman. Plus, it's not like I haven't been through this rigmarole before. From a popular food-and-wine critic to Reid's sous chef to a resort owner on my last mountain getaway, I'm not exactly a newb when it comes to dead bodies.

Still, even with my vats of experience, there's no getting used to murder—to the level of evil required to take a life. It leaves a mark, sometimes visible, like the tiny scar I have on my chest from where I was nearly shish-kebabbed by a corkscrew, and sometimes buried in the subconscious, a primal fear that threatens to swallow you whole if you can't tamp it down.

Suppressing a shudder, I rub my clammy palms on my dress and glance around.

The catering servers linger, their uniforms in various states of disorder, the buttons undone of the college-aged guy's and a brown sauce splattered down the front of the sous chef's. Alternating expressions of alarm, aggravation, and boredom mingle on their faces. As for their boss lady? She is shaken.

Iris perches on a stretcher with a blanket draped over her shoulders while a paramedic shines a light in each eye, peppering her with questions. Iris was responsible for the scream and crash, the wedding cake tumbling out of her hands after she stumbled across Prynne on the way to her van.

At least, that's her version of events.

I recall the heated argument between Prynne and Iris, the latter's threat to take Prynne down with her, and the wedding planner's derisive firing. Could it be possible Iris followed through on her threat? Where had her servers been earlier, and why didn't they help her haul away the cake?

Whoa there, Parker, you're getting ahead of yourself.

The man sitting behind me bumps my chair with his knee. Again. I throw a glare at him but he's too busy messing around with his smartwatch to notice. Disappointed by whatever's on the screen, he lets out an elongated sigh and slouches deeper in his seat, crossing his arms over his chest in a huff.

"Do you have somewhere else to be or something?" I ask snarkily. Because of course he shouldn't have anywhere else to be. We were supposed to be elbow-deep in vittles and cocktails right now.

"Just wondering how long this is going to take," he answers in the polished voice of a car salesman.

I purse my lips, looking from the officer taking down statements to the other blockading the service hallway, down which I know crime scene technicians are scouring for evidence. "I'd wager another hour. If we're lucky."

He cocks one eyebrow. "This a common occurrence at your family gatherings?"

"Of course not," I answer vaguely. It's probably best not

to go into my personal history with murder investigations, which would sufficiently alarm a stranger.

Speaking of, there's something bothering me about this guy—besides his knobby knees, that is. I don't recognize him. And I do almost everyone else here, from bygone reunions or posts from my cousins' social media accounts.

I make a mental catalog of his features. Hair the shade of rust styled with gel, a scar at the corner of his bottom lip as if he'd been fishhooked, and the way he remains aloof, not quite making eye contact with anyone.

"Are you a friend of the bride or the groom?" I prod.

"Um," he starts. He cranes his neck in every direction as if the answer to my very simple question were written on the walls.

I let him sweat, my spidey senses tingling with skepticism.

He clears his throat and I brace myself for whatever lie he's about to feed me, but he never gets to finish.

We're interrupted by a stern voice behind me. "I should've known." The new arrival is in a sleek navy suit with an attitude to match. Eli barely unclenches his jaw as he grumbles, "Ms. Valentine."

I scrunch up my face in an equally aggrieved expression before uttering, with as much distaste as I can muster, "Detective Fuller."

We stare each other down, him from his six-foot-something frame, and me hinging my neck skyward.

Detective Fuller—or, I should say, Eli—breaks first. His lips twitch into a half smile as he shakes his head, crinkles forming around his eyes.

"Well, come on." Eli waves for me to follow him.

With one last look at the mystery man, I jog to catch up.

Eli is my old high school acquaintance and current rock-climbing buddy, who, in a shocking turn of events, evolved from being the renowned stoner of the Boulder Cineplex into a respected detective. His dark hair is neatly parted to the side and you'd be hard-pressed to find so much as a wrinkle in his pressed suit, nor a crumb on his pristine collared shirt. Relief courses through me at his presence.

Eli leads me to the banquet table lined with my wines, far enough out of the way so as not to be overheard. The ice in the buckets has melted, the labels on the whites slowly peeling away, and the reds stand open and waiting for the reception like stood-up prom dates.

I push corks into the bottles with rather more force than necessary; mostly to keep my hands busy, but also because I hate wasting good wine.

Eli rests his hip against the table, directing the entirety of his focus on me. It makes me nervous, just as it did during his first interrogation over a year ago. "Why are you at so many of my crime scenes?"

"I have no idea, but, boy, am I happy to see you," I answer. "Well, not *happy*, given the circumstances, but your expertise is definitely appreciated."

"I hope this means you aren't thinking about investigating yourself."

"Moi?" I give him a mock-surprised face, holding one hand to my chest. "Never."

He snorts in disbelief. "Okay, lay it on me, what happened?"

So, I tell him, including a few more choice details than he probably expected. Like, all of the disasters leading up to the *actual* disaster. It's funny how death puts everything in perspective; a miscreant ring bearer doesn't seem like such a big deal anymore.

Eli pulls a tiny pad of paper from his jacket pocket and jots down a few tidbits. "When was the last time you saw Prynne alive?"

"After she fired the caterer," I say, thinking back to our collision. "I wondered why she wasn't with the wedding party when the music started, but now . . ." I shake my head with a *tut*.

"And how long ago did you observe the caterer take the phone call from a client?" His voice is laced with apprehension. We both know how easily that entire conversation could have been faked, a convenient excuse for her to leave without drawing too much attention.

"A few minutes before the ceremony started."

"Did you see the servers anywhere in the vicinity at that time?"

"No, actually, it seemed the caterer was finishing up on her own. I didn't even know they were still here until, well, now."

He adds another note into the timeline he's piecing together. "How did Prynne come to be your cousin's wedding planner?"

"Chastity."

"I wasn't aware the exorbitance of a ceremony had any relevance to being chaste."

I squirm at his confusion; we're waltzing into dangerous territory, a reminder that Eli at one point harbored feelings for me. Unrequited feelings. Although he's since embarked on a relationship that, from what I can tell, is going very well.

"No, Chastity is my uncle's second wife," I explain.

There's a mechanical note to his tone when he poses his next query: "What can you tell me about your family?"

"That depends. What do you want to know?"

"Just a rundown of who's who, if they were all accounted for before and during the ceremony, if there's a history of violence, that sort of thing."

I bark out a laugh, my eyebrows shooting up into my bangs. "A history of violence? What are you implying?"

"That someone in this room is a killer."

My heart sinks to somewhere around my navel. I focus on my breathing—in through my nose and out through my mouth—looking from my mom and dad to my uncle and Chastity and Grace to my cousins and finally to Great-Aunt Harriet. Her wrinkles are prominent as she stoops to sneak Clyde a treat through the netting of his plush kitty carrier. My chest clenches and I have to drop my eyes to the floor.

Here's the thing: Eli isn't wrong in his line of questioning. But I hate to think of my family on the chopping block.

Investigations are a messy, impartial business. Secrets that may or may not be related to the murder are unearthed and made public. And the media only feeds the fire, the general population quick to read headlines, form their own opinions, and share with anyone who will listen, whether or not they've, you know, actually researched the facts behind a claim. And trust me, it sucks to be on the receiving end of a cruel hashtag.

In short, it's a lot of stress, and I fear the tenuous threads holding us together will snap under the pressure.

"No one in my family did this." I dig my heel into the ground, metaphorically and literally. "They couldn't have."

Pity wells in Eli's eyes.

It only hardens my resolve. "You think I'm naive, don't you?" I ask, letting my hands fall to my side. "After everything I've been through? Scraping to open my own business, defending my reputation, and helping you out on more than one occasion."

"Not naive, no. More like blinded by bias." He tilts his head to the side in challenge, his brown eyes still too kind, too empathetic. "You'd be surprised at how little families really know about each other. I can't tell you how many times a parent or sibling calls us with a tip."

My nostrils flare and flames spark in my vision. "I promise I'll call if I catch any inkling of questionable activity."

"That's how it's gonna be, huh?" Eli asks, pushing himself off the table and to his full height. "Do I have to remind you about obstruction—"

"Of justice," I finish for him. "I'm well versed in legalese, thank you very much." Or rather, I have access to an interpreter in the form of Sage.

Eli isn't ready to give up, though. "There's more than family here," he points out. "Are you willing to go to bat for everyone?"

"Of course not," I snap, and then sigh, giving him a small shrug in apology. "Just . . . can you be nice? Please."

"Hate to break it to you, but 'nice' doesn't catch hardened criminals."

"Fine, be your normal horrible self then." I heave an exasperated sigh. "If you want my opinion, I'd start with the caterer. And that guy over there—" I subtly nod toward the mystery man who kept bumping my chair. "Twitchy, that one."

"All right." Eli flips his notebook closed and tucks it in his jacket pocket, the holster to his gun visible. It's a swift reminder that he does, in fact, deal with hardened criminals on a daily basis. "We still on for climbing tomorrow?"

I level with him. "As long as my family is still in one piece."

"It won't be my fault if they're not," he shoots back. "And hey, be careful." He gives the room a wary appraisal as he walks away, seamlessly transitioning into an intimidating, rule-abiding detective.

Being careful is great and all, but it won't save my family from the dumpster fire of a murder investigation.

Chapter Four

After we're finally released from the Longview Lodge, which earned the unfortunate nickname Longest Day Lodge, no one knows quite what to do with themselves. So, we scatter. Each to our own corner to lick our wounds. Which suits me just fine.

Vino Valentine is like a balm on my psyche.

Located in North Boulder, an area that's a mix of industrial and artsy, it's across the street from a nursery with rows of greenery and bright blooms that are like fireworks along the folds of the front range, and next door are my favorite coffee shop and a co-op art gallery.

The shopping center that houses my home away from home has white cement with charcoal awnings and floor-to-ceiling storefront windows. I've added my own touch to the outdoor decor with oak-barrel planters overflowing with lush petunias, impatiens, and snapdragons.

I open the door to my winery, letting the familiar sounds, sights, and scents wash over me. The happy chatter of customers and clinking of glasses; the full tables and relaxed ambience; the aromas of wood and jammy fruit.

I designed the tasting room so it would be inviting, a brief sanctuary from the chaos of life. Simple espresso chairs surround oak-barrel tables that are decorated with vases of sunflowers and pillar candles, unscented so as not to interfere with the subtle bouquet of my wines. Photos of vineyards from around the world adorn the walls, and in the back is the tasting bar, a gorgeous hard-maple countertop lined with baskets of palate-cleansing crackers, and overhead, floating shelves featuring sparkling crystal stemware.

And let's not forget the star of the show: the wines themselves.

Bottles available for purchase are prominent on a refurbished armoire that's as interesting as it is functional. Painted a midnight blue and festooned with rows of curved iron racks that cradle each varietal for sale, and space in the drawer for sachets of mulling spices, which, given we're in the heat of summer, flavor sangria over mulled wine.

While I created this space with clients in mind, it serves as a refuge for me as well. Even during the Saturday rush, or perhaps especially then. Nothing warms my heart like seeing my craftsmanship appreciated.

I weave between bustling tables and duck behind the bar, stashing my purse beneath the register.

My assistant hurdles through the door that leads to the back of my winery, a vintner haven chock-full of stainless-steel equipment, aging vintages, and a makeshift cellar. She's carrying a case of bottles and starts when she sees me, her long brown hair practically jumping in surprise along with the rest of her.

"Gawd, you nearly gave me a heart attack," Sloan says, pushing the box safely onto the counter before taking a large gulp of air. "I thought you had a thing today."

"Change of plans," I reply. "I decided I'd check in here, even though I know you have things more than handled."

And she does. Not only does Sloan have customer service down pat, but she's also preparing for her final Master Sommelier exam, the culmination of years of coursework, study, and practical experience, honing her tasting skills and learning the industry inside and out. My assistant is basically a walking wine database.

As if to further prove my point, she swiftly extracts bottles from the case and wraps them in recycled brown paper. It should be noted that Sloan has one speed: fast. Luckily, she's smooth to boot, never dropping so much as a rag onto the floor.

"That sounds ominous for a wedding," Sloan says with a grimace. Her mouth is her most notable physical feature, and one she accentuates with ruby-red lipstick and shiny gloss, as if her lips are a frame to her taste buds. "What's the sitch—bridezilla, monster-in-law, sordid love affair?"

I try for an explanation that won't frighten her. "More of a, uh, death-turned-crime-scene situation."

And fail.

Sloan's eyes widen and she stares at me unblinking, even while her hands still methodically wrap bottles. "Are you okay?"

Am I okay?

I'm a tangled mess of sadness, worry, and denial. Only at my shop to escape the images assailing my mind. Of

Prynne lying unseeing on the floor, of my family grouped together in the ballroom, all so innocent and vulnerable, of Eli prying for information. A fierce defensiveness surges through me, and a desperation to guard those I love, if only I knew how.

A tiny voice seems to whisper in my ear, goose bumps forming on my arms. *Find Prynne's killer and this all goes away. Find Prynne's killer and we can get this weekend back on track. Emma can get married and we'll all live happily ever after, if such an ideal exists.*

But can I really go down that road again? Can I afford not to?

Sloan is still waiting for a response, her concern escalating with each passing second.

Obviously, I can't dump the full extent of my crazy on her. I grab a rag and busy myself with wiping down the already-spotless counter. "Jury's still out."

"There's pizza in the back if you want a slice." Sloan is one of those people who thinks food is always the answer, which I'm beyond grateful for. Because even if food doesn't solve a problem, it wards off despair.

I drop the cloth. "Have I told you lately that I love you?"

"Last week when I brought in Voodoo Doughnuts," Sloan says with a wink. "I've gotta run this to table four." She hurries out to a table, exchanges the packaged goods for a credit card, and returns to scan the plastic before I so much as take a step. It must be her shoes, trendy sneakers that she pairs with posh business suits.

In the back, I find a still-warm box from Beau Jo's and my mouth instantly starts watering. I didn't realize how hungry I was.

Beau Jo's is a local gem, notorious for their mountain crust, thick and chewy dough that's like dessert. No, really, they actually serve their pizza with a jar of honey to drizzle on the yeasty perfection. And the toppings themselves are top-notch, satisfying any craving from classic to exotic, meaty to plant-based.

Sloan built her own combo with roasted garlic and olive oil sauce, sliced tomatoes, black olives, bell peppers, mushrooms, and creamy ricotta. There's even sliced fresh basil on top. I let out a tiny moan as I chew my way through my first slice, letting the flavors dance over my tongue.

This pizza would pair beautifully with a crisp sauvignon blanc. A hazard of the trade: mentally pairing everything I eat with a specific vino.

Sloan pokes her head through the doorway as I'm not so gracefully tearing into another slice. "Your mom's here to see you."

I swallow and glance over my shoulder as if Sloan could possibly be speaking with someone else. It hasn't been more than thirty minutes since my mom and I parted ways and I can't fathom what she's doing here, or how she tracked me down.

"Be right there." I shove the last bite into my mouth and wash up, making my way to the front with equal parts curiosity and trepidation.

My mom perches on the last available stool at the end of the bar. The other seats are filled with customers steadily working their way through my tasting menu, from the lightest white to the heaviest red to the port. Swirling, sniffing, and sipping abound. Except for my mom, who shifts awkwardly despite her intimate knowledge of my establishment.

She's still in her formal wear with her tote slung over the

back of her chair, further proof she didn't stay long at home, if she went there at all.

She exhales a puff of air and drums her fingers on the countertop, signs of stress. I know from experience. From the times she's been under pressure as lead chemist at NIST Laboratories, the numerous occasions Liam got in over his head and needed to be bailed out, or when I first told her I wanted to be a winemaker, back before she understood and respected the sheer effort and science involved.

I snag a glass and pour her a generous serving of the Pearl Street Pinot. Sliding the glass across the bar, I ask, by way of a greeting, "What's up, Mom?"

She takes the glass with a grateful nod but doesn't take a sip. "I just spoke with Michael."

I rest my forearms on the countertop. "How's Emma holding up?"

"Okay, I think," she says. "But you know Michael, more concerned about himself than anyone else."

I ignore the dig at my uncle, fully aware of their history—and just how aggravating brothers can be.

Her voice is pitchy as she continues, like she's still piecing together exactly why she's here, "The wedding is postponed, but everyone is staying through the weekend."

My family lives scattered across the state, close enough to make holiday gatherings convenient, but far enough away that we don't see one another much more than that. We usually take advantage of celebrations like weddings, graduations, and, weirdly, funerals to catch up on happenings in our busy lives.

"That's good they'll be in town a bit longer," I say, trying to read between the lines of what my mom is after. Because it's clear she wants something, and my apprehension is growing the longer she's taking to spit it out. "Is there a dinner or other get-together planned? A makeup wedding?"

"Not that I'm aware of." Her eyes flick from me to the guests along the bar.

Dread seeps in and after my morning of playing cat-sitter and dutiful cousin, I cut to the chase. "Okay, what aren't you telling me?"

"Listen, I know how you are with these things," she starts, focusing on the ruby liquid in her crystal bowl. Then she looks up and her eyes meet mine with a penetrating gaze. "Are you going to look into Prynne's murder?"

Ah, there it is.

I'm about to be told to let the authorities do their job and worry about myself for once. Only, if I'd listened to that advice in the past, so much of my life would be different. Vino Valentine would have gone the way of the Angel's Share, evaporated into the wind, and I never would've met and fallen in love with Reid.

No, I have no regrets about doing my part to ensure justice is served—not then, not now.

I grab a dish towel and scrub at a nonexistent smudge on the countertop. "I'll be careful, I promise."

"Oh, I know you will." My mom waves off concerns for my safety with one hand. Which, now that she's done it, I'm not sure how I feel about it. I mean, she believed me *awfully* fast. She adds, "You always are."

She chews on her bottom lip and shifts in her seat again. That's when I realize I've misread her signals. She's not stressed, she's nervous.

I lean forward again, resting my chin on my cupped hands. "What is it, then?"

"I want to help."

* * *

My elbows slide outward and my jaw almost hits the countertop.

I'm not sure what I was expecting, but it wasn't this. Eli's
words float back to me: *You'd be surprised at how little
families really know about each other.* Perhaps he wasn't
entirely wrong if my mom can blindside me like this.

I stand up straight. "Lemme make sure I've got this
straight. You want to help me investigate Prynne's murder?"

My mom lifts her chin, resolved, not unlike the way I do
when I'm trying to imbue myself with confidence. "Yes. I
want in."

"Why?"

"The same reasons as you, I imagine," she says. "For the
family. For my sweet niece, who deserves better."

I consider her. Her stout figure, frizzy hair, and crow's-
feet behind cat-eye glasses. My heart swells with affection.
Sometimes I think I would do as much to protect her as she
would me.

I'm ready to decline her offer, but the steely glint of determination in her eyes gives me pause.

"Okay?" It comes out as a question, and her face, so full
of hope, falls. I try for more conviction, "Okay!"

She perks up immediately. "Really?"

I shrug. "I was planning on poking around a little, see if
I find anything. The sooner we clear this up, the better. For
everyone involved."

"Exactly," my mom says, finally taking a sip of her pinot. "I hate it when things are left hanging."

Here I thought my innate drive for closure stemmed
from events in my life—my Perfect Parker reputation as a
teenager, being dumped by a guy named Guy who never

cared to know the real me, my aunt's car accident and subsequent passing. But maybe I get it from my mom. For some reason, the idea makes me smile. "I understand more than you know."

This could actually be a good thing. With my history with crime scenes and my mom's scientific know-how, combined with our general knowledge of the family, we might actually be able to make a difference.

"So, how do we start?" she asks, right as Sloan returns behind the bar to pour the happy hour partakers their next taster of wine.

I wave for my mom to follow me and lead us through to the back. No need to upset my impressionable assistant or patrons with our talk of homicide.

I lean against one of the towering vats that nearly touches the ceiling, the metal cool through the thin fabric of my dress. It's empty at the moment, at the ready for the fall harvest.

A perk to aging wines in stainless steel: no new flavors are introduced during fermentation, like cherry, vanilla, or smoky notes imbued by oak. In short, the fruit stands on its own.

We could use that rationale now.

"Let's talk through the crime scene," I say, massaging my temples. "Did you get a look at Prynne?"

My mom shudders and takes another sip of her wine, having brought her glass with her. She crosses her free arm across her chest in a fearful manner that makes me second-guess my decision to accept her help. "She was hit over the head."

"Agreed." I bypass that minefield, not wanting to rehash the severity of the gash at her brow, how it likely made her see stars—or worse. "But that wasn't all. Did you notice the other . . . stuff?" I hesitate to use the word *clues*, uncertain how to categorize the mess around Prynne.

"As a matter of fact, I did." My mom nods. "The tulle, the petal."

I pick up her thread, ticking items off on my fingers. "The hair, muddy footprints leading to the door, the rock, the smell. Whoever we're dealing with is either extremely careless or extremely smart." As the words leave my mouth, I feel their truth like a sediment settling deep in my gut. It's dizzying, and more than a little disconcerting.

Narrowing her eyes, my mom turns her back to me and paces a few steps in the opposite direction. She stops before the sealed door that leads to my makeshift cellar, where she pivots again and walks back, all the while staring at the floor. Her lips are moving but nothing comes out.

And I've broken my mother. With all my gory talk of murder.

"If you don't want to do any more today, that's totally okay." I glance around for a change of topic—anything. "Pizza?"

She ignores me, taking another small swallow of wine. "Let's go back to those footprints. Something has been bugging me about them."

And apparently I misread her actions. Again. Curiosity mounting, I give her the go-ahead.

"The stride was off."

I blink in confusion.

"The stride," she repeats with vigor. "The distance between the footprints was short in proportion to the perceived size of the shoe."

She's in her wheelhouse now: science and math. In this case, physics. "How short?"

"Well, I didn't take measurements."

"That's not—" I wince and remind myself we're on the same team. "Touché."

"They just seemed close together. As if whoever left them was shuffling, or had extraordinarily large feet."

I add this to my running catalog of information.

My mom isn't done. She continues, with more confidence, "And it wasn't even raining outside. Where did the mud come from? Those footprints are, what are the kids saying these days, *sus*?"

I silently applaud my mom for using the slang word *sus*. Correctly. "So, someone smart then?"

"Or desperate. Or both. That's my hypothesis." She downs the remainder of her pinot and then looks at her glass as if shocked to find it empty. "External contamination."

"Planted clues," I add.

"How do we tell the fake clues from the real ones?"

"That, Miss Marple, is the question."

"Your dad is the mystery buff, not me," she says, referencing my dad's admiration for Dick Francis novels.

"We'll see about that." I push myself off the vat and to my full height. "Let's start with talking with a few people, see if anyone noticed anything, or anyone, out of place."

"The whole wedding was a complete shambles."

I shift my gaze to the photograph of chartreuse chardonnay grapes hanging over the farmhouse sink.

There's a fungus that attacks grapevines. The first signs are tiny yellow spots on leaves and smudges that resemble burns on vines. From there, the disease spreads to the shoots, but—and this is the tricky part—won't show on the fruit until the grapes are half-grown. Beautifully round and plump grapes will suddenly blacken and wither, collapsing in on themselves. By then, it's too late; the entire crop is ruined.

Signs are always easier to see in retrospect. And if by some streak of luck you do notice them, you still have to choose whether to take action or convince yourself it's probably no big deal, that everything will turn out okay.

I spent the entire morning doing the latter and now someone is dead.

"Maybe some of those shambles weren't on accident. Maybe some were intentional to get Prynne alone in a certain place at a certain time." I let this statement land—breathe—with all its implications. "Although I think it's safe to rule out Harriet and her wayward kitty."

My mom's lips twitch. "Who do we talk with first?" Under her breath, she murmurs, "Please don't say Chastity. Please don't say Chastity."

I snort, shaking my head. "How about we divide and conquer? You get ahold of Grace and I'll check in with Emma at the motel."

She flashes me a conspiratorial grin, rocking forward on her feet. "I've been meaning to have a heart-to-heart with Grace."

Full disclosure, I knew my mom would be positively giddy to chat with her former sister-in-law. Weirdly, the two never got along until Grace's separation from my uncle, wherein Grace became less of a couple and more of a whole person. Now, my mom and her are thick as thieves.

"Let me know if you learn anything," I say. "Also, best to keep it on the DL."

"Is that detective-speak?" my mom asks in a hushed whisper, eyes alight.

"Hardly." I clear my throat to hide my chuckle. "It's the down-low. Essentially, I wouldn't go advertising what we're doing."

"Gotcha. It's in the vault." She mimes locking her lips with an imaginary key. "Now, let's get cracking, the game is afoot!" Then my mom kicks the door open to the front of my winery and charges forth.

Which does little to convince me of her subtlety.

Chapter Five

Come on, Parker, you can do this.
  No really, you've done it before.
  Get a freaking grip and just try.
The steady stream of self-assurances run through my mind as I sit in the driver's seat of Reid's forest-green jeep, my knuckles white as I grip the steering wheel.

I take a deep breath. The interior of his car smells like him, herbaceous and minty with the lingering scent of his aftershave.

When I asked Reid if I could borrow his car while he was out of town, he immediately responded in the affirmative, albeit somewhat perplexed. Because in the year we've been dating, I haven't driven. Not once. Haven't done so since I started experiencing panic attacks in transit following my aunt's car accident.

For the most part, it's manageable. Public transportation in Boulder is far-reaching and readily accessible, and with the rise of ridesharing, my personal needs are satisfied. My business, however, is a different story. With dreams of some-day expanding, this is a pickle I'll eventually need to tackle.

Sure, there are work-arounds, good-natured assistants to fulfill my hauling needs, or begging rides from family and friends. But it's starting to feel like an inconvenience—and a safeguard that may not always be there. Case in point: Reid.

While he'll always be there for me in the grander sense, the physical one will be trickier with him in another state. Which means I need to be able to take care of myself. Admittedly, this is something I've always taken pride in, maybe too much at times. A shelf needs installing? Sign me up! The toilet needs fixing? Look no further! This is another a step I can take—have to take—in my quest for self-reliance.

Besides, I'm sick of being scared. And worrying about being scared. Of experiencing the waves of dizziness and panic. The familiar twisting in my gut, flush of heat, and racing pulse whenever I get behind the wheel.

So, despite every cell in my body begging me not to, I turn the key in the ignition.

The engine turns over and rumbles to life. I glance in the mirrors and make minor adjustments before looking in earnest. The parking lot outside my apartment is completely empty.

My mouth goes dry as my hand hovers over the gear shift.

Even though I've been priming myself for this challenge, it's still hard. Harder than I expected.

I force myself to think happy thoughts. Of my wonder cat, Zin (short from Zinfandel), of Reid and his bottomless well of support, of expanding my winery and opening a second tasting room. It's this last rumination that compels me to put the vehicle in reverse and back out.

With my blinker signaling my intent, I wait my turn. Cars and trucks zip past, the drivers inside nonchalant. A surprising number aren't even focusing on the road, their attention on their phones, dashboards, or passengers, as if they weren't in charge of a ton of metal that could crush and kill not only them, but others.

That's when the prickling starts in my fingertips.

My heart skips a beat and sweat beads on my upper lip. I force myself to swallow and take a deep breath, to put my mind elsewhere.

There's a break in the traffic and I cautiously pull into the street.

And I'm doing it—I'm actually driving!

My elation is fleeting. A van swerves around me and I gasp, my heart leaping into my throat. The sound of rushing blood resounds in my ears and my vision tunnels, wavering with my pulse.

I turn at the next intersection, loop around the block, and pull back into my parking lot.

Forehead resting against the steering wheel, I collect myself. Tears prickle the corners of my eyes at my welling emotions. At my momentary success followed by my colossal failure and the cumulative effects of the day.

I give myself one more minute to wallow before unlocking my phone and ordering an Uber. As disappointed as I may be by my progress, or lack thereof, I have more important things to do—and people to see.

The rooms at the Longest Day Lodge are decidedly cozier than the public areas. The surfaces are clean and the linens fresh, if a little drab, and wooden accents and mountain-themed decor make the space comfortable.

The honeymoon suite boasts a Jacuzzi tub in the bathroom and a view of the CU Boulder campus and, in the background, the Flatirons. A geological formation of giant slabs of slanted rock that look as if they're being expelled from the mountainside. They're basked in pinks and oranges as the sun sets behind them, casting elongated shadows over the town.

Above all, the hotel room is blessedly quiet. The construction crew has wrapped up for the day.

My cousin perches on the end of the bed and her fiancé sits beside her, rubbing circles on her back in a steady stream. I take the armchair opposite them.

Emma is in athleisure wear, sporty shorts and an airy tank, her light-brown hair tamed with a headband. I never saw any tears from her earlier—she was too busy taking care of everyone else to succumb to her own emotions—but I see signs of them now. Puffy eyes, blotchy cheeks, and a general air of shock.

Nash is in shorts, a simple undershirt, and flip-flops that appear to be made out of hemp. All in all, he gives off an upscale, yet environmentally conscious vibe.

Seeing them together in this way is like getting a snapshot of their private life. How they are at home, away from the prying eyes and expectations of the world. And they're one of those couples who just fit. Not unlike a cork and a bottle, the elasticity of each of the materials expanding and warping to accommodate the other.

"Sorry you guys weren't able to get married today," I start, sinking into an armchair across from them, the cushion sagging beneath me.

They look at each other, their gazes tethered by some

invisible thread, and it's as if they have an entire conversation in seconds.

Emma turns her attention back to me. "That's okay." A small smile tugs at her lips. "I'll get him to tie the knot eventually."

"Then she'll be stuck with me forever," Nash supplies.

I chuckle, folding my hands in my lap. "Did either of you notice anything odd this morning?"

"Besides our friends and family?" Nash jokes affectionately.

"Or the ring bearer?" Emma asks with a wrenched laugh.

"Besides the obvious." The level of preposterousness takes me by surprise afresh. Especially because these two don't seem like the type to have wanted any of it. "Anything else that struck you as off? Maybe even earlier in the morning?"

"If there was anything, it didn't register. I was pretty preoccupied," Nash says, his face open and honest. "Till death do us part and all that jazz."

"Understandably." Goodness knows I felt cornered when Harriet even broached the topic with me.

Emma gazes out the window in thought, her silhouette a profile of shock and sadness. "I should've known something was wrong when Prynne was a no-show for the procession." She hiccups. "We shouldn't have gone on without her."

I pass her a bottle of water from the end table. "I thought the same thing, if it's any consolation." I want to absolve her of any guilt she's harboring, but in my experience, that's something everyone has to contend with themselves.

"Carolyn was just so insistent. She gets like that, this tunnel vision trying to pick up the slack."

"Your sister is a force," Nash adds, eyes widening.

"No disagreement here," I say, shifting the conversation. "How was Prynne to work with?"

Emma takes a sip of water and hiccups again. "What you'd expect from a wedding planner, I guess."

Despite her assurance, I catch the glance Nash cuts her way, the way his eyebrows furrow.

"Enlighten me. I have no idea what that process is like."

"She was . . ." Emma scrunches her nose, searching for the right word. The distraction serves to cure her hiccups. "Knowledgeable. About everything that traditionally goes into a wedding—and there are *a lot* of details, like, did you know the groom gets a special cake?"

"No, but I'm all for cake," I say with a wink. "However and whenever."

Nash gives a full-bodied shrug. "Seemed a bit much, but I'll admit, it was tasty."

"I didn't see a second cake and I make note of all available dessert options."

"We had it at the rehearsal dinner," Emma clarifies.

"Did the same caterer make that one?"

"Yeah," Nash says. "When I requested it be vegan, she didn't hesitate. One of the better ones I've had."

"Are you vegan?" Given his passion for the environment and work on carbon-capture technology, it makes sense.

"Nash is, but I couldn't give up cheese—not entirely." Emma shoots me a mischievous grin. "But I'm vegetarian."

"And you guys selected the menu?" Doubt creeps into my voice as I recall the chicken cutlets, charcuterie platter, and casseroles devoid of vegetables.

"Of course," Emma starts. "With input from Prynne and Chastity. They both said there should be options to satisfy everyone, not just us."

Nash gives a tight-lipped smile, one that communicates plenty.

It seems like Prynne had an understanding of everything

surrounding weddings, except for the couple at its center. Because if—and this is a big *if*—I'm ever in the position to plan my own wedding, you'd better believe the food will be exemplary, comprising my and my lucky fiancé's favorite cuisines. Which, naturally, means bottomless glasses of vino and anything Reid cooks.

An ache blooms in my chest and I force myself to focus. "Do you know of anyone who would want to harm Prynne?"

Emma and Nash shake their heads, but my cousin, always wanting to be of service, adds, "You should check with Chastity." There's a peculiar edge to her tone as she utters her stepmom's name, not that Emma or Carolyn would ever recognize Chastity as such. They were both grown and out of the house when the woman upended their parents' marriage. Guess I'd probably have a weird tone, too. "Or with Josie, my bridesmaid. She hired Prynne last summer before her own engagement fell through."

"You mean spectacularly bit the dust," Nash says with a shudder.

Emma tugs on the tail of her honey-brown hair, conceding, "It did get ugly."

Josie was the bridesmaid who needed a tongue-lashing from Carolyn to pull herself together for her friend's big day, apparently caught up in her own heartache. And that wasn't enough to keep her in line. I remember the hostility between Josie and the groomsman as they walked down the aisle and suppress a shiver.

"I'll do that." I swipe my bangs to the side, the rebellious hairs beginning to curl from heat and the bustle of the day. "Any chance you have the contact info for the caterer?"

"Sure, why?"

"Oh, I was just hoping to make a contact in the industry for Vino Valentine," I lie. Better that than tell the truth, which is that I want to solve Prynne's murder before their names and reputations are dragged through the mud.

"Totally." Emma hops up and collects her phone from the dresser, the home screen being a photo of her, Nash, and their two Labradors named Apollo and Darcy. She swipes through until she finds it. "Just texted it to you."

"Thanks," I say, getting to my feet. "I'll get out of your hair and let you get back to your night."

"No problem," Emma says. "Our other plans fell through."

My steps falter and I hesitate, halfway to the door. I should mind my own business. Only, I've never been very good at that. "I don't mean to pry, but was this the wedding you guys really wanted?"

They both answer at the same time. "No" and "God, no."

"I just wanted to avoid a fight with my family," Emma explains.

Nash bumps his knee against Emma's. "And I just want this one to be happy."

Of all the things they've shared, this last bit is what I carry with me when I go. It follows me like my shadow, how far some are willing to go for the people they love.

Another hotel room later, I find myself standing opposite my uncle and Chastity. Standing because there's not enough space for us all to sit comfortably in their room. While the standard accommodations are clean and sport the same mountain-themed decor, they lack breathing room. The dresser is mere feet from the end of the bed, which is wedged beside an end table barely large enough for a lamp and digital clock.

After an obligatory hug from my uncle, he returns to

Chastity's side. And it's clear why. She's a mess, in every sense of the word.

Her blond hair is matted and tangled from product and the style she tried to take down, a rogue bobby pin still attached to a flyaway strand. There are circles of smudged black around her eyes from mascara, and every minute or so, a sob chokes out of her throat.

I immediately regret stopping by.

On my way to the lobby, my optimizing mind realized I could kill two birds with one stop, so I detoured to my uncle's room. Now I wonder if I would've been better off waiting until tomorrow. Or assigning my mom this task, despite the protests it would have inevitably incited.

"I'm so sorry for your loss, Chastity," I start. "Emma mentioned you and Prynne were close."

"She's my best friend," Chastity croaks. "I've known her forever and now she's . . . now she's gone." She descends into a fit of sobs that has me pressing my back against the wall.

My uncle tries to comfort her, rubbing her back soothingly. It takes a minute, but slowly she quiets, slumping against Michael, who shoots me a half-apologetic, half-cautionary look, a combination that takes practice. Not for the first time, I wonder how he became infatuated with Chastity, how this woman enticed him to jeopardize his marriage and family.

"I'm not trying to make things worse for you," I say with a wince. Painful memories of losing my aunt Laura stir in my mind, of the immediate grief and the sorrow that persisted. I soften my tone. "Really, I want to help find out who did this. Did you know of anyone Prynne might have upset—anyone who would have reason to harm her?"

A beat passes, then another, the only sound being the steady drip of the bathroom faucet.

"What's this about, Parker?" my uncle challenges. Typically a tidy man who dresses as if on his way to the golf course, Michael is almost unrecognizable in sweats and an overlarge hoodie, his salt-and-pepper hair splayed in every direction.

His patience has been expended. By the roller coaster of emotions brought on by the day, by the loss of Chastity's friend, who must have been his friend, too, and by the women who outnumber him. Including me.

While we've never been super close, my uncle and I have always gotten along, chatting football or climbing or the latest vintage of cab he's discovered. But now I catch a glimpse of the individual constantly at odds with my mom. The defensive, obstinate, and singularly focused square (her words, not mine).

And yet, I'm the one who barged in unannounced. Maybe there are some lines even family can't cross.

"I'll just—" Using my fingers, I mime walking away, but Chastity cuts me off.

"No one could ever hate Prynne," Chastity says, her voice rough after hours spent crying. "She was the best. Fun and always the life of the party."

This description is so off base from the Prynne I encountered, I do a double take.

I home in on Chastity, taking in her tangled locks (bleached blond), the terry cloth hotel robe fastened at her waist, and her flawlessly tanned skin. The only way you get that sort of tan line–free bronze is through sunbathing. She's not that much older than I am, but it's clear we have very different lifestyles.

What strikes me is her stillness, as if she's waiting for something.

She's watching me, hardly blinking. There's an intention in the way she brings a tissue to her eyes, gingerly dabbing up very real tears, and delivers a pitiful yet final sniff.

Here's the thing: While the tears may be real, the reason for them might be completely contrived. There are those who know how to leverage their emotions to make others feel and behave a certain way. Chastity has always seemed like such a person. Not fake, necessarily, but not entirely real, either.

How accidental was that Facebook post she inadvertently tagged my uncle in that sent his life into chaos? How much of the ritual circus today was her brainchild? What isn't she telling me about Prynne, and more important, why is she holding back?

"She certainly had spunk," I concede. "Could she have offended someone by so naturally attracting the spotlight?"

"Never," Chastity retorts, breathily, shutting me down with that single word. But there's that same penetrating gaze, that challenge to call her bluff.

"I heard she was planning Josie's wedding before her engagement ended. Did Prynne ever mention anything about that?"

Her eyes glitter like sapphires. "She never talked about her other clients," she says. "Confidentiality."

Okay, I would bet a Lafite Rothschild—nay, my entire wine cellar—that Chastity is lying.

I glance at my uncle, but he doesn't seem aware of anything amiss. Or maybe he's too absorbed in his own woes.

Either way, that's when it becomes crystal clear: I've gotten all I'm going to get. For now.

* * *

People and grapes are alike in that we like to hide our weaknesses.

Take fruit that's overwatered or harvested a smidgeon too early. The grapes may look plump and delicious, but the chemistry tells a different story in skewered sugar concentrations which can result in tasteless wine.

Because the truth always comes out in the end.

I was hoping to protect my family by getting the truth out in the open now as opposed to, say, watching it appear on the front page of the *Denver Post*. But Chastity doesn't seem to mind attention.

My mind whirs through possibilities as to what she could be hiding about Prynne. A tulle monopoly, an illicit affair with a groom, A SECRET IDENTITY?!

And I've been watching too many true crime documentaries.

I peer through a window as I march through the lobby, shocked to find it's dark outside. It's later than I realized.

"Parker?"

I turn in place at hearing my name to find Grace sitting on a couch, the coffee table in front of her sprawled with stacks of paper covered in colorful ink. She removes a pair of thick-rimmed glasses and perches them on top of her head. She's in a simple cotton blouse with her hair, mostly silver with hints of its prior gold, cascading down her back. Peppermint permeates the air, steam rising from a ceramic hotel mug beside her.

The lobby is nearly empty, not having much to recommend it in terms of comfort or entertainment. The only other soul present is a late-night employee slouched behind the check-in desk, glued to his phone. Seriously, I'm pretty sure Ralphie, the CU Buffs' very real and very large buffalo mascot, could come charging through and he wouldn't notice.

I know I tasked my mom with reaching out to Grace, but Grace is here now. Surely it would be prudent for me to seize the moment and ask a couple questions. Besides, there's no telling if my mom can yield as impressive results interrogating as she does in her lab. Investigating is a whole different kettle of grapes.

"What are you still doing here?" Grace asks.

"Just stopped by to see how everyone was doing after all the excitement."

"'Excitement' is certainly one word for it." She blows on her tea, sending tendrils into the air, before taking a dainty sip.

"Sorry Emma's wedding was a bust."

She acknowledges my sentiment, setting her mug on the table and folding her hands in her lap. "At least this will give Emma and Nash a chance to think about what they want for their day instead of what will appease the masses."

"Hopefully," I agree, thoroughly unconvinced.

My skepticism isn't lost on Grace. "Emma has always been agreeable, to a fault. Even when she was a little girl, always letting Carolyn boss her around." Her gaze grows dewy with nostalgia. "She didn't learn how to stand up for herself like she ought to. I blame myself for not setting a good enough example."

What Grace lacked decades ago, she has now, and I have to believe Emma will find her own way, too.

"Did you happen to notice anything"—I pause, searching for the right word—"unexpected leading up to the ceremony?"

"I was too caught up trying to get Michael to think about someone else for a change." She clicks her tongue. "You'd think I'd have learned by now how futile that is."

I pivot the conversation away from my uncle and his many faults. "You must've gotten to know Prynne through the planning process. Did anything ever strike you about her? Give any indication that she would end up like this?"

"No," she says through a sigh. "Not really."

"So, something?" I prod.

She shifts on the couch cushion. "I got the impression Prynne didn't see others as individuals, but more as a reflection of herself. She picked up on the bits she understood and ignored the rest. It gave her a significant blind spot."

"That's very astute."

"I've been bulldozed by plenty of people just like her."

More questions burn on my tongue, but I swallow them, sensing I've intruded enough. At least my mom will be taking a stab at digging up intel, and who knows, perhaps her familiarity with Grace will work in her favor.

"What's all this?" I wave at the various piles of paper with telltale formats of school worksheets.

"Grading," Grace says. "It never ends, I'm afraid."

I rest my hand on my hip. "I thought one of the perks of teaching was getting summers off."

"The school needed someone to help with their summer ESL program. I volunteered."

"That's good of you."

"What's good is the curiosity of the kids I have the pleasure of teaching." She smiles, one of those smiles she's wholly unaware of that spotlights her passion for teaching.

"Those are some lucky students."

"I'm the lucky one, trust me." She massages her hand with knobby fingers, pain flitting across her face. Grace has rheumatoid arthritis, has for a few years now. She doesn't let on how much it bothers her, but I know it must.

Sensing my scrutiny, Grace changes the subject. "Your mother called earlier. We're going to get together tomorrow morning for coffee."

I give her my best surprised face, pleased to hear my mom wasted no time jumping on her assignment. "Oh, really?"

"It's such a treat seeing her."

"The feeling is mutual," I answer. *Especially when it's to help solve a murder.*

"Where's that chef of yours?" Grace asks pleasantly. "Your dad was raving about his cooking earlier."

My heart melts and with that melting comes a wave of emotions. It was one thing when Reid swept me off my feet with his perfectly seared scallops and decadent truffles, but it was a whole other kind of romantic watching him prepare a meal for my parents.

For my dad's sixtieth birthday, we decided to surprise him with his favorite dinner: a bacon cheeseburger. Of course, Reid elevated the classic with sliced avocado, chipotle aioli, and tomato relish, serving crispy hand-cut sweet-potato fries on the side. Reid had been so nervous in his quest to impress, he was a flurry of movement that intensified when I mentioned the reason for my dad's partiality to the dish, because my mom didn't do red meat. Reid took it in stride, as he does everything, and prepared a grilled salmon burger just for her.

And then there was the cake he'd "tossed together," a thing of beauty made of doughnuts and maple pecans, all topped with chocolate frosting.

As sweet as all that was, it was nothing compared to the kiss we shared later that night. My entire being was a lovey-dovey puddle that was mirrored only in Reid. We'd snuggled, legs entangled on my couch, as we rehashed how well it went, gently prodding at the subject of our capital-*F* Future. How his mom might get along with mine, how he would prepare the turkey if I ever wanted to host Thanksgiving. There was this unspoken promise of years—decades—ahead of us. Together.

I shake my head, bringing myself back to the here and now.

While I bristle every time the rest of my extended family inquires about Reid, I find I don't mind it so much coming from Grace. Maybe because I know the sorts of questions she was made to answer following her divorce from my uncle, or maybe because Grace has always just seemed so understanding.

"San Francisco," I answer, trying for a nonchalant shrug. "Opportunity calls."

She puts her glasses back on and I get the sense she sees beneath the surface—all the mixed feelings even I can't make sense of. "Well, I look forward to meeting him at the next family get-together."

"Definitely," I say quietly, dipping my chin. "I'll let you get back to work." I turn on my heel and stride into the summer night.

Chapter Six

Zin casually paces by the front door when I return to my apartment. She has silky gray fur and green, orblike eyes that would come across as wise if they weren't constantly begging for food. Her kitty face is veiled by long whiskers and the tip of one ear is missing form a time before we came into each other's lives.

Twitching her tail, she mews as if to exclaim the sheer coincidence of us stumbling upon each other in the entry-way, but her bluff is called when she purrs and rubs against my leg. It's nice to be welcomed home in such a manner.

I scratch behind her ears. "I bet you're hungry for dinner."

She gives a garbled meow-purr in response that I take to mean *Desperately starving, actually.*

"That makes two of us." I toe off my shoes and pad toward the kitchen with Zin trotting at my side. "Where's your pal William?"

I'm watching Reid's fur babe while he's out of town, and yes, his cat is named William Wallace after his favorite movie, *Braveheart*. It works out well for both of us, William gets to stay somewhere he's familiar with and I'm one step closer to realizing my fate of Crazy Cat Lady.

I click on the funky seashell lamp on the entryway table, illuminating my humble abode. Vintage art prints adorn the walls and there are enough plush accents to make it cozy—a russet velvet couch, afghan blanket draped over pillows, and a Persian area rug.

My apartment isn't much, really more of a glorified hallway with my bedroom and kitchen serving as bookends to the living room, barely wide enough to accommodate furniture and a modest flat-screen television.

But it has this view.

French double doors open onto a small balcony that overlooks the Flatirons. The slanted slabs of rock are basked in silver from the moon, the surrounding mountain peaks varying shades of dusky blue. Crickets chirp and the herbs in my potted planters perfume the air, which has cooled to a comfortable level. I leave the door a crack open while I continue my search for William.

I find him in the kitchen, much like his human counterpart would be. A handsome tuxedo cat, William is sleek black except for a triangle of white fur on his chest. He bats at his favorite squishy guitar toy, which has moved considerably from where I positioned it earlier, and from the way he kicks at it with his hind legs, it appears to be giving him a run for his money.

"You get that guitar," I say with an encouraging pat on his head. Then I go about the very important task of filling his and Zin's bowls with kibble.

Zin digs in first, purring and eating at the same time, a

feat I can't quite comprehend, and William follows suit, more polite in his noshing.

Cats seen to, I focus on my own needs, starting with sustenance. I scour my fridge and cabinets for vittles. One perk of dating a chef is fresh produce and pantry ingredients readily available, but the downside to that is I've gotten out of the habit of stocking these items myself. I'm scraping the bottom of the barrel.

Disenchanted, I open the freezer, figuring I'll have one of the emergency Lean Cuisines I keep on hand, and come full stop.

Because this doesn't look anything like my freezer. Stacks of containers line the space, labeled in Reid's tidy handwriting with descriptions and heating instructions. Roasted vegetable lasagna, green pork chili, asparagus and chèvre quiche, chicken potpie—all of them no doubt equally delectable.

I don't know when he found time to do this. Chefs have tight schedules; Reid is always busy menu-planning, procuring the best seasonal ingredients, or, you know, actually cooking for paying guests. The fact that he somehow found a way to take care of me, even from thousands of miles away, makes me feel all warm and gooey.

After I get the chicken potpie warming in the oven and pour myself a hard-earned glass of wine, I call Reid.

He answers on the first ring, "Hey, Parks." His familiar deep voice has my toes curling and me grinning like a schoolgirl.

I sink into an armchair. "So, it seems I've been blessed with a visit by the Food Fairy."

I can practically hear his smile over our connection, all dimples and satisfaction. "You don't say."

"It's true, just when I thought I was plum out of, well,

everything and destined to gnaw on catnip leaves, lo and behold, my freezer is stocked with enough world-class fare to feed a wedding." That last word slipped out, likely from my fried brain and being surrounded by all things old, new, borrowed, and blue. I continue, my heart bobbing in my chest, "Thank you. I have no idea how you pulled it off."

"Eh, I'm just that good," he says, the verbal equivalent of a smirk-shrug.

I shake my head, schoolgirl grin still firmly in place, feigning exasperation. "Always so cocky."

His husky chuckle sends goose bumps down my arms. "Which did you pick?"

"Chicken potpie, paired with a glass of my What Happens in Viognier." I sip on the dry wine, noting how the peach mingles with vanilla and cloves, the flavors dancing on my tongue.

"Wish I were there with you." There's a shift in his tone, hinting at a longing we both share.

"Me too." Zin hops into my lap and I indulge her, scratching behind her ears while she kneads my lap with her tiny kitty paws. "Especially after the day I've had."

"That bad, huh?"

"Whatever you're picturing, add a pinch of pandemonium and a whole lot of homicide." There's a stunned silence on the other end that has me asking, "You there?"

"Yeah, I'm here," Reid says, clearing his throat. "Damn, Parks, you have the worst luck."

"Luck has nothing to do with it."

"Are you okay?"

"I'm still processing, but I think so." I start at the beginning and catch him up on the events of the day. The disaster-fueled wedding, Prynne's notable absence that ended with her demise, the ruling of murder and subsequent investigation.

"Now I wish I were there even more," Reid says through an anguished sigh. "I'm booking the next flight home."

"No, really, I'm okay. Just talking to you is enough." It's true; this conversation—our banter, which has always been there—gives me a taste of normalcy.

"But I kinda feel like it's my boyfriend duty to be there for you in times of distress."

"You are here for me—only, there," I argue. "And it's my responsibility to make sure you're following your dream."

There's no playful quality to our words now, just what we are—and more important, need to be—to each other. "Are you sure?"

"Positive."

"If you change your mind, I'll catch the first plane out there."

Reid means it, which is more than enough. Has to be enough. I refuse to be the reason he misses out on his fantasy restaurant location. "How goes the venue hunt? See any promising listings yet?"

"A couple," Reid admits. "One overlooks the water, but needs a ton of work—borderline too much. Another is downtown and seems like it was designed for me, but it's over my budget." He sighs, giving me an audible glimpse of the stress he's under, of the vulnerability and fear he's experiencing. "It's overwhelming."

Before Reid opened his restaurant, Spoons, he struggled to take the plunge. To risk a job that was fine to pursue something that might not pan out—or might lead to something incredible.

Now I wish I were there with him.

"You've never shied away from a challenge." I readjust in my armchair, Zin having melded to my lap. "Does one have better space for live music?" A drummer in his spare time, music is another of Reid's passions, and he loves playing host to local artists at Spoons.

"For sure—" He cuts off, cursing in the background. "I just saw the time. I've gotta run."

"Oh," I say, trying not to sound too disappointed.

"I'm meeting the investors for dinner," he explains, his voice muffled as I imagine him pulling a shirt over his head. "You'll call me if you need me, right?"

"Of course." I clear my throat, mustering a "Go dazzle them."

"Love you, Parks."

"Love you, too."

The line goes dead and silence closes in, opening a pit in my stomach.

Sulfur dioxide is a chemical added during fermentation to prevent spoilage. All it takes is a couple drops to change the makeup of a four-hundred-gallon batch of wine. The same happens with uncertainty. Drops plop into my subconscious, sending out ripples of unease.

Reid and I have proven our relationship is strong enough to survive the potential pitfalls of a professional partnership (Vino Valentine being the primary label sold at his restaurant), family drama (mostly his, although it's not like mine is a walk in the park), and a less-than-stellar vacation (after which we needed another vacation). But this distance sets me on edge.

I'm not a traditional gal, per se. I haven't given much thought to whether or not I want the white picket fence, kids, the whole nine yards. Maybe it was all the marriage talk today, Great-Aunt Harriet needling her way into my psyche, but I find myself grappling with it now.

Even if Reid and I weather the stress of opening and operating a restaurant out of state, what would our future look like? What do *I* want it to look like?

These questions aren't only for me, but for Reid, too. Once I have a better understanding of my own answers. Fortunately, I have plenty to distract me in the meantime.

As often happens with Google, one search leads to another as I follow curiosities into obscure corners of the internet with results barely related to my original query.

I started by typing "Prynne Pearsall," took a detour on YouTube with the latest viral flash dance down the aisle to ABBA's "Take a Chance on Me," and wound up reading about the fascinating and unexpectedly brutal origins of wedding traditions.

Bridesmaids were initially recruited as decoys to confuse exes and evildoers, groomsmen were put in place to coerce cold-footed—or reluctant—brides, the wedding cake began as humble barley bread the groom crumbled over his bride's head, and the tossing of the bouquet used to be a free-for-all where guests tore at the floral arrangement and even the bride's dress, hoping to snatch up a piece of her good fortune.

Suddenly, murder doesn't seem like that far of a stretch.

I shovel another forkful of potpie into my mouth, savoring the creamy béchamel, succulent roast chicken, and root vegetables, the dill, thyme, and parsley adding nuance. Not to mention the crust, which is a thing of beauty, flaky and buttery. It almost feels as if Reid could be in the next room.

The food rejuvenates me and the research distracts me, the perfect recipe to dispel doubts.

I chase my bite with a sip of Viognier, swishing the wine around my mouth and noting how the flavor shifts from sweet to citrusy to herbaceous as it rolls over my tongue.

I turn my attention back to my computer screen and click on my original search tab, currently open to Prynne's website. It's professionally designed, which makes her seem legit even if her conduct spoke otherwise.

Her wedding-planning company is called Blush, and it's still relatively new, having been started the prior year. Which explains why she doesn't have many reviews. But the ones she does have are divisive. People either loved working with her or . . . not so much.

A user by the name of DollyLlamaMama says: Prynne was a train wreck. She didn't listen and pushed her own agenda, which was ridiculous—and expensive! We had to stay on her and double-check everything. Hire at your own risk!!

Whereas MrsPrestonFields writes: Prynne is THE BEST. Couldn't have gotten through our special day without her. Her attention to detail was impeccable and her ideas unique and perfectly tailored to me and my now-husband.

I like to think I know which camp Emma falls in, but I wonder about her bridesmaid Josie. If she's Team Dolly-LlamaMama or Team MrsPrestonFields. Why her own engagement came to an end and if she had reason to want to harm Prynne.

That's when I recall the flower petal. The silky coral clamshell that rested near Prynne's leg, a complement to her ivory pantsuit, if she hadn't been splayed lifeless on the floor.

Emma's bouquet comprised roses and calla lilies, and a lavish display at that. That petal could have only come from one of the bridesmaids' bouquets, either Carolyn's or Josie's.

Although whether the petal was intentionally or accidentally placed remains to be seen.

I take another bite of potpie as my phone pings. Munching, I grab it from the end table and find a text from Sage.

Pretty sure there's a rule that if your day involves a dead body, you're supposed to check on your bestie. So, this is me checking on you.

I help myself to a swallow of wine as I mull over a response. If there's one person I can be honest with, it's Sage, and yet, the full range of my emotions—vulnerability, fear, shock, and doubt—would take an eon to type. Hence, I opt to keep it simple.

Me: *I'm okay. Eating dinner. You?*

Sage: *Comforting my delicate state with a* Lord of the Rings *marathon.*

I snort; Sage is the fiercest person I know and would probably drop-kick anyone who dared to call her *delicate*.

Me: *You just wanted an excuse to watch Orlando Bloom, admit it.*

Sage: *Hey, today was traumatic—meeting your extended family AND a murder.*

Sage: *But also, yes, a thousand times yes to Orlando Bloom.*

Me: *Knew it!!!*

Zin trots up and, lifting her kitty face, sniffs at my plate from where it's perched on the coffee table. I nudge her away with my toe and she turns with a huff, tucking her paws beneath her in bread pose, with her back to me. No one does passive-aggressive like cats. I'm tempted to snap a picture when a thought comes to me.

Me: *BTW, please ask my dear brother if he caught anything in the photos he shot today.*

I could have texted Liam directly, but I've found if I want

a timely answer, it's best to go through my friend. As long as I do so sparingly, Sage doesn't seem to mind participating in our little game of telephone.

Not even a minute passes before she responds.

Sage: *Liam already looked and he didn't get any shots in the service hallway or of Prynne.*

Me: *None with Prynne at all??*

Sage: *Unless she's a vampire, no. Also, Liam says you need to stop attending parties. He doesn't want to get sucked into any more investigations.*

I roll my eyes and send an equally flippant retort, one that will hopefully make her smile. *Tell him to mind his own business and fawn over you until you regain your composure.*

She shoots back a thumbs-up and I set my phone down, understanding that to be the end of our conversation.

I polish off the rest of my dinner with Zin glaring at me over her shoulder. After setting my plate in the sink, I squat down and scratch behind her ears. Unable to resist, she leans into my palm, a purr rumbling through her chest.

"See, there's no reason to be a grouch."

Zin tumbles onto her back, paws held adorably at her chest, and blinks up at me as if understanding perfectly. Amends made, I give her head one last pat before tucking back in with my laptop.

In earlier tabs, I dipped my toe into the vast well of social media. I submerge myself entirely now with an ungraceful belly flop.

Prynne has a Facebook page, but that proves to be mostly a continuation of her website, featuring pretty pictures of lacy dresses, flowers, and embellished frosting. That's not what interests me, though.

I find Prynne's private account through Chastity, but apart

from a couple posts she made public—mostly relating to how she's living her best life by opening Blush and, oh, by the way, would you please spread the word?—she shares information only with friends.

I navigate to Instagram and do a double take, sure I've accidentally logged in to someone else's account. Sponsored ads for engagement rings, ball gowns, and hand-drawn calligraphy invitations overwhelm my feed.

Great, I think, *thanks to my investigating, I'm going to be plagued with targeted ads for wedding paraphernalia.* Which is the last thing I need, for so many reasons.

Swallowing my annoyance, I search for Prynne, then Blush, finally striking gold with the account @BlushWeddings.

With a meager following, influencer she is not, but Prynne has a decent number of posts, from dress fittings to cake tastings to snapshots of choice events. And I've gotta hand it to her, she knows how to sell herself. Maybe it's the filters, but everything has a sheen to it, a polish.

I hover over a picture of Emma shopping for bridesmaid dresses for Carolyn and Josie. The three pose together before a rack of frilly pastels, Emma appearing uncertain, Josie tearful, and Carolyn repulsed. Prynne's caption: #FriendshipGoals.

I continue scrolling through her timeline, back through the variety of events she's orchestrated. Through dainty teas in parks I recognize to formal affairs in establishments I don't. I swipe until I come to the post I'm looking for, only discernible from the tags: Josie's would-be wedding.

The cover image is of a table setting; a place card embossed with calligraphy, a cloth napkin folded into a swan, and a centerpiece of violet tulips. The text reads: The final touches make all the difference.

I sit up ramrod straight in the armchair, leaning over the screen.

Final touches.

That means Josie's engagement ended—or rather, spectacularly bit the dust, according to Nash—during the final stages of planning. Like, right before the big day.

There are no comments, no other hints as to what happened, but there must be a story there. A plump, juicy one. And I intend to find out what it is.

There's professional attire and business casual, but no precedent for entrepreneur with a side of sleuthing.

Zin and William, sadly, provide no answers. After scarfing down their respective breakfasts, William took up his post to stare down a rambunctious squirrel and Zin settled in for a lengthy bath.

Tapping one finger against my chin, I sift through hangers, considering various combinations—graphic tees and airy blouses, pencil skirts and wide-legged capris, dresses and posh suits—until I come to a recent purchase. An olive utility jumper with pockets galore and a wrap belt. The price tag is even still attached.

I drape the piece on my bed, disrupting Zin's diligent licking.

"What do you think? Too funky?"

She cocks her head to the side and twitches her ear with the missing tip.

"You're right, it's perfect."

I change quickly and slip into a pair of Birkenstock sandals. Before my antique brass mirror, I comb my fingers through my A-line bob, leaving my dark hair wavy, and apply neutral eye shadow and mascara. I finish with jewelry, clasping my beaded necklace so it drapes just below my collarbone and securing tiny silver hoop earrings.

With one last pat on Zin's and William's heads, I bid my kitties adieu, tuck a paper-wrapped bottle in my bag, and catch the bus to Vino Valentine.

Downtown Boulder passes by out the window. While every season has something to offer, summer is especially beautiful—or maybe that's because it's here and now.

The parks are lush and green with prominent leafy trees that offer shade to picnickers. Time seems to slow, with students out of school and more languid hobbies on the rise, like ultimate frisbee, tubing down Boulder Creek, and slacklining.

Pearl Street is the crowning jewel, dotted with performers, musicians, and vendors selling everything from artwork to kites to Italian soda. And flower beds feature extravagant displays in literal rainbows, rows of red that blend with orange, yellow, and through the rest of ROYGBIV.

Of course, North Boulder isn't to be discounted. The rocky outcrop of Flatirons transitions into green, rolling hills that rise into the surrounding mountains as the bus trundles along. A burgeoning area for galleries, microbreweries, and wineries, it's industrial chic, giving off an urban vibe that's wholly unique.

My parents were skeptical when I first picked the location—and they weren't the only ones. But my gamble paid off.

I tug on the rope to signal my stop and disembark with a thank-you to the driver. After the bus pulls away with a hiss and a screech, I take a minute to appreciate the view from the far side of the parking lot.

The inviting storefront with its clean cement siding, welcoming planters, and elegant windows, all capped off with

the blue lettering that brands it as Vino Valentine. I'm
grateful every day that it's mine—that I somehow pulled
off this crazy pipe dream. While I harbor fantasies of opening another tasting room, I can't imagine anywhere else
being as fitting or picturesque.

The bell jingles when I open the door. As anxious as I
am to question the rest of the wedding party, I have a business to attend to and a commitment to uphold.

I'm ready for Sloan when she arrives promptly at eleven
o'clock.

"G'morning," Sloan says. She's in pin-striped slacks, a
sleeveless blouse, and trendy sneakers the same ruby red as
her lipstick.

In seconds she's in front of the tasting counter. She sips
her coffee, the rim stained with her shimmery gloss, as she
takes in my setup.

A single glass rests on a tray, filled a third of the way
with a wine so jammy and dark it looks almost inky.

"I'd get yourself a palate cleanser," I say with a clap.
"Pop quiz."

An important term in Sloan's agreeing to work for me
was that I sporadically test her wine-tasting skills to help
her prepare for her final Master Sommelier exam. Because
not only do sommeliers need to know the ins and outs of
the industry and which varietals to pair with certain dishes
and flavors, they also need to pinpoint where a grape origi-
nated from based on a tasting alone.

This specific label I'm trying to stump Sloan with was
recommended to me by my competitors turned mentors,
who spent a stint in France last year to get inspired. They
stumbled across a hidden gem of a winery run by nuns in
the Madiran region and haven't stopped raving about it.

Not that Sloan knows any of that. The bottle is safely

wrapped in brown paper and I'm eager to see how close she can get.

Sloan stashes her purse beneath the counter, tosses the remainder of her coffee, and goes for a palate-cleansing cracker. She munches as she begins her analysis, holding the glass up to the light and tilting it this way and that. The colors, viscosity, and legs are all clues to the wine itself.

"A garnet color that runs clearer around the edges," she starts, "which means it's been aged, but not for long since it hasn't lost too much pigmentation. Impressive legs so slightly higher alcohol content, and it's thick."

I wear my best poker face, nodding benignly along while resting my elbows on the counter. I wait patiently, giving nothing away.

Palate cleanser seen to, she sticks her nose in the glass and breathes in. "Ooh," she says, her tone growing excited. "Buckets of blackberries and vanilla and"—she hesitates and turns away to take another big sniff—"yep, espresso. Had to make sure there wasn't any interference."

The last part is the actual tasting, and Sloan does so, eyes narrowed in thought as she gives the telltale gurgle that comes from simultaneously breathing in and swallowing.

"Mmm, that's good." She smacks her lips together. "More blackberries and dark fruit and even a hint of cardamom."

I shift on my feet, unable to contain my curiosity any longer. "And?"

"Give me a minute." Sloan cycles through the steps again—swirl, sniff, sip, repeat—creases forming in her brow.

The bell jingles, alerting us to a new arrival, three, in fact. A trio of bicyclers beaming with endorphins from their ride down the Diagonal Highway. They traipse in, their shoes clicking against hardwood, water bottles in tow, and claim an oak-barrel table near the front.

"I've got this," I say to Sloan, gesturing between her and her glass. "You stay focused."

I see to the bicyclers, bringing them a basket of crackers, three flights of tasters, and extra water. Then I serve a glass of my infamous Chautauqua Chardonnay to a favorite repeat customer, Libby Lincoln.

Libby is a food-and-wine blogger with a flair for adrenaline and an edgy style to match. She brought my business back from the brink last year and as a thank-you, I give her extra-large pours. Which is probably why she continues haunting my winery, never ordering anything but the chardonnay that was, until I set the record straight, rumored to have killed a man.

All the while, Sloan paces, it not being her nature to remain still, murmuring grape regions under her breath.

I'm ready to break for lunch when she finally exclaims, "Southwest France! Tannat and cabernet franc!" Her eyes are alight and there's a fervor in her movements as she gauges my reaction.

"You nailed the region and you're close, so very close, with the grape," I say. "It's pure Tannat, not a blend, aged one year in oak."

She takes another sip and nods. "Right, there it is." She dumps out the remainder and places her glass in the commercial dishwasher with a dejected sigh. "Maybe I'm not ready."

"Don't beat yourself up, that was a tough one."

"The exam will be tough," Sloan frets, rubbing her palms over her eyes.

"You're ready," I insist. "And now you have one more varietal in your repertoire."

"But this week . . ." She trails off, grabbing a dishrag

and polishing the nearest surface, more to channel her energy than to actually clean.

Sloan is planning to attend the exam in Aspen on Wednesday, which has come up faster than I thought possible. It consists of three grueling portions: theory, blind tasting, and service. In the entire history of the Court of Master Sommeliers, only fourteen people have passed on their first try.

I don't remind Sloan of this, though; she's plenty aware of her chances. Further proven when she gives voice to her fears. "What if I completely bomb and embarrass myself and am blacklisted forever?"

"Then at least you'll be memorable." I flash her an encouraging smile. "And you try again, and again, and as many times as it takes to get you certified."

She nods more resolutely, hand on her hip.

"You've got a job here as long as you want."

"Thanks, P," she says, snagging a couple tasting menus for a couple that hasn't even come through the door yet. "Don't go easy on me next time just because I blundered this tasting."

"I would never." I lean back, hand flitting to my necklace. Sloan isn't the only one I won't be going easy on.

Chapter Seven

During my lunch break, I make my way once more to the Longest Day Lodge.

It's a ride away from Vino Valentine on the Skip RTD line, which circumnavigates Boulder by looping around campus. There aren't as many passengers as during my normal commutes, mainly students sporting headphones en route to class, straggling professionals making their way to the office, and fellow drive-challenged individuals on their way to appointments.

Legs crossed in the cushioned seat, I leverage the time by texting my mom for an update.

My phone buzzes with an incoming call a moment later.

I answer with a question: "What do you have against texting?" Seriously, I hate talking homicide in public.

She speaks in a weird, breathy voice. "Don't want to put anything in print, or say too much over the phone." There's an imminent pause. "Can we meet up later at Vino Valentine?"

Confusion bubbles like acid in my stomach. I lick my lips. "Where are you?"

"Work."

"Oh."

This shouldn't come as a surprise. My parents have always taken their jobs very seriously, as they should, given their roles. My dad is head of the Computer Science Department at CU and my mom is a lead chemical engineer at NIST Laboratories. Long hours and getting called into work on weekends was the norm growing up. Which could explain my own work ethic. And yet, she was the one who was so eager to get involved with the investigation.

I slump back in disappointment. Outside, we pass by the engineering building at CU with its sloped rooftops that mimic the mountains. Absently, I wonder if my dad is inside, reviewing notes for an upcoming lesson or meeting with desperate students.

My mom shifts into a whisper. "It's something relating to *you know what*."

"*Oh*." Intrigue creeps in as I try to imagine what my mom could be up to, what she could be using the elaborate tools and measuring devices at her disposal for. I come up blank. "Stop by the shop when the, uh, *Eagle* has landed."

"Ooh, I've always wanted to be an astronaut."

"Right. Same thing," I say. "Just let me know whenever you're done doing whatever it is you're doing."

"Roger that."

Next, from the contact info Emma gave me, I dial Iris Catering. An excuse is on the tip of my tongue, omissions hidden by a half-truth, that I long to break into the wedding industry, despite recent events. Only, it goes to voice mail.

"Hi, this is Parker Valentine," I start when prompted. "I, uh, had a couple questions I was hoping to ask Iris, so give me a call back whenever you get a chance." I rattle off my number and hang up with an awkward, "Okay, see ya."

To curb my immediate fretting over my vague message, I walk the last block to the motel, relishing the warm sunshine on my face. Whenever I travel, I miss the vastness of the Colorado sky, a robin's-egg blue that seems to stretch forever, unobstructed by soaring buildings or dense forest.

On a whim, I pull out my phone and snap a selfie from a low-enough angle that my face is in the bottom of the frame with the sky overhead. *Sending you a bit of Boulder xoxo.*

Reid pings a response immediately. *How'd you know that's exactly what I needed?*

Me: *Feeling homesick?*

Reid: *Nervous.*

Three bubbles appear and disappear on the screen. I reach the entrance to the lobby, the glass doors sliding open and closed until I step out of range of the sensor, when he finally sends his tome of a text.

Reid: *On my way to meet the realtor to look at the two properties again. Investors are keen to hear more details and I don't want to miss my window of opportunity.*

Me: *I take it dinner went well?*

Reid: *Very.*

Me: *No surprise there. You wowed them, just like you do everyone.*

Reid: *Thanks, Parks. You always know how to boost my ego.*

Me: *Like your ego needs boosting;-) Trust your gut and let me know if you need a second opinion.*

Reid: *Will do. Love you, Parks.*

Me: *Love you, too.*

My chest swells with elation for my guy. Reid is crushing it, making his dream a reality, and I couldn't be prouder. It's only a moment later, when I register a tiny pang of sadness, that I remember the questions I still don't have answers to, what the reality of him achieving his dream will mean.

Everything is happening too fast, like a climbing rope slipping through my fingers, and me, desperate to hang on and regain my footing.

I tilt my head back and breathe in the sky, as if I could capture a sliver of the expansive azure to save for later. Then I brave the dark lobby and the murderer that may be lurking there.

I don't like Josie.

And I don't say that lightly. Usually I can find something positive about everyone I meet—you don't get far in the service industry without being able to do so—but Josie rubs me the wrong way.

When she answers the door to her hotel room, she scans me from head to toe, her forehead wrinkling in confusion. I watch as she struggles to place me, even though we've met dozens of times over the years, she and Emma being childhood friends. Sure, I'm not a part of her inner circle, certainly not privy to major events in her life like her broken engagement, which is the real reason I'm here, but I would've expected at least a whiff of recognition.

I let her languish for a beat before coming to her aid. "Parker," I remind her. "Emma's cousin. I was hoping to talk with you."

"Of course," Josie says as if she knew all along who I was. She has a round face, eyes that are a little too close together, and wide nostrils, which I know only because she has this habit of sticking her nose up at the world. The smile she gives me is completely phony, a sneer meant to be taken as such. "I was just on my way out. Can't this wait?"

This would, of course, have been more believable had she been wearing shoes.

I stare pointedly at her bare feet and then back into her eyes. "It'll only take a couple minutes. It can be while you're getting your things together."

She turns with a groan. "If it's really that urgent."

"It is."

I follow her into her room, which is strewn with clothes, accessories, makeup containers, and what looks like a month's supply of chocolate. Not that I'm one to judge. I once had to explain to an Apple technician, straight-faced, how chocolate ended up in the charging port of my phone.

I lean against the wall, stuffing my hands in the deep pockets of my jumper.

Josie searches through her mess of belongings until she finds a lavender sandal with a decorative flower on top. She slips it onto her left foot and continues digging for its pair.

How people pack says a lot about them. If they plan ahead or fly by the seat of their pants, account for unexpected delays and inclement weather, neatly fold and stack their garments or haphazardly toss everything in.

What does it say about Josie that she lugged her entire wardrobe here and let it explode all over her room? That she's a disorganized slob and hardly a mastermind.

Although, as I've repeatedly learned, looks can be deceiving.

"Have Emma and Nash made up their mind about a redo?" Josie asks, midscoop.

"I'm not sure," I answer. "I get the impression they just kinda want to get married, no matter how it happens."

"Then what did you want to talk to me about?"

I cock my head to the side, studying her. "Your bridesmaid bouquet, to start."

"Did you know peonies are my favorite flower? I was going to have them in my bridal bouquet, really lush, with baby roses throughout." She pauses her search and cups her hands in front of her midsection to illustrate. I catch her glance in the opposite mirror as if she could see the image there.

"Sounds pretty," I say with a sad smile. "I'm sorry you didn't get to walk down the aisle with yours."

"Me too." She drops her gaze to the mess coating the carpeted floor.

"You seemed awfully upset yesterday." Which is putting it lightly considering the sheer level of distress I witnessed in the lobby. Really, it's a miracle Josie managed to pull herself together as much as she did.

"It brought back some painful memories."

"Right," I say, infusing my voice with sympathy. "I heard you were engaged."

"We would be celebrating our one-year anniversary next month if he—" She shakes her head, her ponytail coming loose, the hair tie disappearing into the pile. "You don't want to hear my sob story. No one does."

"I don't mind. Really." I try not to sound too eager, my hands balled into fists in my pockets. "Sometimes hashing it out can help."

"It was right before our rehearsal dinner," she starts with a sniff. "Bob told me we needed to talk. He said planning a wedding together made him realize we had different priorities, how miserable we'd be if we married."

Tears well in her eyes and she reaches for a Hershey bar. She unwraps it and stuffs a square into her mouth with a speed that takes practice.

She speaks around her mouthful. "I tried to talk sense into him, remind him of all the good times we'd had, but he wouldn't hear it." Her tone turns bitter. "He said I'd changed. When really, it was him."

"Breaking up that close to the wedding must've been brutal." The wound—her grief—seems fresh, even though it happened almost a year ago. With heartache still that raw, it must have come as quite the shock.

She nods, breaking off another square, but she just stares at the morsel in her palm. "I told him that, asked why he waited, if it was to cause me even more pain. He denied it. Offered to handle everything, notify family and guests. As if I'd give him the satisfaction." She pops the chocolate in her mouth and chews with relish.

"I heard Prynne was planning your wedding."

Her eyes flit warily to mine. "Y-yeah."

"How was she to work with?"

"Prynne was . . ." Josie trails off, setting her chocolate bar aside and taking up her shoe search again. "Lovely."

"Really?"

"Absolutely, she was so understanding, even waived part of her fee."

"Did she help contact everyone, cancel everything?"

"Mostly, but it was more than that. Prynne felt for me, gave me a hug, said she was sorry the event she'd planned wouldn't go on."

"How generous," I say, clicking my tongue. I change gears, hoping to keep Josie on her toes, metaphorically speaking, since she finally found her wayward sandal. "Did you set your bridal bouquet down anywhere?"

"No way," she scoffs. "Why would I? It complimented my dress."

I move on from that dead end. "So, at the ceremony yesterday, I couldn't help but notice you and the groomsman Jack didn't seem to get along. Is there history there?" It was an idea that just came to me, recalling their undiluted animosity as they walked down the aisle. Friend circles are tight, after all, and not always sensitive to breakups.

Josie barks out a laugh. "As if." Her face scrunches up in pure spite, accentuating a smudge of chocolate on her cheek. "Jack and I went out once. Emma thought he might make a good rebound, a way to get me back in the dating saddle. No way, nohow. Not with that jerk."

"Blind dates can suck," I agree with a shudder. "What's so bad about Jack? For the most part, he seems all right." *When he isn't guzzling coffee to banish a hangover.*

"Take it from me, don't believe a word that comes out of his mouth," she snaps, grabbing a purse slung from the back of a chair. She unclasps the front pocket and tosses in the rest of her chocolate bar and a hotel key. "Now, if there's nothing else, I should really go."

Josie doesn't wait for a response before striding to the door and holding it open for me.

"Right, to your thing," I say.

"Exactly."

I pick my way across her room, scanning for anything that seems out of place. You know, like shoes that are too big, torn tulle that matched the strand draped around Prynne's neck, blood-soaked gloves. There's nada, and I've only further aggravated Josie.

"Have a good"—the door shuts in my face—"afternoon."

For someone who was in such a hurry, Josie sure took

her sweet time. It wasn't until I mentioned Jack that she seemed to remember she had somewhere to be at all.

After being unceremoniously booted from Josie's room, I duck around the corner and wait.

Josie never emerges.

If there was any doubt in my mind she was lying about having somewhere to be, it's gone now. The question is *why*. Either I'm that intolerable of a person, which I refuse to believe, having plenty of evidence to the contrary, or she has something to hide.

And now I have a grimy, exposed feeling. Not of being watched, necessarily, but of being in close proximity with someone so disingenuous.

Spotting my next target waltzing across the lobby, I squelch my discomfort and straighten to my full five feet, four inches.

Jack appears to be in better shape today. There are still bags under his eyes with such deep grooves they might as well be permanent, and facial hair tinges his upper lip. But he's alert—poised, even. His blond hair looks windswept and his clothes, while casual, are clean.

"Hey, Jack," I start, giving him my best buddy-buddy tone. "Not sure you remember me, but I'm—"

"Parker," Jack finishes. "Of course I remember you. How's it goin'?"

I camouflage my surprise at his friendly greeting. "Fine, all things considered. You?"

"Same." He shrugs. A rustling sound draws my attention to the paper bag in his hands. I recognize the logo on it as being from one of my favorite sandwich dives.

"Gotta love Snarf's. Did you get their hot peppers?"

"There's only one right answer to that," he says. "Are you here to see Emma?"

"You, actually," I answer, trying not to sound like a total creeper.

He lifts his eyebrows. "In that case, join me. I was gonna eat alone in my room. This is better."

Will he still feel that way when I'm probing him with morbid questions?

Jack leads the way to a couch across from the main desk, the same one I saw Grace at the night before. Only now, instead of student papers, the coffee table is covered in local magazines and advertisements for nearby tourist attractions. I make note to bring a stack of Vino Valentine brochures the next time I stop by, which seems like an inevitability at this point.

Jack sinks into the couch and unwraps his sandwich. I take the adjacent armrest, my stomach panging in response to the aromas wafting toward me. Toasted bread, bacon, and gooey cheese. Maybe I can swing by Snarf's for lunch on my way back to Vino Valentine.

Focus, Parker.

Jack opens a snack bag of chips and offers it to me. I gladly accept, munching on sweet and tangy BBQ crisps while Jack dives into his sub.

He lets out a moan. "Never disappoints."

The way he says that pegs him as a regular. "Do you live around here?" It strikes me that of the entire wedding party, Jack is the one I know the least about.

"I have an apartment in Denver, but I'm a man of the world."

I help myself to one more chip and return the bag, wanting to leave him more than crumbs. "What does that mean?"

"I'm a pilot."

"As in *We are now cruising at thirty thousand feet and please enjoy your complimentary bag of peanuts* pilot?"

He takes a break from his half-demolished sandwich and points at me with a chip. "Those peanuts have sustained me more than I care to admit."

I smile and venture, "That must be exciting."

"And exhausting." He wipes his hands on a napkin, head sagging. "My dad was a pilot, always made it seem exotic and romantic, bringing my mom and me trinkets from around the world. It never dawned on me until I followed in his footsteps that it was all an act." He purses his lips to the side. "One I fully perpetuate, now that I think of it."

I study Jack, from his mussed hair to his smooth Lacoste shirt to his Vans, uncertain what to make of that last statement. No doubt, he's a meticulous packer. "It doesn't seem that way to me."

"My guard must be down from, well"—he gestures broadly—"usually I'd be yammering on about my foreign escapades and bizarre anecdotes from a mile high. Truth is, I was in Paris Wednesday, Hong Kong Friday, and I don't even know what time zone I'm in now."

"Mountain Daylight," I supply cheerfully.

"Ah, that's why my wake-up call didn't come through," he quips.

I fan myself, the air-conditioning lagging behind as the temperature outside climbs toward triple digits. "The hangover yesterday?"

"Jet lag." He takes a swig of water from a bottle. "It makes everything hit you harder—elevation, booze. But I wanted to give my buddy a proper send-off."

While hangovers rarely imply innocence, I've gotta cut him some slack for putting his friend first.

"The perfect storm." I give him a sympathetic wince. "Speaking of storm, what's the deal with you and Josie? There seemed to be some history there."

He waves Josie off as if she were nothing more than a gnat. "She's just overemotional, like women get." He hurries to add, "No offense."

In my experience, whenever someone says *No offense*, it means they're wholly aware they are, in fact, causing offense but don't want the burden of responsibility.

Pity, I was just starting to warm to Jack.

Maybe Josie wasn't lying about *everything*. She warned me not to trust a word out of his mouth; I wonder what Jack lied to her about.

"She mentioned you two went on a date."

"Don't remind me, I'm trying to eat here." He exaggerates a feigned gag. "Can't believe I let Nash talk me into that."

"What was so terrible about it?"

"She wouldn't shut up about her ex, blubbered through the entire meal, and then got bent out of shape when I didn't call for a second date."

That sounds so much like Josie, I can't help but believe him. "How did you meet Nash, anyway?"

Sometimes there's no explaining friendships. Opposites attract in much the same way they do romantic couplings, balancing each other and creating a dynamic that's challenging and fruitful. Just look at Sage and me. She's the stereotypical indoor kid to my alfresco enthusiast, always partaking in the biggest fandom crazes whereas I can barely distinguish between Marvel and Tolkien, and, until recently, blasé toward grapes of any form while I make them my livelihood. But we come together on what matters.

For some reason, I can't picture the sweet and brilliant Nash being friends with Jack, let alone choosing him to be a groomsman.

"I've known Nash since college," Jack says. "He was on my floor in the dorms at Berkeley. I took it upon myself to make sure he got out of his room and had a good time once in a while."

Now *that* I could see. "Nash is a good guy."

"The best." His eyes flit to mine, shrewd and curious, as he licks a drop of mustard from his finger. "What's with all the questions?"

A dribble of sweat trickles down my back, making me shiver. "Just trying to wrap my mind around what happened yesterday."

He considers me with a nod. "Did my answers help?"

"We'll see." I get to my feet and shoulder my bag. "Enjoy the rest of your lunch."

I have a choice to make: get lunch or finish questioning the wedding party. I don't have time for both, my break already veering on excessive.

I must really love my family.

The maid of honor and best man are lounging beside an empty pool. Empty because it's under construction, but luckily, not at the moment, Sunday being a day of rest for some.

Patio furniture in various states of upkeep surround the tiled pool. Trees offer patches of shade and weeds creep their way through cracks in the concrete. A stale scent like tar mixed with chlorine hangs in the air, a fence blocking what would be a welcome breeze. I breathe through my mouth to counter the acrid scent, making my way to the deck, basked in sunlight.

Carolyn is lying on a lounge chair, her sunglasses on, her head tilted back, soaking up the rays in shorts and a tank top with the straps pulled down around her shoulders. My cousin is more relaxed than I've maybe ever seen her. I almost hate to interrupt.

While Xavier isn't quite as carefree, he's trying, clearly one of those people more at ease working than playing. He's in shorts and a T-shirt, his pale limbs scrawny and unaccustomed to sunlight, one arm draped across his thick-framed glasses to protect his eyes from the brightness.

It's interesting that they're together. Not *together-together*, mind you, just hanging out. I wonder if it was intentional or accidental that they both found themselves here.

I clear my throat to announce my arrival, rocking back and forth in my Birkenstocks, loose concrete sticking to the patterned tread.

Carolyn barely stirs, acknowledging my presence with a tart, "I hope you brought that giant glass of wine you owe me."

I snap my fingers. "I knew I forgot something."

She clicks her tongue and perches herself on her elbows, eyeing me over the rim of her sunglasses. "What are you doing here, then?"

"Sticking my nose into everyone's business."

"So, the usual?" she asks, smirking.

Carolyn is a successful product manager, a role that requires her to keep loads of details in her brain and cajole teams into getting their work done. Her demeanor gets her ahead in her professional life, but leaves her rather lonely otherwise. She's never had many friends, and even fewer lovers. Has never seemed all that interested in either, to be honest.

Xavier sits up, his back naturally curving into a hunch that bemoans hours spent tapping away at a keyboard. He rubs his palms on his shorts and gives me a half smile.

"We didn't get to chat much yesterday," I say. "You work with Nash, right?"

"Y-yes," he stammers. "We're partners."

"It's cool what you guys are researching—what you're trying to do." Removing carbon from the atmosphere could be a game changer in terms of climate relief. And who knows what other areas the technology could benefit? Like, say, winemaking.

"It won't fix everything," Xavier says modestly, pushing his glasses up his sweaty nose. "And it's only cool if we can pull it off."

"If there's anyone who can lead the front, it's you guys," Carolyn interjects. It's an uncharacteristically kind comment, although there's undeniably something about Xavier that makes one want to rush to his defense.

I plop down into a chair on the other side of Carolyn and instantly regret it, the plastic straps of the seat so stretched my bum nearly hits the ground. I readjust as nonchalantly as possible.

"What did you two make of everything yesterday?" I purposely leave my question vague to see how they interpret it, whether they direct the attention to or away from the murder.

"It was so sad about that poor woman," Xavier says. "Not that I knew her well, but you hate to see anyone go like that. Or go, period."

"Yeah," Carolyn agrees, lips pinched together so tightly

there's obviously something on the tip of her tongue. Something she's trying not to blurt out. Given this is Carolyn, the battle is soon lost. "Although Prynne didn't help her case."

I jump on that like a book club does a bottle of wine. "Meaning?"

"Why is it when someone dies they become a saint?" Carolyn asks. "The sadness of their death makes everyone forget what a nightmare they were."

Xavier, instead of looking stunned, nods thoughtfully beside Carolyn. "It's true. My perception of her has already shifted."

Has my own judgment been equally clouded? What could that mean for my pseudoinvestigation? I've seen Eli suffer a similar fate, witnessed firsthand how detrimental it can be. But in the end, it doesn't matter if someone is likable or not when it comes to justice.

"Honestly, I feel worse for Emma and Nash," Carolyn says.

"They were really eager to get married," Xavier says, running a hand through his curly hair. "Still are. Who knows when that'll happen now."

I tug on my jumper but desist for fear of tangling myself again in the chair. "Have they talked about trying to organize something else this weekend?"

"Oh, my dear stepmother has been filling their pretty little heads with all sorts of ideas," Carolyn says, her use of the term *stepmother* laden with sarcasm. "They don't seem to have bought into anything yet. Thank God."

"I just want them to be happy." Xavier is the solitary voice of reason in the wedding party, even my own cousin too jaded to see the forest for the trees.

"Me too." I flash him a warm smile. "Did either of you notice anything else odd yesterday?"

"Wow, you really are sticking your nose in it," Carolyn says, but then continues. "The caterer didn't seem too happy. Stormed out of the ballroom and nearly barreled into me and Harriet's cat. Didn't even apologize, or look twice at the cat, which you think she would."

"The caterer may have had other things on her mind," I muse. Like, how to compensate for the loss of ingredients and time, taking on a new client, committing murder. "Was she on the phone?"

"Not that I recall, but I could be mistaken. Everyone has their phones in their hands these days, it's easy to breeze over something so commonplace."

So, hardly a vote of confidence. I turn, hopeful, to Xavier.

That's when I catch it. A whiff of something piney and spicy in the stagnant air, as artificial as tar, only far more unsettling.

I lean forward, my butt sinking closer to the cement, downwind from Xavier. And nearly choke with recognition. Because he reeks of the cologne that was hovering over Prynne's dead body.

There's no mistaking that pungent aroma, and the physical reaction my body has to it. My fight-or-flight instincts trigger. My breathing grows erratic and goose bumps break out on my forearms. Every fiber of my being is longing to flee.

I let out a long exhale, calming my features into mild curiosity instead of escalating horror. Because if his cologne was around Prynne, that means he was, too.

"I missed all that," Xavier says, bringing me back to the present. "I was just trying to tie my tie correctly. And it still ended up crooked." He shakes his head, a curl springing loose from behind his ear.

"Was anyone with you?"

"No, Jack and Nash abandoned me, said to catch up with them after I finished wrestling with my tie. Blasted formal attire."

"At least you only had a tie to worry about. Imagine all the accessories women have to deal with," Carolyn says with an aggrieved sigh. "Heels, dresses that only an acrobat can zip, mascara wands!"

I nod along with her venting. "Statement jewelry, clutches, bouquets," I add, the latter uttered with purpose, side-eyeing Carolyn. "Did you ever lose track of your bouquet?"

"Wow, random, but of course. Everything was in chaos, I kept setting it down and having to go back for it."

"So, anyone could've gotten to it?" *And pilfered a petal to leave at the crime scene.*

"I guess," Carolyn says. Her phone pings and she checks it with an audible, "Ew."

"What?"

"Just another desperate attempt by Josie to gain approval by commandeering the bridal Slack channel." Carolyn flashes the screen at me and from the sheer number of exclamation points and emojis, she's not wrong.

"Wait, you set up a Slack channel for the bridal party?" I ask.

"What? It's efficient." She checks beneath the strap of her tank for a tan line. Seemingly satisfied, she nestles back. "For more intel, we will require payment. In the form of wine."

"Fair enough." I struggle to extricate myself from the chair, every limb needed to finally push myself free. "I'll come better prepared next time. For now, I'll leave you to this . . ." I trail off with a meandering gaze, uncertain how to describe the barren pool.

"Slice of paradise?" Carolyn suggests, to Xavier's obvious amusement.

He lets out a guffaw that morphs into an ungraceful snort, not remotely villainous, but startling all the same.

"Sure," I concede. "Let's go with that."

I pause in the doorway to the hotel, glancing back at the odd couple, who have settled into a hushed conversation.

There are unexpected food and wine pairings: Goldfish crackers and cabernet sauvignon, banana bread and chardonnay, tacos and Riesling. It takes desperation and resourcefulness to find those sorts of complements. People are no different; I wonder which united the unlikely duo behind me.

Chapter Eight

As soon as I return to Vino Valentine, I'm sucked into a whirlwind of motion.

I collect discarded stemware, pour tasters, and chat with customers about my winemaking process. The grapes harvested from Palisade on the Western Slope, fermenting techniques, and aging in steel versus oak. It's all so natural to me—comforting, even—that the afternoon passes in a blur.

Sloan helps, moving through the space double speed, having shrugged off her disappointment from the pop quiz earlier.

The crowd has thinned by the time my mom arrives. Her periodic table tote is clutched in one hand, a Tupperware in the other, and her hair bounces with unconfined energy.

"I did it. I found something," she says over the tasting bar countertop, bluish-gray eyes wide behind her cat-eye glasses. "About *you know what*."

"Okay, Miss Marple, give me a sec, then we'll go in the back." I deliver a tray of wine flights to an oak-barrel table in the middle of the floor, naming each varietal for the quartet of bubbly girlfriends chattering animatedly.

I fall in stride beside Sloan, practically having to jog to keep up. "I'll be in the back if you need me."

"Take your time," she answers, twirling a tray between her hands. "Things are *wining* down out here, anyway."

"Everything happens for a *Riesling*." I shoot her a wink.

Then I lead my mom into the warehouse space that serves as the grape equivalent of a Batcave. Vats stretch like giant stalactites to the ceiling, barrels containing aging reds line the perimeter like rounded rock fixtures, and my other equipment—crusher de-stemmer, winepress, and state-of-the-art bottling system—create a meandering path across the smooth cement. After the bustle of the last few hours, the silence is welcome.

Once we're settled, me perched on a metal stool and my mom in a spare folding chair, she passes me the Tupperware. It's warm to the touch and smells faintly of tomatoes, chilies, and cheese. "Is this what I think it is?"

"You know I can't make a batch without sharing with you, even with your father hovering like a vulture."

I retrieve a fork from a box of cutlery I keep on a utility shelf with my lab equipment. My mom's specialty—and really, only meal she knows how to make—is chicken enchiladas, spicy, savory, and satisfying. It's the ultimate comfort food for me, which I'm very vocal about.

First Reid plies me with food, and now my mom. It's

almost as if I'm being watched over. Conspiracy theorist? Possibly. But it seems too good to be true.

Utensil hovering over the dish, I narrow my eyes at my mom. "Did Reid put you up to this?"

"Absolutely not." She sets her tote on the floor, a fan of papers peeking out of the top. "But I know it must be hard with Reid out of town."

"You know I'm a grown woman, right? Fully capable of taking care of myself."

"I never said you weren't." My mom gives me a gentle smile. "You are independent and strong and I love that about you, but that doesn't mean you can't get lonely. That you can't struggle."

I shift my knees, my forgotten fork clinking against the container. "I want us to be able to do this." What I'm really saying is I want *me* to be able to do this.

"Do what?"

"Support each other, no matter where it takes us."

She nods in understanding. "One of the hard parts of relationships is figuring out how to grow together."

"Even if we're physically apart?"

"Especially then. You'll figure it out." There's something about a mother's reassurance that makes it feel true, like maybe everything will work out okay. She runs the backs of her fingers across my forehead like she used to do when I had nightmares as a child. "Until then, eat your enchiladas while they're still warm."

I waste no time tucking in. "Thank you," I say, although it comes more as "Aink ooh" around the bite in my mouth. If you could taste the heavenly tortilla-filled gooeyness, you'd understand my lack of decorum. Once I swallow, I say, "So, I ran into Grace."

My mom bristles, lines forming in her brow as she opens and closes her mouth. "But it was my job to talk to her."

"It's not like I sought her out," I say defensively, enchiladas momentarily forgotten as guilt sloshes in my chest. "I bumped into her at the motel and we had a quick chat. If you could even call it that."

My mom knows me well enough to read between the lines of my veiled explanation. "Did you ask her about Prynne?"

"Yes," I admit with a wince.

"I see." Her eyes drop to the floor as she exhales through her nose. "Parker, you accepted my help. I want to do my part, to at least have a shot, if you'll let me."

My mom excels at guilt trips and this one hits hard, exposing me for the control freak that I am. "I want your help. I do. It's just hard. Letting go."

"Oh, I understand that."

"I didn't mean to step on your toes, promise."

"We just can't help ourselves sometimes." She flashes me a knowing smile that only somewhat eases the shame prickling through me.

"Pray tell, what did you learn from Grace? I bet it was loads more than I did."

"Well, there's drama in the Cooper house."

"Isn't there always?" I gesticulate with my fork before taking a small bite.

"To some degree, but this is different. Chastity has been bossing Emma around and even Grace has had it."

I twist the lid off my water bottle and take a sip, my mouth on fire from the chilies. "Wow, that is serious."

When my uncle's affair came to light, Grace took the high road, which, for her, meant the quiet road. She decided the best revenge would be to emerge strong enough to not have to rely on anyone ever again. Only, when she achieved that, she forgot how it all started. Now she's a teacher and happy as a clam.

Not only did she regain her self-dignity, but also the respect of my mom (and trust me, that's not easily earned). It's hard to believe there was once a time we had to consciously separate them at family gatherings. That I had to listen to my mom gossip about how weak and shallow Grace was. Now we just have to abide her rants about my uncle.

"Grace has been encouraging Emma to stand up for herself, like she wishes she'd done while she was married to Michael."

My uncle wasn't an overbearing man, just a selfish one. Even during our conversations, it was often me broaching topics of mutual interest, not him. Which is saying something, given he's my senior by thirty years.

My mom continues, "Grace even cornered Michael yesterday to try and convince him to step in."

"Did he?"

"Doubt it," she says. "My brother doesn't like to make waves."

I raise my eyebrows at the hypocrisy of this statement after the tsunami he shocked his family with.

"The thing you have to understand about your uncle is sometimes he does things without realizing the rippling effects they could have." She hesitates, eyes drifting to the posters of heaping grapes on the wall behind me. "While he tries to steer clear of drama, it often finds him."

How ironic, I think. *That's how I feel about murder.*

"I bet Grace hated Prynne planning her daughter's wedding," I speculate, shoveling another forkful of enchiladas into my mouth.

"That's an understatement." My mom lowers her voice

to a whisper, even though no one else is within earshot. "It was Chastity's idea to hire her, and Grace has a hunch she orchestrated more than that."

"The huge ordeal, the dress, the decor."

My mom taps her nose while I polish off the rest of my lunch-slash-dinner, musing. I'd sensed as much, but the confirmation makes me nervous. How much was Eli likely to pick up on, and which target would he home in on?

I set the empty Tupperware aside. "What were you doing at work?"

"Ah, right." My mom wiggles in anticipation. "I had a theory about the perfume at the crime scene."

"Perfume? I assumed it was cologne. It had that sorta spicy, pine undertone." I don't add—not yet, not without knowing where she's going with this—that I'm fairly confident I know to whom it belongs.

"Nomenclature is irrelevant," she says. "I ran some analysis with an olfactometer."

A perk of my mom's company is access to the latest measurement doodads, NIST standing for the National Institute of Standards and Technology, from temperature to atomic clocks to smells, apparently, they offer the best in scientific tools.

"It looks at the dilution of odors by capturing chemical molecules that trigger the olfactory receptors."

Memories of middle school science fair projects flash through my mind. Times when I was equal parts frustrated and awed by my mother, her intellect a deep ocean I can scarcely imagine. "In English, please?"

"It's a way to quantify smell." She naturally shifts into chemist mode. "Perfume—or cologne—is a combination of essential oils and a water-ethanol compound. When you spritz your signature scent into the air, moisture droplets and vapor are expelled into the atmosphere. It's how these interact when they come into contact with skin and the atmosphere that leaves behind a detectable odor."

"Okay, I'm following, I think, and wholly impressed."

"You're only saying that because you feel bad about talking to Grace."

"I mean it," I scoff. "I didn't even know this was a thing and it legit sounds cool."

She reaches for the papers in her bag, shoving the top one into my hands. "This is a graph of how scent dilutes over time." She points to a scatterplot and trend line reminiscent of algebra. "This red trend line shows a natural course of diminishing concentration, when the water-ethanol and oils evaporate, leaving behind the vapor."

I take the extended paper in my hand and study it, rubbing my chin. The red line is a gentle slope downhill, a bunny hill compared to the other one. "And the blue line?"

"Shows the levels at the crime scene. Reenacted with the olfactometer, for directional purposes."

"Does this mean what I think it means?"

"The odor we detected around Prynne was too strong to have been a lingering whiff attached to the killer."

And finally, I understand. "It was added after Prynne was already dead?"

She immediately does that annoying scientist thing where she qualifies her findings, wobbling her head back and forth. "That's impossible to tell without knowing the exact time of death, but based on the experiments I ran, yeah. It could only be a matter of minutes."

"Another planted clue."

I deflate, letting the paper fall to my lap.

This doesn't mean Xavier is off the hook by any means, but it offers another explanation as to how his god-awful cologne might have ended up on the scene. Only, who else had access to it?

"What now, Nancy Drew?" My mom asks, sitting up straight.

At her eagerness, I find my voice. "Can you call the caterer? I left a voice mail and never heard back, which seems weird since you'd think she'd jump on any potential business."

"You can count on me."

You know the saying: *Keep your friends close and your enemies closer.* But what if they're one and the same? Even only temporarily.

My preferred climbing gym features a bouldering cave and lofty climbing walls with routes of varying difficulty, all framed by bright murals of notorious Colorado peaks. There's an oxygen chamber in an adjoining room that mimics higher altitude—higher than our already impressive 5,280 feet, that is—along with a series of grips to strengthen fingertips.

The Spot, which is its actual name, caters to professional climbers, aficionados, and beginners alike. Rock music plays over speakers and a tang of sweat and chalk permeates the air.

An instructor teaches a lead-climbing class, a skill even I'm not qualified for, sporty coeds swap belaying ropes—and gossip—at a bench near the locker rooms, and people clamber on and off walls. All told, there's a general hubbub that gives the impression of privacy—anonymity.

I find Eli in the bouldering cave, a smaller space with a black mat stretched across the floor and lower ceilings. He maneuvers from one hold to the next, the lean muscles in his arms and back flexing as his legs shift to support him from below.

Bouldering is pure climbing. No ropes, no harness, no safety net. With routes that don't go too high, it's just you and the bright-colored grips that depict various paths, more about the puzzle than the adrenaline rush.

I plop down on the cushioned floor and lace up my shoes. They're snug on my feet, borderline too tight, perfect for wedging into crevices or summiting mountains. Along with the flexible leggings and tank I changed into, I'm ready to traverse the most rugged terrain. At least, theoretically.

Eli reaches the end of his route and dismounts. I applaud and whistle, to his embarrassment. If I can keep him off-kilter, perhaps I can glean information about the case. About where he sees my family fitting in.

Eli dips his chin against his worn tee. Outside of work, his attire primarily revolves around bands from his misspent youth, this one being Pearl Jam.

"Must you always make a scene?" he asks, his neck tinged pink.

I strap my chalk bag around my waist. "No, but it's more fun."

He shakes his head, a dark strand of hair falling over his forehead. "So, should we address the elephant in the room?"

"What elephant?"

"The real reason you insisted on climbing tonight." He crosses his arms over his chest. "There haven't been any new developments in the investigation."

What he's really saying is this: there haven't been any new developments *that he can share*.

I change tactics. "Honestly, I'm hurt you think that's why we're here. When what I really want is a game of eliminator."

Eliminator is a bouldering game where climbers take

turns removing holds from a route until someone falls. The purpose is to encourage creativity and explore new ways of moving your body. It also serves as an appropriate segue to the conversation I intend to have with Eli.

"Okay," he says. He rubs his thumb across his eyebrow in obvious disbelief. "Purple, then."

My eyes dance over the route, making mental note of potential pitfalls, of which there are plenty.

I sashay to the start, hunch myself into a ball, and place my feet on the grips, mere inches above the mat. While starting in a compressed position, this trek will soon be challenging for how far apart each grip is, even without any eliminations. Eli was smart to pick a route that would favor his height.

My muscles are taut as I careen from one hold to the next, shifting my weight and stretching my legs from pointed toe to hinged hip, until I reach the other side.

I hop down and tap one of the grips near the start, signaling to Eli which one he has to avoid.

While his back is to me, I ask, "How are things going with Alyssa?"

Alyssa came climbing once, I suspect to make sure the woman belaying her boyfriend wasn't romantic competition (spoiler alert: I'm not). But she held her own on the wall, ribbed Eli more than I do, and sent a few of her design clients to Vino Valentine. In short, I approve.

"Great. We're taking a trip next month, our first together."

"That's a big step," I say, impressed. "I've always thought traveling together is a good indicator of a relationship, like a canary in a coal mine. Where are you going?"

"San Francisco," he grunts as he dismounts, tapping a grip at the end.

"Reid's there now." I pull myself and my emotions back onto the wall.

I wonder if Eli can sense the weirdness in my voice, all the things I'm not saying. That I'm not sure how I feel about the physical distance between Reid and me and what it might mean for our future. Probably. That's one of the downsides of being buddies with a detective; very little escapes their notice.

"Ah, I wondered why he wasn't at the wedding," Eli says. "Pass on any recommendations."

"Will do." I finish the route and point to a hold at the beginning. So far, we're going easy on each other. Which means it's time to steer this conversation into the danger zone. "You know what I like about this game?"

"What?"

"It challenges your perspective, makes you think about which grips are really needed and which you can do without."

Eli heaves a sigh as he steadily crosses the wall, staying focused until the end. He dismounts and smacks a grip in the center that will be tricky to bypass. No more Mr. Nice Guy. Then he whirls on me, pointer finger extended in my direction. "I knew it."

"Fine, I *might* have an ulterior motive for wanting to climb tonight," I admit. I straighten my back and roll my shoulders in exaggerated circles. "I have a lot of pent-up stress."

"And you thought you could needle details pertinent to the case."

To delay answering, I take my turn. I sense Eli's gaze on me as I climb, adding extra chalk on my fingers before attempting a lunge over the recently eliminated hold, the next one well out of reach.

Sometimes, in climbing and in life, you just have to go

for it. Take a leap of faith, against all logic and reason. As long as there's a cushion to land on.

I lead with my foot, leaning into the bumpy surface as I shift my weight. My toes slip as I strain to find purchase and I lurch backward. A swooping sensation turns my stomach upside down, and I ram my side into the wall. I double down; it's now or never. I throw my hand out, my fingertips grappling for the bit of protruding plastic.

And I nail it.

Elated—and more than a little stunned—by my success, I finish the route with ease. My heart is still pounding when I land on the mat. A mischievous grin blooms on my face, I pat the next grip to be ignored. Avoiding it will definitely spell doom for me on my next turn, unless it knocks Eli out first.

"If you thought that's why I asked you to meet me, why did you agree?"

He considers my query, and the nearly impossible feat I've set for him.

I've gotta give him props for effort. Eli gives it his all, swinging back and forth by one hand to gain momentum like a human pendulum, but when he tries to stick his landing, he flails and falls flat on his back.

I extend a hand and he takes it, gingerly getting to his feet. "I'm here because we're friends." He rubs his side, limping slightly toward a bench. "At least, I thought we were before you made me do that."

"I made you do nothing," I quip, fully aware his competitive streak rivals mine. "And we are friends. And they're my family. Can you blame me for doing all I can?"

The fire in his eyes dims. "I guess not."

I readjust my headband, my muscles smarting from exertion. "Now that we got that out of the way, what did you make of all the clues at the crime scene?"

Climbing is an exercise in trust. You rely on your belaying partner to spot you. To check the fastenings on your harness, feed enough slack into the rope so you can scamper up the wall, and react quickly should the worst happen.

The worst happened to me last year. My harness was tampered with and it's purely thanks to Eli's skill and quick reflexes that I'm still standing. He's proven to be not only trustworthy, but someone I want to have watch my back. Given that he continues climbing with me, I can only assume he feels the same way. Despite my more annoying habits.

We stand before a climbing wall in the back room, below a loudspeaker, to camouflage our conversation. "Of course I noticed the sheer amount of evidence," Eli says. "I am adept at my job, you know."

"Oh, I know. This has nothing to do with your skill and everything to do with wanting to protect my family."

I step into my funky orange harness, two loops that are snug on my upper thighs with a belt that secures around my waist. I click my chalk back into a gear loop with a carabiner. Then I work on the two figure-eight knots that connect the lead ropes to my harness and, in turn, to Eli.

Eli checks over each knot and buckle, and grunts his approval. "Even planted evidence can reveal clues as to the identity of the culprit. What red herrings they chose, where they want to direct our attention; they're all pieces to a grander puzzle."

"Different clusters, same vine." I look into his brown

eyes—warm, intelligent, and worried. "The footprints, the cologne—"

"Scents are hard to rely on since they're subjective and dissipate so quickly."

I think of my mom and her reenactment of the crime scene with the olfactometer, the graphs of data that, while perhaps not admissible in court, prove odor interference. Not that Eli needs to know that; if he disapproves of me snooping, I can't begin to imagine what he'd say if he found out my mother was involved, too.

Eli runs his end of the rope through the belaying device that attaches to the front of his harness. "The footprints, however, tell me the killer wants us to believe it's an outside job."

I check his handiwork and nod, my brow furrowed. "But the flower petal . . ."

"Insinuates it was internal, someone in the wedding party."

I take a step away from Eli and turn toward the wall, chewing on my lower lip. "I can't picture any of them doing it, though."

"I understand," he says hurriedly, placating. "Whoever did this is smart. They knew they wouldn't have a lot of time and carefully planned their crime to cause confusion, to blur fact from fiction."

A shiver snakes up my spine as I pull myself onto the lowest holds.

As I climb, I muse over what Eli imparted, my arms and legs seemingly moving of their own accord, ropes dangling below me. Entropy is the universe's natural tendency toward chaos. But sometimes it's helped along. By natural disasters, politics, mischievous pets, or, in this case, a murderer.

If the clues at the scene of the crime are still helpful, that means none can be discarded. Including the one I haven't wanted to consider: the strand of silvery-blond hair.

Because I only know one person with hair like that who was in attendance, and it couldn't have been her. Grace would never . . .

Only, she did confide in my mom that she was sick of Chastity bossing her daughter around. Was it possible that after everything, Grace finally snapped? That the calm and accepting front she put on was nothing more than that—an act?

I reach the top of the route in a daze, the dizzying height and my smarting biceps the only indications I'd actually climbed. Music blaring, louder up here than on the ground, I flash Eli the signal—a thumbs-up—and start back down, taking care to pay attention as I bounce off the wall in gentle arcs until my toes reconnect with solid ground.

"Let me ask you a question," Eli says. "Do you know an Earnest Merriwether?"

I go about the routine of untangling myself from ropes. "Should I?"

"Not necessarily," Eli replies, his gaze calculating. "An agent noticed a disparity. Mr. Merriwether was questioned with the other attendees but wasn't on the supplied guest list, nor is he in our system."

"Earnest Merriwether?" I ask again. I read something once that if you repeat a name you're less likely to forget it, and this is a name I want ingrained in my brain.

Eli nods in confirmation. "Thought you might be able to shed some light."

"Sorry I can't be of help," I answer. "But it is interesting . . ."

"Undeniably."

The name sounds old-timey, made up, or like a cruel joke on a kid. "I'll ask around and let you know."

Eli clenches his jaw and gives me a hard look. "Let the record show I asked you to do no such thing."

My lips tighten into a grim smile. "Noted."

We don't talk much the rest of our session, alternating climbing and belaying until we're worn out, each of us lost in our own muddled thoughts.

As I leave the gym and make my way to the bus, I text Emma, inviting her and Nash to meet me for dinner on Pearl Street. My treat. Although, as any budding entrepreneur worth their grapes will tell you, there's no such thing as a free lunch—er, dinner. And there's something I'm very much hoping to get in return.

Chapter Nine

If millennials have a phobia of phone calls, that's nothing compared to how we feel about spontaneous drop-bys. Which is why I practically pull a button loose from the blouse I'm changing into at the knock on my apartment door later that night.

I look to Zin and William, as if they could have been responsible for the noise. Zin is fast asleep on the end of my bed and William is giving his squishy guitar toy what for in the kitchen.

Goose bumps prickle my arms and unease seeps through my veins. Possibilities flit through my mind, each more alarming than the last. Package delivery, solicitor, murderer.

I snag my pepper spray and press one eye against the peephole. And feel completely ridiculous.

I stash the pepper spray back in my purse and unlock the dead bolt. The door swings open to reveal Sage.

She's in short overalls with a *Star Wars* crop top underneath, her hair pinned into a bun on top of her head by sticks I suspect are actually wands. She clutches a bottle of wine in her hand, one of my favorite pinots with a label that features mug shots from crimes committed in yesteryear.

"What are you doing here?"

"Nice to see you, too," Sage says. She nudges past me and makes herself at home.

I glance outside in either direction before closing the door. Crickets chirp lazily and the evening air is warm, humid, and calm. *Jeez, Parker, don't be so paranoid.*

I pad into the kitchen to find Sage wielding my corkscrew like the newb she still is. She takes the twisted metal to the cork in such a clumsy manner, I fret over the amount of debris that will end up in our glasses.

"Here." I gesture for the wine and opener.

Sage acquiesces and, while I twist, flummoxed by her presence, words pour out of her mouth in a steady stream. "So, I thought we could start with some *Grey's* then move on to that cheesefest of a romcom that will inevitably make me cry." She procures two glasses from my cabinet, plunking them down in front of me. "Food, of course, will be involved. Preferably delivery because I don't plan on moving once I plant myself over there." She points to the couch, where William has retreated, his tail twitching at the newcomer.

"Objection," I say, unsure how else to get her attention.

"Overruled." She riffles through takeout menus in my junk drawer. "Whatever your objection is, it can't stretch so far as McDreamy."

I peer at her. There aren't any signs of stress that usually prompt a girl's night—bunched shoulders, clenched jaw, undercurrent of rage—so it must be something else. "While that's usually the case, I've gotta ask, Why are you really here?"

"To spend quality time with my best friend." Only, it's clear from how her blue eyes dart from the coffeepot to the balcony doors to a spot over my shoulder, that isn't the full story.

"And?" I raise an eyebrow at her.

She blows out an exhale, wisps of strawberry-blond hair flying away from her face. "Because I thought you might like some company, and I knew if I texted, you'd say you were fine and turn down my offer."

"You're not wrong." I pour us each a glass of wine and lead the way to the couch. I settle in beside William, scratching behind his ears soothingly. To be honest, I'm not sure which one of us needs it more. "First Reid, then my mom, and now you. Does no one think I can handle a few days on my own?" *If no one else thinks I can, who am I trying to kid?*

"Stop it," Sage snaps. "That's not it at all. You have people who care about you and want to be there for you. Especially after the trauma of yesterday. Suck it up, lady."

"Ouch." I sip my wine, chastised.

"Sorry, seemed like you needed some tough love." Sage sinks back into the cushion and indulges in her own glass of pinot. "Is that chocolate I detect?"

I take another sip, swishing the wine around in my mouth. "Spot on," I agree after swallowing. I clink my glass with hers. "The student becomes the master."

"Well, I did learn from the best." She basks in our shared glory for a moment before piercing me with the laser focus of her blue eyes. "Now, fess up, why all the self-doubt?"

"It's just, I can't help but think about Reid and me and

where we'll be in five years, ten years, et cetera." I twirl my hand in the air and William mews for me to continue showering him with attention. I oblige, petting the silky fur along his back.

"Ah, I see," Sage says, well, sagely. "Liam went through the same thing. All the marriage talk got to you."

She tilts her head to the side, unblinking, and I crumble, much like I assume witnesses do under her cross-examination. "Ugh, you might be right."

"I'm definitely right. Your brother isn't the type to instigate relationship talks and he was in a tither after your great-aunt Harriet put a bug in his ear."

Despite the circumstances, my lips twitch into a smile. I can't wait to rib Liam about that little tidbit. For now, though, I have my own problems to hash out.

I lean forward, rubbing my palms on my skinny jeans. "The thing is, I think it's the right time for Reid and me to talk through some of this stuff. Make sure we're on the same page and want the same things."

"That's totally fair," she grants. "Just remember relationships look different for everyone, and it's no one else's business what you and Reid decide to do, or *not* do." She tugs at the frayed denim hem of her shorts. "Heck, I don't know if I ever want to get married."

"Really? But you were engaged." I think back to her ex-fiancé, the guy who was wrong for her in so many ways, and how it almost shattered her—and our friendship—to figure it out.

"Yeah, and that turned out great," she says with a sarcastic snort. "The more I think on it, the more I wonder, what's the point? And this has nothing to do with my mama drama."

My heart pangs for my friend, whose mama drama, as she likes to call it, surpasses the norm. Growing up with a mother who saw herself as a doormat for men and a force to be heeded by her daughter left deep scars. No wonder Sage turned to fantasy worlds as a kid.

Sage tilts her glass to the side, the ruby giving way to blush before turning translucent at the edge, continuing, "I mean, I know there are legal benefits, but there are other avenues to those. And for some, it's about making a commitment in front of family and friends, which I don't know if I need."

I feel like I'm seeing a fully grown version of my friend. My eyes grow misty with pride and maybe something else, until I remember who her significant other is. "Did you say all this to Liam?"

"Yeah. Pretty sure that wasn't what he expected, and something tells me he might want the whole shebang, whether he realizes it or not." A bemused expression flits across her face. "But we'll figure it out, just like you and Reid will." She gives my leg a hearty pat. "You're good together. Don't get in your head too much."

My throat clenches. "Where have you been the last twenty-four hours?"

"At the other end of a text or, gasp, call." She brings her free hand to her cheek in feign horror. "You don't have to be Miss Independent about everything."

I suppress a groan. How many times am I going to have to learn that lesson before it finally sinks in? But now that she mentions it . . .

"Hey," I say. "What are you doing right now?"

"Hanging out with you, duh. I thought we already covered this."

"Yes, but there's another component to my objection. I have dinner plans with Emma and Nash. Why don't you tag along? We could use your rationale." This idea is growing on me by the minute. "Maybe you can convince my cousin to speak up for what she wants." *And camouflage my snooping.* I add the cinching factor, "My treat."

"That depends," Sage says, waffling. "Where are we going?"

As if my friend would ever turn down free food. "Don't worry, it won't disappoint."

Spoons is many things: upscale farm-to-table restaurant, live-music venue, and trendy happy hour scene. But to me, it's a sanctuary.

Reid's restaurant is an extension of him, and I see and feel him everywhere. In the seasonal menu printed on re-cycled paper, rustic decor tinged with musical influences, stage where bands perform on weekend nights, and, natu-rally, the bedecked-yet-comfortable kitchen.

It's quieter than usual, it being Sunday night, but given "the usual" is fit to bursting, most of the tables are full. The chatter of well-tended and happy diners floats through the space. Flickering lanterns painted with staves and trumpets repurposed into sconces give off ambient light. And the smells are heavenly, an ode to the five tastes: sweet, salty, sour, bitter, and umami.

Emma and Nash are waiting when Sage and I traipse through the door. They're dressed to slay, Emma in a mini-skirt and loose tank with layered chain necklaces, and Nash in fitted khakis and a dark tee that leaves little to the imag-ination. They seem at ease in the chic environment, proof that my cousin is more capable than most give her credit for.

"Thanks for meeting me," I say by way of a greeting. "You remember Sage. She was *desperate* to hang out with me so I invited her along."

Sage elbows me in the ribs. "Hope you don't mind me crashing your party."

"The more the merrier," Emma says, and Nash nods beside her, perusing a menu. "This place is fantastic."

"That it is."

Given I'm basically the First Lady of Spoons, I'm treated like royalty. The hostess seats us at a prime table with a view of the kitchen, and a server I'm friendly with gives me a hug along with our water glasses.

"Did I know you were coming in?" Katie asks. Since she has to hear an order only once to remember it, we both know she didn't forget. The server gig is purely to finance her master's degree in art therapy, which she's steadily been working toward.

"Spur-of-the-moment outing to show my cousin and her fiancé a good time."

"Well, you've come to the right place," Katie says, tossing her festooned hair, bejeweled with sparkly barrettes, over her shoulder. "Can I get you something to drink?"

The wine list may be small, but it's impressive, showcasing mostly Colorado labels, primarily Vino Valentine. "A glass of the Campy Cab for me."

"Same," Emma says.

"Better make it a bottle," Sage adds, gesturing at me with her thumb. "This one's buying."

Nash rounds out our order with a pale ale from a local microbrewery. "Hazed & Infused, please."

"You've got it," Katie says before disappearing behind the bar, adjacent to the stage.

I glance around, absorbing the sights and sounds. All in all, everything seems to be running smoothly in Reid's absence. Which is another mark in favor of his expanding.

Katie returns with our drinks. She deposits Nash's frothy

beer in front of him and then, with an added flourish, opens and pours our wine. "So," she starts as she deposits a glass in front of each of us, "how adventurous are we feeling tonight?"

"We're always up for trying new things," Emma responds, wriggling in her seat in anticipation.

"Good answer." I rub my hands together and answer for the table, "Chef's choice. As long as it's vegan. With a cheese plate." I throw Emma a wink.

A devilish grin spreads across Katie's face. "That can be arranged."

"Wow, is service always this good?" Nash asks.

"Always." I swirl my glass of wine on the table and then sniff, familiar aromas tickling my nose. "I propose a toast to Emma and Nash. To your future." We clink glasses and I take a sip, letting the smoky and fruity notes roll over my tongue.

"How did you two meet?" Sage asks.

"Through friends," Emma starts, blushing adorably. "Neighbors in my old apartment building invited me to go out with them to meet some guys they knew. Nash was there and the rest is history."

"Although," Nash cuts in, "technically we met before that. In the stairwell months earlier when I was on my way to see them and you were on your way out. You pointed out gum on a step and I joked about how that would've made the climb to the sixth floor even harder. When you laughed, all I could think was that I wanted to keep talking to this girl."

Sage lets out an audible sigh. "Sounds like it was fate."

"It sure started that way." Emma purses her lips, obviously thinking of recent events.

"Have you considered rescheduling your nuptials?" Sage asks.

"We've talked about it," Emma says, "but I feel like we've been living in wedding madness for so long, I just want it to be over and done with. Which doesn't really seem like the time for what's supposed to be the happiest day of your life."

"It'll be a happy day, no matter how or when it happens." Nash laces his fingers through Emma's.

"And what matters are all the days that come after, not the day itself," Sage says.

I nod as if this were new advice Sage was dispensing and not the exact same wisdom she bestowed upon me last Valentine's Day.

Nash cuts a look at Emma in a way that says, *I told you so* and Emma tilts her head as if to reply, *I hear you*. And, if I'm not mistaken, coursing between them is a flicker of something resembling hope.

Or maybe it's just hunger.

Our cheese board comes ridiculously fast. No doubt the kitchen put all other orders on hold to accommodate our table. I would scold them for giving us preferential treatment, but I—or rather, my stomach—is too appreciative.

The assortment would make angels sing. Brie, cheddar, chèvre, and blue cheese, interspersed with rustic crackers, fresh and dried fruits, and a balsamic glaze for drizzling.

While the girls dig in to the creamy offerings, Nash helps himself to a date.

"Carolyn and Xavier sure seem to be hitting it off," I say around a nibble of sharp cheddar. "Who would've seen that coming?"

"You sure it was Carolyn?" Emma asks.

"They were lounging poolside earlier."

"Should I warn Xav?" Nash shoots Emma a worried glance before explaining for Sage's and my benefit, "He tends to get attached rather quickly where women are concerned."

"And Carolyn isn't the type to attach herself to anyone, or put up with being an attach-ee," Emma says. "It wouldn't hurt, just so Xav doesn't end up heartbroken."

Nash whips out his phone and unlocks it with a swipe. His fingers fly across the screen as he composes and sends a message. "Done."

It's funny how notoriety can build. With actions, sure, but also a few choice words. Take the movie *Sideways*; its jokes about merlot nearly toppled the varietal. Pity needles me for Carolyn. But I know where she'd tell me to shove that, so I tamp my emotions down with a wedge of Roquefort.

"Josie has enough heartache for the lot," I venture, not so subtly changing the topic. "I had no idea her engagement ended the day before their wedding."

"Ohmygod," Sage says. She licks a drop of balsamic from her finger so it isn't abundantly clear if she's exclaiming over the food or my revelation. "I can't imagine how tough that would be. Was it recent?"

"Last year," Emma says, eyes downcast. From the way she rolls her lips together, I can tell she longs to say more, but unlike her sister, she possesses restraint.

I take another swallow of wine, a pleasant buzz settling around me and spurring me onward. "And I bumped into Jack over lunch."

"You were really making the rounds." Nash directs a nervous chuckle toward Emma.

"You get used to it," Sage supplies cheekily, sitting up straight in her seat.

"Thanks, friend." I focus on Nash, across the table. "Jack said you two have known each other since college." I leave the statement hanging, inviting him to elaborate.

"We were on the same floor in the dorms. He was a wild man. Still is, for that matter." Nash flashes us his dazzling smile and takes a swig of ale. "Not who I usually gravitated toward as far as friends go."

"What made you, then?"

"He was determined to show me a good time, said I was making everyone else look bad with all my studying." Nash shrugs. "But I suppose it was the night we got to talking and I learned he lost his dad, too. We have that in common."

"I'm sorry," I say.

"It was a long time ago."

"I'm still sorry."

"Now Jack's our go-to for travel advice, always knows the best places to visit and sights to see," Emma says, slathering goat cheese onto a cracker. "He even helped us pick where to go on our honeymoon."

"Ooh, where are you going?" Sage asks.

"Peru." Emma sighs dreamily. "To hike Machu Picchu."

"And mountain bike through the Sacred Valley," Nash finishes.

These two were clearly made for each other, and are way more adventurous than I expected.

"That sounds incredible." Sage hurries to clarify, "For you. Take me to Comic-Con and I'll be yours forever."

"Noted," I say.

Our food arrives, putting a hold on conversation. The

chef's choice is a smorgasbord of regional ingredients and a cornucopia of vegetables. Flatbread dotted with garlic, rosemary, and halved grapes; grilled Palisade peaches tossed with peppery arugula and curried chickpeas; and a citrusy spin on succotash with legumes, corn, and blistered cherry tomatoes that burst like fireworks over my taste buds.

It's served family style and we act like family, shamelessly going back for second and third helpings until we've scraped each platter clean.

We chat about small nothings: the food, the best places to go on Pearl Street for a nightcap, the drought plaguing our state.

Katie whisks away the ruins of our devoured feast and Reid's world-class pastry chef appears a moment later, balancing four plates on a tray.

Britt's desserts are as impressive as her toned arms. While I used to find her intimidating, I've since learned she's as layered as the cakes she bakes, an arresting exterior that yields to soft buttercream. She has a platinum pixie cut, steely-gray eyes, and a tattoo of cursive along her neck that reads "Time is undefeated," wisdom courtesy of Rocky Balboa.

A woman of few words, she deposits our desserts on the table with a curt description. "Berry crumble with coconut sorbet."

"This looks incredible, Britt." I lean over the plate and breathe in the jammyness of the raspberries and blackberries, tang of orange zest, warming cinnamon and nutmeg, and creamy sorbet.

Britt lingers near my chair while the others dig in. "I didn't take you for the sentimental type."

"Huh?" I'm the epitome of eloquence with my mouth stuffed full of crumble.

"You're missing Reid, aren't you?" I've always suspected Britt saw more than most, and her unwavering gaze now leaves me feeling exposed. "That's why you came here tonight."

"And because it's where all the cool people are."

"Yeah, right." Britt pats my arm as she walks by, saying louder, "Y'all enjoy."

Britt returns to her domain and I turn my attention to the real reason I invited Emma and Nash out tonight. "Do either of you know an Earnest Merriwether?"

Sure, I could've asked this question via text, but so much is missed that way. Like frowns, sudden twitches, flushing cheeks, eye contact or the lack thereof. Physical reactions portend lies. And emojis, while adding nuance and humor to messages, go only so far.

I study the couple now, my gaze flitting from one to the other. They appear equally perplexed, and at ease.

"No," Emma says.

"Never heard of him," Nash says. "Why?"

"He was at your wedding yesterday." No need to burden them with my inkling that this unexpected guest could be responsible for the tragedy that derailed their vows.

"Could've been a plus-one," Sage offers.

"True." I drum my fingers on the table, far from satisfied with that answer.

At some point in the evening, Reid tried calling. I notice only when I'm back at my apartment, cozy in pajama shorts and a hoodie.

I dial him back but it goes straight to voice mail. I opt for a text: *Sorry I missed you. I was busy being lauded over at Spoons. Everyone says hi btw <3*

Too wired for sleep, I nestle into the couch, draping my favorite afghan blanket around my shoulders, more for security than warmth. Zin and William soon flank me, curling up on either side for a good night's sleep. You know, because the hours of naps they undoubtedly took weren't enough.

I pet each furry head in turn and, to the soundtrack of faint kitty snores, open my laptop. Hopefully the screen will illuminate more than my living room.

I start with a simple Google search for "Earnest Merriwether" but there are too many hits. Then I try "Earnest Merriwether Colorado" which yields nada. Perplexed and growing somewhat desperate, I type "Earnest Merriwether wedding." That's when I strike gold.

I know who Earnest Merriwether is.

I know why he isn't in whatever system Eli referred to, and why his name sounds like a figment of someone's imagination.

The Earnest Merriwether I've been looking for doesn't exist.

He's fiction. An alter ego created by the host of a podcast titled *Earnestly Crashing Weddings*, wherein a guy named Kyle Garcia picks a wedding to crash each week and then rates his experience.

And this Kyle Garcia? I recognize him as the knobby-kneed, harried guest who kept kicking the back of my chair while we were waiting for the authorities to question us. I recall his rust-colored hair and the scar at the corner of his lips, and his twitchiness. What I took for impatience as he checked his smartwatch over and over was really frayed nerves.

He thought he was about to be found out—or worse, accused of a crime.

Eagerly, I click on the most recent episode to find it's titled: "The One with the Murder."

My jaw drops. Literally drops. Then clenches again. Because this guy has some nerve.

How dare he crash my cousin's wedding! And then narrate the disastrous event for entertainment's sake!

A cold fury roars through me.

I slam my laptop shut, smoke practically spouting from my ears.

But then Zin and William gaze at me in that loving-yet-accusatory way of cats. Zin lets out a mew, nuzzling her head against the corner of my computer.

"Oh, fine." I scratch behind her ears and she lets out a rumble. The purr calms me, making me wonder if perhaps there is something to the research claiming cats lower stress.

I reopen my laptop and click play, snuggling deeper into the cushion.

Kyle Garcia's voice is deep and gravelly and oddly soothing. There's a cadence to how he speaks. He's a natural.

I listen as he describes the venue, decor, vendors, wedding party, and guests in ingratiating detail. He really noticed everything.

He talks about the construction and the dust, the ridiculous amount of tulle and vases of peonies (which apparently give him the sniffles). The bickering match between the mother and father of the bride, flighty wedding planner, canoodling bridesmaid and groomsman, and rebellious ring bearer.

My ears perk up as he mentions me. Not by name, thank God, but by conversation.

"Apparently," he says, "this sort of drama isn't out of the norm for this family, as one rather attractive guest was quick to impart her experience with law enforcement."

Which, admittedly, isn't so bad. I've been called worse than attractive.

Only, he continues, "With gate-crashing, I've come to expect some theatrics, but not ones that threaten my life. That's why, for the first time ever, I'm giving a wedding a negative score."

"How rude!" Red clouds my vision. I mean, this guy must have a brass pair of something. It's not Emma and Nash's fault that everything went to hell in a tulle-lined handbasket.

I throw my head back and take a deep breath, stroking Zin's soft gray fur. She peers at me with one eye, contorting herself into a spiral with her paws facing the popcorn ceiling. William, not to be left out, gives a doleful mew. I pet him, too, hoping the additional cat is enough to calm me down. *How many cats am I going to need if this keeps up? Where's the research on that?*

Silence presses in around me, seeping in and lulling my rage into a low simmer.

I press play and start the episode from the beginning and, once it finishes, I listen again. And again.

Three things stand out to me.

First, the canoodling bridesmaid and groomsman must have been Carolyn and Xavier, whom I've seen together since, especially considering the bad blood between Jack and Josie. Did Nash's warning to his business partner come too late? Could we all have misjudged Carolyn?

Second, Grace was more vocal than I realized in her malcontent with the control being exerted over Emma. She knew her daughter, and knew the wedding wasn't her at all. It was Prynne and Chastity and maybe even a little bit Harriet with her cat. Basically, everyone had a say except for the bride and groom.

And third, the prevalence of peonies in the ballroom. Anyone could have snagged a petal and left it at the scene of the crime. Which was already the case with how careless Carolyn had been with her bouquet, but still . . .

I grind my teeth in frustration. How am I still floundering about with meaningless evidence? How am I not further along in solving this thing?

So, I tell myself the lie I do at the end of hard days: Tomorrow is another day. The case will still be there for the cracking and future Parker has got this. Good luck, future me.

I grab my phone and discover a series of texts from Reid. *Glad you got first-class treatment at Spoons. I'd have to kick some ass if that wasn't the case.*

I snort, knowing full well that Reid is only half-kidding.

I decided on a location. I can imagine you sipping wine on the patio.

A picture accompanies this text. Of an aging wooden deck, the planking splitting in places, paint peeling from the side of a decrepit structure. It's the location on the water, the one Reid said would need borderline too much TLC, and he wasn't exaggerating. But that view. It overlooks the bay with its vast waves, rocky outcrops, and, if I'm not mistaken, seals basking in the sunshine.

Even as a knot in my throat bobs at what that could mean, I can't help but smile. I can see myself sipping wine there, too. Well, to be fair, I can picture myself with a glass of wine almost anywhere, but especially there.

And his last text, sent thirty minutes ago: *Miss you. Love you.*

I tap out a response and listen to the *whoosh* as it flies over the Rocky Mountains and state lines and all the way to Reid. *Looks incredible! Can't wait to see it in person. Any*

chance for bacon-wrapped dates to pair with the wine? ;-)
Love you, too.

See, I could do this. Be cheery and supportive.

A pit unfurls in my stomach. This is us now. And it works. We have no responsibilities apart from our work and our cats. But that may not always be the case. In fact, I'm starting to think I don't want it to always be the case. As Ariel so eloquently sang in *The Little Mermaid*, I want more.

My laptop screen goes dark and I wave my finger over the touchpad to wake it back up. I copy the URL of the podcast into two more texts, sending one to Eli and one to my mom. Then I drag myself to bed for what little sleep I can get.

Chapter Ten

I yawn as I open the door to Vino Valentine.

The sky was lightening outside when I finally fell asleep, rusty rays of orange and red permeating my eyelids. It felt like mere seconds before my alarm sounded. The one on my phone I could—and did—snooze. The furry ones, however, were relentless in their quest for breakfast. Zin and William prodded at me until I finally tossed my covers aside. It's a good thing they persisted, though, otherwise I would be running even later than I already was.

Which is why Sloan beat me to opening the shop. Baskets full of palate-cleansing wafers are perched on the counter and tables, a fresh vase of daisies adorns the tasting bar, and the unscented candles are lit. Soft music wafts from the speakers.

I take a large gulp of my vanilla latte from the Laughing

Rooster next door, ignoring how it scorches my tongue, willing the caffeine to give me a boost of energy.

Sloan is behind the tasting bar, rocking on the balls of her feet and mumbling to herself as she flips through a hefty stack of fluorescent notecards.

"Studying?"

"Always," she responds. "I keep forgetting all six of the vines outlawed in France. There's the Herbemont, Jacquez, Noah, Isabelle, Clinton, and . . ." Her face twists in a pained expression until she lets out an aggrieved sigh and peeks at her notecard. "Othello."

"Ah, the forbidden grapes." These American vines have been banned for nearly a century for supposedly producing subpar wines. They've recently resurfaced because of their resistance to drought and insects, albeit, in secret. "Maybe the law will finally be changed."

"If it hasn't happened since 1934, I doubt it'll happen anytime soon."

"Look at you spouting that date like it's no big deal." My compliment loses all meaning thanks to the giant yawn accompanying it.

"Late night?" Sloan bounces on the toes of her highlighter-yellow trainers, in contrast with her slate slacks and cream ribbed tank.

"You could say that." Late night that stretched into a long morning.

My phone pings and I glance at the screen. It's a text from Reid.

I open my messages to find an accompanying picture. His green eyes are still blurry with sleep and his hair is perfectly disheveled, the light cascading through his hotel room tinging it amber. There's a smirk on his lips and a mug of coffee in his hand.

His text reads: *Morning. The only thing missing in this picture is you. And William.*

I grin, snap a selfie with my to-go mug, and type back: *Cheers! With William in the other chair, where will I sit?*

His response is complete with a wink-kiss emoji: *I'm sure we can come up with something . . .*

My cheeks flush and I change course before either of us combusts: *Tell me more about the new digs.*

Reid: *Outdoor seating over the water, enough space for a stage. But with all the work it needs, it could be a money pit.*

Me: *Or it could be perfect. Sometimes you just have to take the plunge and hope for the best.* Those are the same words I told Reid when nerves nearly kept him from opening Spoons and they seem even more imperative now.

Reid: **Groan**

Me: *Wait, did you just type groan?*

Reid: *Yes, in concession that you talked me down. Again. It was an endearing groan.*

Me: *Oh, I'm sure. And endlessly attractive.*

Reid: *The investors are meeting me there today. If all goes well, we'll start the paperwork and get this show on the road.*

Me: *And where, pray tell, will you be staying during this show? I know you can't last more than a week without your own kitchen.* Granted, this is a conversation we probably should have already had, but neither of us wanted to cross the bridge until we needed to. The whole *bushel of grapes before the harvest* kind of thing.

Reid: *VRBO until I can find something more permanent. There are a few near the train that goes north to Napa. Hoping I can convince you to join me for a weekend.*

Me: *Only if you can promise truffles.*

Reid: *Forever.*

"What has you all glowy?" Sloan asks.

That's when I realize I've been conducting this flirtatious text tête-à-tête in the middle of my tasting room.

"Nothing," I say hurriedly as another text comes in. Buzzing with giddiness, I sneak a peek at the screen. And immediately deflate when I see it's from Eli.

Eli: *Thanks for the tip on Earnest Merriwether/Kyle Garcia. Please do NOT take this as encouragement to continue snooping.*

Me: *Is anything he doing illegal?*

My mom shared my shock and horror at the podcast— and the opinion that no one else in the family can ever find out about it. However, that doesn't mean I can't try to put a stop to Kyle's/Earnest's gross invasion of privacy.

Eli: *If you're asking if I have any authority to make him stop, the answer is no. He's not breaking any laws.*

Frustrated, I shove my phone in my bag and turn to Sloan.

"Hey, what wines would you recommend to serve at a wedding?"

"Another pop quiz?" she asks eagerly.

"Of sorts."

Sloan stashes her notecards on top of a pile of folders overflowing with aroma diagrams and flavor profiles. "Champagne, obviously." She purses her lips in thought and then taps varietals out on her fingers. "Then probably a chardonnay, merlot, and rosé. An assortment that will please as many palates as possible without breaking the bank."

"Very good." I empty my to-go cup and toss it in the rubbish bin. "That's what I'll take with me to pitch to the caterer." Who conveniently neglected to get back to me and my mom.

"Still hoping to break into the biz?"

"A girl can dream, right?"

Truth is, I haven't forgotten my desire to dip my toe in the lucrative wedding pool. The fact that the caterer might also have intel on Prynne's murder is icing on the cake.

The bell to the storefront jingles. "But first, let's take care of business."

Iris Catering is located off of Twenty-Eighth Street, the main artery flowing in and out of Boulder. It's more commercial, lined with shops and restaurants that become increasingly generic the farther you travel from Pearl Street. I briefly considered it as a location for Vino Valentine. While garnering the attention of daily commuters, the views of parking lots and bumper-to-bumper traffic hardly inspire relaxation and indulgence.

But maybe it works for Iris.

I alight from the bus with a tote of wine bottles clinking at my side.

I really should have driven, I think to myself as I pant along on the sidewalk, *or at least tried to*. If I actually want to improve, I have to get back behind the wheel, and transporting wine is ridiculously cumbersome, even with only four bottles like I have now.

The building I'm targeting is at the end of a shopping center. I push the door open and take in the space. It's small, nay, quaint. A bookcase rests against the storefront wall, full of binders and laminated pictures. A bistro table and chairs are front and center, with a computer and food warmer perched on the opposite counter, adjacent to a swinging door that must lead to the kitchen.

There's no one in sight, not even a bell to ding to garner attention.

That's no way to treat potential customers. How is someone supposed to get ahold of Iris if she refuses to return phone calls *and* doesn't oversee her store? How did Emma and Nash manage to secure her services? Or is there another reason for Iris's avoidance?

"Excuse me," I say. There's no answer, so I try again, raising my voice. "Hello!"

I may as well be shouting into the void.

Setting my hefty tote on the counter, I nervously approach the swinging door and peek through the slit of a window.

Iris is in her kitchen. Stainless-steel appliances are wedged along the perimeter with an island that doubles as a staging zone in the middle. The space is cramped, with barely enough room for two people to cook without bumping elbows. Seriously, the sous chef stands so close to the saucepan she's stirring I worry she'll singe her torso.

I recognize the sous chef as one of the servers from the wedding. She's petite with a narrow face accentuated by the braid of dark hair draped down her back. Small operations like this require employees to wear multiple hats, the event coordinator doubling as the chef, bartender as the busser, and so on. This young lady seems weighted down by the toque perched on her head. She glances at me through the slitted window and then hurriedly back down at her whisk, color dotting her cheeks.

So, at least the sous chef knows I'm here.

Iris carefully sprinkles herbs over a bowl, a square of

rolled dough at the ready beside it. Smells of garlic, fresh basil, and yeasty flour reach my nose.

I push open the door and announce myself, "Um, hi, Iris?"

"Yeah," Iris grumbles as if disappointed by this fact.

"I was hoping to talk with you."

She barely looks at me. "Give me a minute to finish this and I'll be right with you. Feel free to take a look at the menus out front."

For the record, it's not one minute. It's twenty.

I keep myself occupied by perusing her binders, full of pricing and bundle options in addition to dish selections. There are pictures of each appetizer, entrée, and dessert for gatherings from brunch to supper. There are age-old classics that, from the faded font on the page, are decidedly *aged*. She doesn't update her offerings often. If ever.

I imagine myself sitting here with Reid. What he would say, and the possible occasion we would be planning for. Shaking out my hands, I get to my feet and set the menus aside.

A framed photograph catches my attention. It's hanging beside the front door and shows Iris on opening day, arms splayed wide and face full of such excitement she looks like a different person. A man stands on the other side of the door from her, eyes glistening with tears of pride and hands midclap.

I spin around at the sound of the kitchen door swinging open. Iris emerges, wiping her hands on a towel. The hitch in her step tells me she expected me to give up and vamoose. Her eyes narrow as they shift from me to the bottles of wine I unpacked and displayed on the bistro table.

"I'm Parker," I say, mostly to fill in the silence.

"I recognize you." It's clear from her tone that this isn't a point in my favor.

"I was at the event the other day."

She grunts, smacking the towel against the countertop and leaving it there, crossing her arms over her chest. "The event I was fired from."

How interesting she's chosen to remember it that way instead of the event where someone lost their life. "Right, sorry about that." I flash her my most winning smile. "I was hoping to talk to you but didn't get the chance. You see, I'm hoping to break into the wedding business."

"Why would you want to go and do a thing like that?"

"Because it's insanely lucrative."

Iris heaves a sigh, her shoulders slumping forward as if gravity impacted her more than the rest of the world. Premature streaks of silver line her hair beneath the net and stains mark the front of her chef's coat, the embroidered iris flowers and name of her company fraying at the seams. "It's not worth it, kid. All you'll get is drama."

Maybe it's being referred to as a kid, or maybe it's having my aspirations so thoroughly dismissed, but I prickle. "Drama like when you threatened to take Prynne down with you?"

Iris stares at me, aghast. Her face drains of color as she sinks into a chair. "What do you want?"

"Answers."

A dullness enters her muddy-brown eyes and her voice grows hoarse. "Fine, you win."

Wait, is Iris confessing? If so, that was easy. Too easy. And I'm woefully ill prepared.

My phone is deep in my purse and digging for it might make her reconsider whatever it is she's about to tell me.

While I freeze like a deer in headlights, Iris continues in an empty husk of a voice, "That's not my proudest moment."

I pull myself together and peel my tongue from the roof of my mouth. "What did you mean by it?"

Iris wrings her hands in her lap. "Reviews are everything. A bad one from Prynne could have ruined me." A spark enters her eyes and a cruel smirk plays at her lips. "But then I realized the same could be said for her."

I recalibrate. Because confession, I think not. "Tit for tat?"

"It seemed like my only move at the time." She gives the smallest, most defeated shrug. "Instead, I should have counted myself lucky to get out of there."

Understanding washes over me. I know how brutal reviews can be, how subjective taste is, and how much it can hurt when someone tears down years of hard work with a few keystrokes. But the thing is, reviews can be helpful, too. Even bad ones boost the chances of someone discovering your product. Not that Iris wants to hear that.

And Prynne clearly upset her. Struck a nerve that had been eroding over time, like caustic liquid through insufficient piping. Upset her enough to make her lash out with a threat. Which makes me wonder: When Prynne didn't take her seriously, could Iris have lashed out in another way?

"Who called when you were in the middle of packing everything up?"

"A client."

"When is their event?"

"Job fell through," Iris answers, unblinking. "It happens a lot, especially on cold calls."

I sink into the chair opposite her and cross one leg over the other. "So, you do answer your phone."

"What are you talking about?"

I level with her. "My mom and I both left you messages. Neither of us heard back."

"You have to give me at least twenty-four hours to respond."

"We did." I soften my tone. "You might consider hiring some more help."

"You might consider minding your own business," she snaps, proving once again that she can certainly bark. But what about bite?

I raise my palms up in front of me. "Touché." I give her a benign smile. "How did you get the job for my cousin?"

"Prynne," Iris answers. "She put us through the ringer, made us prepare samples of every dish, multiple times, and negotiated down my standard pricing. I was barely going to break even before having to cut it as a complete loss." It's clear the sting of her dismissal still smarts, and probably would until she recouped, both her pride and investment.

"Any chance I can chat with the servers who were working that day?"

"What d'you want with Mischa and Don?" Wariness crosses her face, from her scalp to her chin, like blinds being drawn.

Thinking quick, I bring my palm to my forehead. "You see, I lost my wallet and have been trying to track it down."

She stares at me like I'm a complete moron, which, to be fair, isn't wholly unjustified. "Mischa's in the back. She can give you Don's number."

"Awesome."

Iris makes to stand but I stop her. "Do you have a go-to wine provider?"

She sighs the sigh of a thousand long days. "Why would I need one?"

"Because nothing pairs better with romance than a glass of vino. And bonus, my label offers a touch of local flair."

She clicks her tongue, entirely unimpressed—and unconvinced.

"It can be on a referral basis for now, clients who ask for recommendations." I nod at the bottles I brought along. "These are a few of my most popular varietals, free for you to try, no strings attached."

"Hate to break it to you, but I'm getting out of the wedding biz."

I sag in my seat. "But why?"

"Too much drama. If it's not a bridezilla, it's an overzealous wedding planner, controlling family, or all of the above. I can't take it anymore." She shakes her head and barks out a sardonic laugh. "You know, this used to be my dream. Providing nourishment for the happiest day of someone's life, being a part of the celebration and memories."

"And now?"

"Turns out, to most, the happiest day of your life means making everyone else miserable."

I cock my head to the side, studying her. "That's not true. It can't be."

She scrutinizes me in a superior fashion. "Keep telling yourself that, kid. As for me, if you know anyone who needs a caterer for professional summits, graduations, hell, even funerals, I'm their gal."

I take a long hard look at Iris. At the flyaway strands

escaping her hairnet, the curve of her spine, and the lines around her toadlike mouth.

Disillusioned. That's what Iris is. And exhausted.

I glance at the framed picture on the wall again. At the girl beaming, on the verge of achieving her heart's desire, and sharing the moment of her success with a loved one.

Iris went for her dream, with everything she had—or perhaps didn't have. Only to discover it wasn't what she wanted anymore.

Some say it's the fear of failure that keeps you from pursuing your dream. But I think there's more to it than that. Like support, resources, or not knowing what you want to begin with. Even if you take a leap of faith, there's always going to be this fear, this stark realization that the thing you've worked so hard for—possibly centered your life around—could crumble, taking everything you've ever known with it.

The thought chills me to my core. Especially when I consider the woman in front of me. To Iris, Prynne was the embodiment of her dream gone sour.

"You can keep the wine," I say, gesturing once again to the bottles between us. "I'll just go check if Mischa has seen my—er—wallet."

Mischa proves to be as chatty as her boss, which is to say, not very.

I wedge myself beside the stovetop and the island. "Mind if I ask you a couple questions?"

Mischa practically leaps out of her clogs at being addressed. "I—I guess," she stammers with a baleful glance toward Iris, who's still in the front of the store. "If it's okay with my boss."

"It is."

She moves the saucepan she's been doctoring to an unlit burner. There's a thin, brown liquid inside that makes my nostrils prickle. Maybe Prynne wasn't off base with her criticisms of the food.

Mischa leads the way out a back door, checking over her shoulder as if I were a rabid dog nipping at her heels. The alley is host to a dumpster and a parking spot with a van sporting Iris Catering's logo on the side. Somewhere in the distance, a car alarm sounds.

I repeat my fib in hopes of lulling Mischa into a conversation. "Did you happen to find a wallet at the hotel the other day?"

Misha tugs at her braid. "No, sorry." Her voice is so quiet it makes me feel like I'm shouting.

"Darn," I say, snapping my fingers. "Did you happen to see anyone acting suspicious, skulking around where they shouldn't have been?"

She leans away from me, a suspicious look on her face.

"Because maybe they have my wallet," I hurry to add, which seems to appease her.

"I didn't notice anything, but we weren't there all that long." Her eyes flit to mine and it strikes me that she's beautiful, just lacks confidence.

"What about in the service hallway as you guys were tearing everything down?"

She rubs her arms as if chilled, only it's ninety degrees outside. "There were people everywhere."

Ah, an introvert. "Was Prynne one of them?"

"I can't remember. I don't do well in crowds."

"Gotcha," I say. "I don't do so well myself. How do you like working for Iris?"

If you want to know someone's true colors, ask their

employees. Mischa perks up a bit. "Oh, Iris is great. Lets me help with the cooking and I get paid well enough."

"What about your coworker Don?"

She rolls her eyes, warming to me. "Students are always a pain to work with. They're never very permanent, though."

"Do you have his contact info?"

"No, but I can get it for you on your way out."

She does just that, halting before a whiteboard tacked up in the kitchen. His name and number are written in blue marker, already half-erased. Mischa's, I notice, is intact at the top corner, just below Iris's.

Mischa shows no sorrow at seeing the back of my head. There's no heartbreak on my end, either. I have what I came for: an assurance that at least the sous chef wasn't culpable. If her demeanor wasn't convincing enough, her strength— or lack thereof—made it clear she couldn't have knocked Prynne hard enough on the head to kill her.

Talking with Don proves equally fruitless.

I dial his number while I wait for the bus. He doesn't answer the first time and instead of leaving a vague and rambly voice mail, I try again.

"Hello," he answers groggily.

"Hi, Don?"

There's a shuffling of fabric. I've woken him. At noon on a Monday. "Who's this?"

"A guest from the wedding Saturday morning. Iris gave me your number."

"What wedding?"

Any hope I had of Don providing answers evaporates. I choose my words carefully. "The one you guys were fired from."

"Oh yeah," he grunts. "What do you want?"

"I lost my wallet and have been phoning around trying to find it. Anything you may have seen or heard would be helpful."

"Look, lady, I don't got your wallet and I'm late for class. G'luck."

The line goes dead.

Chapter Eleven

As wines age, oaky notes are introduced through barrels, tannins polymerize and soften, and flavors meld, becoming smoother and more complex. Of course, much can go awry—elevated temperatures, oxygen inadvertently introduced, microbial spoilage, all of which can render the wine unpalatable.

The same can be said for passions. They can—and should—grow with you or risk disappearing entirely.

That afternoon, I try to put myself in Iris's shoes. Through every taster I serve to customers; through every explanation of my process; through the update from my grape grower and the number crunching that follows. I wonder how I would feel if winemaking ever became rote, or no longer brought me joy.

It would be back to square one, at least professionally, which, while difficult to swallow, would be better than turning to vinegar.

I flip my shop sign to CLOSED and turn my attention to something else. Namely, if there's any way I can get out of my evening plans. All I really want is to go home and snuggle up with my kitties, indulge in a glass of wine, and help myself to a dose of McDreamy and one of Reid's culinary masterpieces.

But I made a promise to Liam, and he would be all butt-hurt if I bailed now.

He's been hounding me to meet his new rock star friend for months and tonight is finally The Night.

Now, normally I don't mind being a third wheel. Heck, I'm great company with or without a date. It's just that, in my current state, I'm afraid it will serve as a reminder that my relationship is on the fritz. That I'm alone.

At least it will give me the opportunity to practice driving, a task I've avoided since my last failed attempt. But I'm not one to give up easily. Not with the future of my business on the line. Plus, a part of me wonders if having Sage and Liam as passengers might give me the edge I need. Both with their constant support and the added responsibility of being their ride for the evening.

I pull into the parking lot that houses Liam's apartment complex. While it can't have been more than two miles by back roads, I momentarily applaud myself for making it this far.

My brother's apartment is in a shoddy building next to campus that appears as dirt cheap as the rent boasts. There's no security system, a questionable shopping cart in the stairwell, and a perpetually burnt-out lightbulb in the hallway.

But it's his own place, outside Mom and Dad's basement, and, oddly, it's grown on me.

I knock on his door a few minutes earlier than our planned meet-up time.

"It's open!" Liam shouts from somewhere inside.

I let myself in, breathing in the scent I've come to associate with my brother: a mixture of dill pickles and Windex from the chemicals he uses to process film, his spare bedroom a makeshift dark room.

His entryway is littered with props. Cardboard backdrops from brick walls to forests to beaches lean against the closet door. Plastic instruments, hollow books with golden spines, picnic baskets full of fake food, and silk plants galore overflow from a trunk. He's slowly amassed this collection for photo shoots.

The rest of the furnishings are more commonplace, cast-off furniture from our parents and his pride and joy, a massive flat-screen TV I know to be one of his first—and finest—purchases.

Liam emerges from his bedroom, buttoning up a blue collared shirt that matches our eyes, his dark hair still wet. "You're obnoxiously early."

"I'm just shy of punctual. You're running late."

"My last shoot of the day decided on an extra costume change," he answers. "It was at Boulder Res, I just got home a few minutes ago."

"Senior photos?"

He checks his reflection in the black TV screen, swiping his hair to the side. "Seems like I'm working my way through all of Boulder High."

"That's gotta be good for business, right?"

"Yeah, when I'm not already booking a month in advance."

"Have you thought about backing off your hours with the city?" Liam works on a landscaping crew and is responsible for many of the gorgeous displays on Pearl Street.

He gives a lazy shrug. "I would, but I've found I've grown rather fond of health insurance."

"Who would've thought?" I ask sarcastically. "You know there are other ways to get that, right?"

"Yeah, yeah." He waves me off. "Why are you here early, again?"

"Thought I'd look through the photos you took from Saturday."

"I told you, there's nothing there but frills and family candids," Liam says.

"I believe you, really. Just like I believed you when you told me snipe grant you three wishes if you can catch them." Snipe were the make-believe birds Liam convinced me were real as kids. A roadrunner-like creature who supposedly possesses magical powers and comes out only at night.

He chuckles at the memory. "You were so gullible. You spent hours wandering around the backyard with a pillowcase and a flashlight."

I make grabby-hands with my fingers. "The photos, please."

"Someone's cranky," Liam says. "Are you and Reid going through a rough patch or something?"

"What makes you say that?"

"Whenever something's wrong in your personal life, you find ways to distract yourself. Like investigating a murder. With our mother. Which, first off, how did that even happen? And second, doesn't it seem like, I dunno, *maybe* a bad idea?"

This is exactly why I told Mom to keep it on the DL. I roll my eyes at him. "She begged me. I couldn't say no."

"And here I thought I was the sibling with poor judgment." There's good humor in his ribbing, which means he's more amused than concerned.

"I was gonna let you off the hook and not ask how you feel about Sage never wanting to get married, but now . . ." I trail off meaningfully.

He rocks forward on his feet and coughs to clear his throat. "I'll just go grab my laptop so you can look through those photos."

I crinkle my nose at him. "Good idea."

Liam disappears into the spare bedroom and returns a second later, booting up the screen of his computer. "I haven't had a chance to give them more than a once-over, but have at it."

I perch on his/my parents' old sofa, eagerly skipping through the images. There are artful shots of the decor, banquet table, candids of family and friends (including the infamous wedding crasher), even a few decent shots of yours truly. But Liam was right. He didn't get any in the service hallway, or of Prynne.

For someone who commanded so much attention, Prynne sure managed to dodge the spotlight.

I close Liam's laptop as Sage arrives, giving them privacy to greet each other before I make my presence known.

"Hey, stunner," I say in the entryway.

Sage twisted her hair into an elegant updo and applied more makeup than usual, blush to accentuate her cheeks and dark eyeliner that makes her eyes pop. She's wearing an airy floor-length skirt, a tank sporting the USS *Enterprise* logo, and combat boots. Protective footwear is of the upmost importance where we're going. Which is why I paired my jeans and camisole with closed-toe flats.

"You sure you're okay driving?" Sage asks. She's fully

aware of my, for lack of a better word, phobia, but not of my recent resolution to get back behind the wheel.

"Absolutely." I try to sound more confident than I feel.

Liam engulfs Sage in a hug from behind. "Shhh, don't talk her out of being our DD."

"Hey now." I round on him. "There will be no shenanigans. Reid's car will be in pristine condition when he gets back. Or else."

"Spoilsport," Liam says, punching me lightly in the upper arm.

And just like that my apprehension disappears. At least for the moment. Which was probably Liam's goal.

I snag my purse and keys and usher them out the door. "Let's get this show on the road, we have a bona fide rock star to meet."

Sage climbs into the front of Reid's jeep while Liam makes himself as comfortable as he can in the middle of the backseat. I cue up Jimmy Mickelson on the Bluetooth to get us in the right mindset.

Jimmy Mickelson first topped the charts in the early 2000s as a member of a popular boy band, but has found arguably even more success as a solo artist. With his catchy melodies, poignant lyrics, and soulful vocals, it's no wonder he's a worldwide sensation. Imagine our surprise when a few months ago, he contacted Liam—*Liam!*—to take shots for posters, flyers, and social shares for his upcoming tour. Jimmy being an advocate for showcasing local talent, Liam got the job, and they apparently hit it off; my brother has always been a smoothie.

While my musical preferences sway more toward T. Swift, I've gotta admit, there's something calming about Jimmy

Mickelson's music. Which makes it the perfect soundtrack for this little escapade.

Putting the jeep in gear, I pull out of the parking lot and onto a frontage road. Sage and Liam are quiet—too quiet—and it sets me on edge. My stomach churns with the vegetable lasagna I had for dinner and my palms grow clammy.

I swallow my nerves and divert my spiraling thoughts, asking, "So, how were your guys' days?"

"Same old, same old," Sage responds. "Revolutionizing the justice system one case at a time."

"While she was saving the world, I juggled fixing irrigation on Pearl and shot a series of portraits."

"Does that make us a power couple?" Sage asks, swiveling toward Liam.

"Only if we're powering a lamp, possibly a panini press."

She nods, facing forward again. "A panini-press couple, I can work with that."

They fall silent and my heart hammers in time to the click of the blinker. This is going to be a long ride if that's the best they can offer in terms of distraction. I focus on my breathing, on the gentle vibrations beneath my fingertips and the soothing scent of Reid's jeep. With a surge of determination, I turn onto the main avenue through town.

And immediately get stuck in traffic.

Oh no. Oh no. *Oh no.*

I lean into the window to get a better view around the truck in front of me. "How is rush hour still going on?"

"Because people work too hard," Liam says.

"Adulting," Sage says with a shake of her head. "It's a killer."

We crawl through Boulder. My knuckles are white and my gaze is fixed on the truck in front of me. One of its brake lights is out, and it has a personalized Colorado license

plate that reads RDRH8R, hinting at the football rivalry between our revered Broncos and the Las Vegas Raiders.

We reach the edge of campus, the few students partaking in summer sessions easily outstripping us, and then,
finally, hit our turnoff. Highway 93 winds along the front
range, past the Rocky Flats and through Golden, all the
way to our final destination. Some twenty miles away.

Suddenly, it's too much. Stars break out in my vision and
I pull into a gas station.

I can't even look my brother in the eye as I ask, "Would
you mind driving the rest of the way?" Given it's Reid's car,
I assume he'd feel more comfortable if his friend took over.

"Sure thing, sis." Liam hops out and is at the driver's side
in an instant. He claps me on the shoulder after I extract
myself, whispering, "You did good. It's gonna take time."

Thoroughly defeated, I climb into the backseat and buckle
myself in, chewing on my lower lip to keep from breaking
down.

"I hate driving in rush hour." Sage gives my knee an
encouraging squeeze. "You got us through the worst part."

I nod numbly, unsure what I loathe more: my failure or
their pity.

The Red Rocks Amphitheatre is a Colorado landmark. A
majestic outdoor venue carved into the mountainside. Smooth
angled rocks tinge the trademark red rise on either side and
enclose the space. Tiered stone seating arranged in arcs overlooks the stage. Beyond that, the eastern horizon is visible,
downtown Denver a smattering of tall buildings that sprawls
into suburbs and rolling hills. And to the west, the park
bleeds into Mount Falcon and the surroundings Rockies.

Liam parks Reid's jeep in the lower lot and we clamber

out, the sun casting the dirt and rocks in an orange glow that only intensifies the red. The waxing moon hangs suspended in the sky, just shy of full, and a slight breeze stirs my hair. All in all, it promises to be a good night.

We start our trek to the entrance, a glorified hike up winding paths and staircases lined with fellow concertgoers.

I'm slightly out of breath when we finally reach the summit. Despite our lengthy commute, we're on the early side, people filing into rows of rocky benches, spreading blankets and opening picnic baskets. Concession stands at either end offer snacks and beverages to the less prepared. Aromas of buttery popcorn and grilled hot dogs mingle with smoke—both the skunky haze of marijuana and the sweet bite of cloves.

The stage itself may not look like much, dwarfed by the majestic surroundings, but legends like the Beatles, U2, and Radiohead have graced its surface. And the venue hosts more than musicians. Graduations, Film on the Rocks, Easter service, and even sunrise workout groups are held here.

Liam leads the way to the stage, where an intimidating bodyguard glares down at us. "General seating is over there," he says gruffly with a nod toward the seats behind us. He's clearly used to being mistaken for an usher.

Liam flashes him three badges. "We're friends of Jim's," Liam says, taking immense pleasure in this name-dropping.

The bodyguard scrutinizes our passes, and each of us, before breaking into a grin that's only slightly less disconcerting than his frown. "Well, that's a horse of a different color. Go on back." He steps to the side and waves us through.

I can't help but marvel at his biceps as we pass, thick as the metal pillars holding up vast speakers.

We weave between scaffolding holding spotlights and

around cases and cords, the all-weather roofing casting a shadow across the slate ground.

"Liam, my man," a shout comes from behind us.

And there's Jimmy Mickelson, in the flesh.

In black skinny jeans and a baseball tee with thick leather bracelets adorning his wrists, he's seemingly unaffected by the soaring temperatures. Although he must be at least ten years my senior, he has this ageless quality about him. His hair is a mane of red curls, his nose is slightly crooked, and he's shorter than he appears on camera. Like, at eye level with me. But he has this aura that pegs him as an A-list celebrity. He oozes confidence like I do sweat.

"Hey, Jim, thanks for the invite." Liam holds out a hand in greeting.

Jimmy takes my brother's hand and pulls him into a hug, planting a kiss on either cheek. If Liam is taken aback by the gesture, he doesn't let it show.

"The pleasure's all mine," Jimmy says in a Southern drawl, smooth and silky as port. "You must be Sage." Jimmy welcomes Sage the same way, a hug and *la bise*.

My friend is too stunned after he pulls away, touching her cheek lightly with her fingertips, to respond with more than a stammered, "Y-yeah."

Then Jimmy turns his full attention on me. "Parker, right?" He swoops in, his lips soft and brief on either side of my face. From the ease with which he partakes in this very European custom, it must be the norm for him. A reflection of his worldliness, or perhaps simply his warm personality.

"That's right," I say, grappling for words. "Nice to meet you. This is incredible." I wave around me.

"Red Rocks is my favorite venue to perform at," he says. "I insist it be included in every tour." Like the current one, which led him to hiring my brother.

"We should have good weather, too," I say, and then flinch. Am I really talking about the weather? With an actual celebrity?

"Rain or shine, doesn't matter one bit to me," Jimmy says. He has this infectious smile, my own lips maniacally mirroring his. "Last year, I played in a downpour and it was epic. Wet, for sure, but man, the crowd and energy was so intense. It was like lightning."

This guy must be some sort of social genius. Seriously, he could sell raisins to a grape grower.

Which is probably why I find myself agreeing. "I've sat through concerts in the rain here," I say. "You're right, there is something special about it—the willingness of the musician to play through anything, the fervor of the fans."

He nods and flashes me a peace sign. "That's what I'm talkin' about."

"I'm a big fan," Sage finally manages to interject.

"I'm a fan of yours, too, babe," Jimmy replies without missing a beat.

A sound technician shouts for Jimmy from the front of the stage.

"I've gotta get ready but enjoy the show. See you at the after-party." He waltzes away, all swagger.

"So, that was Jimmy Mickelson." I shake my head to come to, feeling like I've been in a whirlwind.

"That's Jimmy Mickelson," Liam confirms.

"He seems nice." Sage touches her cheek once more.

"And then some," I say. "Come on, let's get a drink."

The evening is the picture of perfection. Two of my favorite humans, stars twinkling overhead, a magnificent view, solid live music from beyond-incredible seats, and a margarita that's just the right amount of sweet and sour. So, why wasn't I happier?

The logical answer is I miss Reid, heightened by the proximity of a happy couple. But there's a falseness to that, like chemicals added to enhance the flavors of low-quality wines. The reason for my malaise is more complicated.

I feel unsettled—agitated.

I'm no closer to figuring out what happened to Prynne, despite pounding the pavement to untangle the mess of clues and talking the ears off anyone tangentially involved. Every second that ticks by increases the chance of my family being sucked into a colossal shitstorm.

Not to mention, I'm letting Emma and Nash down. They're so obviously in love and desperate to get hitched but seem to be waiting for something. For closure from their ruined ceremony, or perhaps for Emma to realize she deserves the wedding of *her* dreams.

And don't even get me started on my own failures. Me and my wine hover on the outskirts of the wedding industry, which I'm not even sure I want to be a part of anymore, and my attempts at driving have remained just that: attempts.

I focus on the moment, on the remarkable scene in front of me. Spotlights cast Jimmy Mickelson into a silhouette. He's as talented a performer as he is a socialite, commanding attention as he dances across the stage, song after song pouring out of him. The packed amphitheater goes wild with cheers.

The bass vibrates through the soles of my feet, which is probably why it takes me a minute to notice my phone buzzing in my back pocket. Switching my plastic margarita cup from one hand to the other, I grab my phone and check the screen. It's my mom, and this isn't the first time she's tried calling.

"Mom, what's up?"

But it's useless; I can't hear a thing.

"Hang on," I shout into the receiver.

I tap Sage on the shoulder and gesture with my phone to let her know I'll be back.

I jog to the far side of the stage, carefully cross the hallway of cords and scaffolding, and skip down the steps, stopping only when the music has faded into the background. I find myself near the restrooms and a balcony overlooking the parking lot.

Then I press the phone to my ear, plugging the other one with a free finger, my margarita dewy against my cheek.

"Sorry, I'm at a concert," I explain.

Fans jostle me on their way to the bathroom, many flushed and sporting Jimmy Mickelson shirts, mouthing along with the lyrics of a lesser-known song, the melancholy notes drifting through the air.

"That was tonight, wasn't it?" My mom's voice sounds weird and shaky, which sets me on edge. "I didn't mean to interrupt your fun."

"It's fine. Really." I nudge my way to the railing, wedging myself beside a girl angling her phone to take a selfie. "Is everything okay?"

"No." She shudders an exhale through our connection, and sniffles.

She's crying. Which jolts me straight into panic mode. Because I've seen my mom cry only once. In my entire life. It was after the police called and informed her that her little sister—my aunt Laura—was killed in a car accident. So, whatever this is, it's bad.

"Mom, tell me." My mouth goes tannin dry and my legs wobble. I lean on the cool metal railing, fearing my frayed nerves might flee my body and escape into the night.

My mom swallows and says in a tone of utter disbelief, "Grace has been brought in for questioning."

"What?" I ask. "Why?" Although, somehow, I already know the answer.

"They think she had something to do with it. They think she killed Prynne."

Chapter Twelve

I get off the phone with my mom with instructions to stay put, promising to call as soon as I have more information. Then I leverage my contacts, namely one.

Eli answers on the first ring with a curt, "I can't discuss the investigation with you."

I ignore him. "Why did you haul Grace in?" A loud raucous swell of applause erupts behind me as Jimmy strums the opening chords to his most popular song.

"Where are you?" Eli asks.

"It doesn't matter," I say, blocking out the escalating noise. "How could you do that? Grace doesn't have a mean bone in her body. My family is in pieces."

Even though I've only chatted with my mom, I can picture the rippling effect, how it will slowly impact Emma, Carolyn, my uncle, even my great-aunt Harriet, and, by extension, Clyde. They'll be completely beside themselves when they find out.

The only silver lining is Grace hasn't been arrested. Yet.

"That's classified," Eli says.

"Come on," I choke out. "You've gotta give me something. Or else, no joke, I will give my mother your cell number and you can brush off her many, *many* calls with vague nonanswers, capisce?"

He sighs, so softly I can barely hear it, especially with the audience chanting along with Jimmy to the chorus of a song. It's a steady roar that has me pressing my finger into my other ear so hard it hurts.

"Look," Eli finally says. "We found DNA evidence at the crime scene linking directly to Ms. Bostwick. It's suggestive."

After her divorce from my uncle, Grace reverted back to her maiden name. Even now, it's weird to hear her referred to as a Bostwick instead of a Cooper. Formal, detached, unbiased. Which is exactly what Eli is going for.

"What DNA evidence?" Then it comes to me, the clue I've been avoiding, haven't been able to explain away. "The hair?"

"Possibly."

Read: definitely.

I don't even care about the faint clinking of glasses and clattering of silverware in the background on his end, that I'm likely interrupting a date with Alyssa.

"We both know the evidence at the crime scene has been stacked," I argue. "The cologne was too strong, we can show you with data from an olfactometer, the footprints weirdly close together, and now this?" I'm shouting now and scaring passersby. I offer them a silent apology, continuing more steadily, "It's too convenient. It could've been from when Grace was walking by earlier that day."

"Do you recall seeing her near the service entrance?"

"No," I say hurriedly, not wanting to give Eli any more reason to detain Grace. "It's just . . . there are other ways for it to have ended up there. It could've been nicked from her hotel room and planted to cause confusion."

"Parker, remember who the expert is." His tone is mildly threatening and completely infuriating. "There was more than the hair."

This stops me short. "What do you mean?"

"There were a series of emails, sent from Grace to the deceased. The alarming subject matter along with the number of witnesses who overheard the accused argue with Michael Cooper"—I was wondering when my uncle would be dragged into this—"about Prynne, in addition to the rest of our dossier, builds a case. A strong one."

"What emails?" I push my bangs away from my face and blink rapidly. "Grace would never . . ." I trail off.

A weight drops in my stomach and curdles with acid.

My mom said Grace had reached her threshold, had had enough of seeing Emma bossed around. Even the wedding crasher had made note of her fight with my uncle. Maybe Grace really did snap.

No, I refuse to believe it. *Can't* believe it.

"Parker, I don't pretend to understand how difficult this must be, but you have to trust me. Let me do my job." The reassurance in his voice does nothing to ease the knot in my stomach. "If she's innocent, she'll answer our questions and be released."

Until they find something else to come after her with. In my experience, once they reach the building-a-case stage, there's little that can be done. "But you've made a mistake. Please, just—"

"No," Eli says gently but assertively. "Alyssa is waiting for me."

Because apparently everyone's relationship is on solid ground. Except mine.

He continues, "Go, be there for your family. Let the authorities handle this. Let *me* handle this." He exhales and I can picture him rubbing the back of his neck. "And brace yourselves."

I bite the inside of my cheek until bile pools inside my mouth. "I can't." Family is there for one another, through thick and thin, and that includes Grace.

That clearly isn't what he wanted to hear because he says, disappointed, "Goodbye, Parker."

I climb back up the stairs in a daze. Music and applause reverberate around me, but all I hear is a dull thrum in my ears. I register everything as if from afar, the smooth stones, the swaying backlit phones, the smoke. My feet could belong to someone else for how disconnected I feel. Head down, I ignore the people pressing around me and let my thoughts spiral.

Wedding interrupted, Prynne murdered, Grace suspected.

Each thought is more surreal than the last and my heart wrenches at the injustice.

Step after step, the harsh predicament thunders through my mind until a new thought eclipses all others. *A killer still at large.*

My brain alights with worry—and plans.

Because as bad as things may be, I still have a few tricks up my sleeve.

It's a miracle I make it backstage without injuring myself. Seriously, I can't even remember passing the intimidating bodyguard. But somewhere in my blind hike, I realized what I have to do.

Sage flashes me a smile when she sees me, she and Liam jumping up and down to the beat. Her face is as flushed as her hair, a Golden Snitch bobby pin hanging on for dear life.

"You missed the best song," Sage shouts over the music.

"I'm going to miss more because I've gotta go."

She twists in the air and lands her last jump angled toward me. "Is everything okay?"

"Not really," I say. "But you guys stay, have fun, enjoy the after-party."

Her brow furrows as she catches her breath. "How will you get back?"

I flash the screen of my phone at her where I've already pulled up the Uber app, a driver a mere button-push away.

Sage tugs on Liam's hand to get his attention and whispers something in his ear.

Disappointment flashes in my brother's eyes and he chides, "You have better places to be? Cooler people to hang out with?" Liam glances meaningfully around him.

"Never," I say, not having to exaggerate my hurt at his brash defensiveness.

Liam widens his stance, halfheartedly lifting a hand in the air before letting it fall back at his side. "What then?"

I clamp my mouth shut. I was hoping to shield them from the bad news, let them savor this evening before getting sucked into more family drama, but if he insists . . .

"Aunt Grace is the prime suspect in Prynne's murder investigation and Mom's a mess, so I'm gonna go see what I can do." This comes out in a rush, like wine being poured too quickly, all gushy with drops splashing onto the tabletop.

Sage grips my shoulder in support, which is more than Liam does.

His mouth opens into an O and he rubs his chin. "They

don't actually think she did it, though. It's only questioning.
Eli dragged me in last year and it turned out all right."

Of course, Liam is twisting this based on his own experience, implying that I'm overreacting or somehow mistaken. Irritation bubbles beneath the surface.

I raise my voice to be heard over the swelling drums.
"Yes, it's *only* questioning, but not all of us view that as just
another Monday night."

"And not all of us seize any chance to go gallivanting
around with a killer on the loose."

"It's a good thing I do or your questioning may have led
to more," I snap. If I hadn't interfered last year when a food-
and-wine critic met a bitter end at Vino Valentine, who knows
what would've happened? To my business, my brother, me?

"You're . . ." Liam grimaces, struggling with the word.
"Right."

"And don't you forget it." I get back to what matters,
Sage shifting awkwardly between us. "They really think
Grace is guilty. Eli confirmed as much. It's only a matter of
time before she's arrested."

Liam deflates, running a hand through his hair. He casts
a wistful gaze toward the stage before turning back to me,
resolved. "Then we'd better hit the road."

"What about Jimmy? The after-party?"

"Family comes first," Liam says with a shrug. "He'll
understand. We'll catch the next one."

I throw my arms around Liam. No matter how much we
bicker and razz each other, he's still my big brother. And in
that instant, I need him. My fingers grip the soft fabric of
his T-shirt and I let out a long sigh.

He hugs me back, hesitantly patting the top of my head.
"Come on, sis, you're embarrassing me in front of my rock
star friend."

I release him with a snort. "It would've happened, with or without my help."

Liam grins, his standing mission of spreading cheer complete. He shoots Jimmy a text explaining our sudden disappearance while Sage gathers our things.

Then, we jet.

My mom did *not* stay put.

And I mean, fine, it's only fair. I wouldn't. Guess this apple really didn't fall far from the tree.

The car ride back to Boulder is tense, only because we each fall into our usual coping mechanisms. Liam tries to break the tension by cracking jokes about anything and everything: other drivers, the gaming podcast he cued up, anecdotes from past concert interruptus. Sage shifts into productivity mode. She wields her lawyerly expertise, ringing her many contacts and securing Grace legal representation in the event she doesn't already have someone, which, let's face it, why would she?

As for me, I fold within myself, staring out the window.

Everything looks different at night, cloaked in shadows, and even though I've driven this way countless times, I have a hard time tracking our progress. The mountains are almost navy in the moonlight and the trees dotting the slopes look like smudges of paint. Reflective eyes of animals peer out of the underbrush.

We pull into the Longest Day Lodge, the *L* of the neon sign flickering dismally. The motel lobby is deserted, except for the same bored attendant from the other night, once again glued to his phone.

No complaints here. The less attention we draw to ourselves, the better.

Somehow, I know where to go, as if pulled by a strange Valentine magnetic field. I navigate the dreary hallways and tarped construction, the layers of dust on the ground masking our footsteps. All the way to the ballroom. Where everything started.

Sage's phone rings at the double doors, the opening bars of the theme song for *Star Wars* echoing through the cavernous space. As naive as I am about various fandoms, I at least recognize John Williams.

"I'll be right behind you guys," Sage says before swiping to answer with a professional, "Sage Bennet."

My mom, dad, and cousins are sitting in folding chairs they've scooted to the middle of the empty room. Mom is in capri yoga pants, a tunic, and slippers, clearly having shuffled into whatever she could find on her way out the door, and my dad's hair is sticking up in the back like he just woke up.

My cousins aren't in any better shape, their hoodies and shorts so wrinkled, they must be nearing the bottoms of their suitcases.

At Liam's and my arrival, they get to their feet.

"I can't believe it," I say, dispensing hugs to Emma, Carolyn, and ending with my mom, who gives me an extra squeeze.

"She didn't do this," Emma says. "How could they think she would do this?" There's a frantic edge to her voice, frustration bubbling to the surface in a way I've never seen on Emma. Her vast well of patience must finally be running dry.

"We know, honey," my mom says.

"What exactly happened?" I ask, my gaze on Carolyn, the more rational of my two cousins.

To my surprise, it's my mom who answers. "Grace was over at our house. We were visiting and enjoying a glass of wine while we poked away at the puzzle."

My mom is notorious for picking almost impossible-to-assemble jigsaw puzzles, arranged on their rarely used formal dining room table. The one in question is of the Milky Way that I have yet to land a piece on.

She continues, "Grace's phone rang and when she answered, an officer asked her to come down to the station. I offered to go, too, but she wanted me to be with you girls." My mom looks glumly from Emma to Carolyn.

Carolyn's gaze is cool and calculating. "Could've been worse," she says. "Mom could've been at school, teaching a classroom full of impressionable young minds."

"Ah, Carolyn, always the ray of sunshine," Liam says, flopping into a spare folding chair and sprawling his gangly legs before him.

"She's not wrong, though," I point out. I could picture the nightmarish scene, summer school students aghast as their teacher is being handcuffed and Mirandized. "We'll get this sorted." I wish I felt as confident as I sound.

Emma, at least, appears comforted by my words. Carolyn, not so much. But before she can open her mouth and impart whatever witticism is on the tip of her tongue, Sage enters.

"Good news or bad news first?" she asks, slipping her phone into the pocket of her skirt.

"There's good news?" I ask hopefully.

"Yes; there haven't been any formal charges yet."

"That's the good news?" Liam asks. "I mean, don't sugar-coat it on our account." Sage swats his shoulder; Liam grips her hand and plants a kiss on her palm.

"You'd better give us the bad news," my dad says in his commanding lecture tone, the one that makes college freshmen tremble in their boots.

"They have probable cause," Sage says. "They'll likely solidify their case. And soon."

Fear looks different on everyone, but there's always something primal in the eyes. A defense mechanism that springs, a kind of shock mixed with denial. While Emma lets out a sob, Carolyn scoffs, but their gazes lock, holding the same guttural reaction—a plea for this to not be real.

I hate to think about Grace stuck in the cold interrogation room. I've been there. I've sat in the metal chairs that make your butt scream in protest, traced the etched carvings in the tabletop, and shuddered under the harsh fluorescent lighting. And no balm in sight to ease the ache of Grace's arthritis.

"So, Counselor, what do you suggest?" I ask Sage.

"That we get her out of there before they can make their move." She paces back and forth, easing into her courtroom persona, even with her flyaway hairs and concert attire. "They can hold Grace legally for twenty-four hours. There's nothing we can do about that except use that time to discover the truth. Prove her innocence, or at least plant a seed of doubt."

I rub my hands together. "Okay, so, based on my resources—"

"Eli," Liam interrupts, feet twitching.

"Not that it's pertinent, but correct." I throw a pointed look at my brother and he mimes zipping his mouth shut. "One of the major things they have on Grace are some emails she supposedly sent to Prynne." I pivot on my heel toward my cousins. "Does that ring a bell for either of you?"

Emma and Carolyn shake their heads simultaneously, more in sync than they maybe have ever been.

"Mom hardly ever sends emails," Emma says.

"Yeah," Carolyn snorts. "Pretty sure she's still using dial-up."

I shift the spotlight to my mom. "Did Grace say anything to you?"

She pushes her cat-eye glasses up her nose, her frizzy hair splaying in every direction. "No, but she was upset with Prynne—and Chastity. There's a chance she wrote something out of anger."

Liam audibly clears his throat.

"Something you'd like to add?" I ask.

He points to his closed lips, blinking at me with undisguised satisfaction.

I roll my eyes and nudge his toe. "Spill."

"Well, we live in the digital age, do we not?"

"Get to the point," Carolyn says in a singsong voice. Having grown up with Liam's antics, Carolyn might as well be another sister.

"Why don't we try to access her email account? Take a gander at these hypothetical messages."

Liam's suggestion is met with silence as we all consider.

Now, I'm used to Liam's harebrained ideas. Building a jump out of couch cushions for our bikes to go over (which resulted in a trip to urgent care). The party he threw in high school while our parents were upstairs (pretty sure he's still grounded for that one). And pouring the entirety of his savings into day trading (which ultimately landed him back in Mom and Dad's basement).

But this could actually work.

I look to the person in the room with the most skill

at computers: my dad. "Could we hack into her email account?"

"With the personal details we know as a whole, probably," he concedes. "But as Mary Shelley eloquently showed in her groundbreaking masterpiece, the question isn't *could we* but *should we*."

Frankenstein has been a centerpiece of my moral compass since before I was aware of the sensationalized adaptations of the monster. But he isn't wrong.

I leave it up to Emma and Carolyn.

Emma shakes her head adamantly, chewing her lower lip. "Wouldn't that, I dunno, be an invasion of Mom's privacy?"

Liam tilts his head to the side. "The police have already read every gory detail."

"But police are *police*. This is us," Emma implores. "We have to see each other at family dinners, look each other in the eye."

"Only if we can prove her innocence," Liam says. "Hence, the emails."

Emma and Carolyn look at each other, Carolyn with one eyebrow cocked in question.

"I don't like it," Emma reiterates.

"There's nothing about any of this to like," Carolyn states. "There's only what we have to do to make it right."

"Why don't you two take a minute to chat," my mom proposes.

"That would be great," Carolyn says, leading the way to the front of the ballroom, where the wooden altar is still erected, a sad reminder of what could have been.

Emma trails behind, looking more weighed down than she did in her hefty wedding gown.

* * *

Emma and Carolyn debate quietly in the corner. To be honest, it gives me hope for Emma. On principle, I've learned never to disagree with Carolyn, especially in public. That Emma is able to speaks to her backbone. If only she could leverage it for herself instead of her mom.

The rest of us linger awkwardly, pretending not to eavesdrop.

My dad seems the most at ease, leaning back in his chair and swiping at something on his phone. I take the seat next to him, curious. "What are you doing?"

"Playing Scrabblebots."

"Never heard of it."

He peers up at me, his eyebrows especially bushy over his glasses. "One of my students made it for a project and uploaded it to the App Store." Pride shines in his eyes. While not easily impressed, if accomplished, my dad is a total softy. "It's very popular, a mix between Words with Friends and *BattleBots*."

"Sounds cool," I say, sneaking a peek. The screen bursts with bright colors and a smattering of letters and tiny animated robots. By the looks of it, he's crushing his opponent. "Who are you playing against?"

"Reid, actually."

I start, my hand fluttering to my beaded necklace. "What? When did this start?"

"After the dinner he made for my birthday. I mentioned it to him and he sounded interested." He waves it off as if this is no big deal, his attention on the letters he's assembling into the word *xi* and the robot he'll secure with the points. "We go back and forth a few times each week."

"I had no idea you guys did that." My mind immediately leaps to why. It's not that Reid doesn't love a good match-up, but his interests sway more toward billiards, not a logic puzzle against the guy who taught the developer.

"Don't act so surprised, Parker." My dad finalizes his move and presses send. Then he turns to me, his gaze softening when he notices my genuine confusion. "The boy wants to make sure we know he's serious about you. Which we already know." His head bobs in that studious way of his. "But I like Reid, I like this game, and I like winning. So, we play."

I'm not sure which part of his statement takes me the most aback. That what's so apparent to my dad is so *not* to me, or his transparency. Either way, a warmth radiates through my chest, barely making a dent against the brewing sense of despair. "Your secret is safe with me."

"Good girl." He pats my knee. "Now, what else has you looking so glum?"

A cluster of reasons clamor for attention, but my failure on the road stands out like a sour grape, the subconscious always so quick to focus on personal flops. "Do you know the real reason I don't drive anymore?"

It's not like it's a huge secret, but my pride has kept me from divulging the entirety to my parents, not wanting to make it a capital *T* thing or further burden them with the loss that drove me (pun intended) to this point.

"Because you're environmentally conscious," my dad supplies. "At least, that's what you told us when you sold your car."

I fiddle with the lace hem of my camisole. "It's more than that."

"I had a suspicion. The timing was significant."

"Right after Aunt Laura's accident." Coming up on three years ago.

He nods somberly, willing me to continue.

"I've been trying to get back on the road and"—I blow out a puff of air, shoulders slumping—"it's not going well."

"Why the sudden urge?"

"Because I want to be able to take care of myself. To not have to rely on others to move my business forward." But even as I say all this, I know it's not the full truth. "Because I'm sick of feeling helpless."

"Parker, I want you to listen closely." My dad leans forward, his gaze locked on mine. "There's a difference between feeling helpless and being helpless. And you, my dear, have never been helpless."

I blink, startled to find tears pooling in my eyes. How is it that my dad knows exactly what I need to hear?

He continues, "You have Reid, your friends, and family." He gestures with a wave at the amazing humans chattering softly around us. "We would all rush to your side at the drop of a hat." He leans back, chair squeaking, and gives me a warm smile. "You're made of too sturdy of stock to let this hold you back."

"Thanks, Dad," I whisper, my throat tight.

"Anytime, kiddo."

The ringing of Emma's phone echoes through the space, a lively show tune that has my cousin sagging with relief. "It's Mom." She hurries to answer, remaining in her semiprivate nook. "Are you okay?"

Carolyn rejoins us and Liam, being Liam, breaks the silence. "Hey, not that I mind being one of the sole Y chromosome representatives, but where are Nash, Xavier, and Jack?"

"Nash and Xav had some important call," Carolyn answers.

I check the time, forehead creasing. "It's, like, eleven o'clock."

"It's with New Zealand."

"The country?" Sage asks.

"A company working on synergistic technology," Carolyn says with a nonchalant shrug, reminding me, once again, that even though we got in trouble for cutting our own hair as children, she now operates in the upper echelon of corporate America. "I guess it was a big deal. And Jack is probably driving Josie crazy, he said he was going to see what she was up to tonight."

"Are you sure it's safe for those two to be in the same room together unsupervised?" I ask.

"Yeah," Sage interjects. "That could lead to a *Captain America* versus *Iron Man*–level showdown."

Emma returns, hands at her side. "They released Mom. She's on her way here now."

There are sighs of relief all around, and a choice expletive from Liam.

"Mom can stay with me tonight," Carolyn says. "She won't want to be alone." It's a kind offer, and yet, there's something in the way she averts her eyes that leads me to believe it isn't entirely selfless.

"But I have the suite," Emma argues.

"The honeymoon suite, where you're staying with your fiancé. I, however, remain a spinster."

Emma shakes her head, her expression doleful. "Don't call yourself that."

"Being a spinster is only seen as a negative by those sensitive to it." Carolyn crosses her arms over her chest, daring a response. "I embrace my independence."

I have to give Carolyn girl-power props. But after observing her easy camaraderie with Xavier, I can't help but wonder if she's so focused on her autonomy that she could be missing out on something great. Takes one to know one, I guess.

"So you say," Emma mumbles.

"Tensions are high," my mom intercedes. "Let's call it a night and regroup in the morning."

We trudge toward the door, exhaustion settling over us like sediment at the bottom of a wine bottle.

"Call if anything changes," I say before we part ways. "I have the detective's number and won't hesitate to phone at all hours. Incessantly. In fact, it would bring me no small amount of joy."

Chapter Thirteen

Wired, stressed, and exhausted, my nerves have been frayed, squashed, charred, and then frayed some more. Life has taught me caution in these situations. To be mindful whom I sob to, which is why I hesitate with my finger over the call button. The only thing that can really heal—or help make sense of things, if any sense is to be had—is time.

But if I can't call Reid, what does that say? Besides, he would be hurt if I didn't tell him about the latest developments.

Perched in bread-loaf pose on my couch armrest, William cocks his head to the side as if to say *Go on, we both know you're going to.*

On the cushion opposite him, Zin licks her paw lavishly, blissfully unaware of the rest of the world.

I go out onto my balcony and, with a view of the Flatirons bathed in moonlight, I finally dial.

Reid answers on the first ring, a clash of background noise accompanying his greeting. "Parks, I'm glad you called." His voice is deep, rough, and like a balm. The background ruckus fades as I imagine him finding a quiet place.

My throat clenches. "Me too."

He's immediately on guard after hearing the tremble in my voice. "What's up?"

I let it all come gushing out. My mom's and my efforts in the investigation, Eli's infuriating accusations, and Grace being the primary suspect in Prynne's murder.

To his credit, Reid listens in silence. Lets me spill out all of my disbelief and fear and anger. At some point I wander inside. The movement helps, makes me feel like I'm doing something, even if it's only making myself a cup of tea.

"It's going to be okay," Reid eventually says.

I sink into the couch, setting my steaming mug on the end table. I wrestle a corner of my afghan blanket from Zin and pull it into my lap, picking at a loose thread. "You don't know that."

"You're right, I don't," he says through an exhale. "But this is you we're talking about, and I know better than to underestimate you."

My throat clenches again. "I miss you."

"I miss you, too, Parks." There's something weird in his tone, something almost accusatory.

I play it cool—natural. "What's the haps with you?" And wince. Because did I really just use the word *haps*? I may as well wave a giant red flag that says, *I'm not okay.*

"The investors are on board with my vision for the expansion and are eager to move forward. I already contacted the owner of the space about leasing and she sent over the paperwork. I'm meeting with an old chef buddy tonight to try and convince him to leave his current gig to work with me."

"Wow, it's all really happening," I say, stunned by the speed of everything. "That's incredible, Reid."

He chuckles, bemused, and I can practically picture him running a hand through his mussed copper hair. "It almost feels too easy."

"Easy is good, right? It can mean something's meant to be."

"The same could be said for hard things."

And suddenly, we're not talking about his future restaurant anymore. We're in the realm of relationships—of The Talk.

There's a beat before he continues, "Do you want me to come home?"

My response is immediate, like an involuntary reaction. "No."

"Why not?" he challenges. One of the things I've always appreciated about Reid is he says what he means, sans drama, passive-aggressive nonsense, and veiled implications. "Why haven't you asked me to? Asked me to stay?"

To stay? That's never been in the equation. "I want to be supportive."

"Come on, Parks, we both know there's more to it than that. You're pulling away and I deserve to know why."

I get up and start pacing, chewing on my bottom lip, tea forgotten. Chamomile can't help me now. I'm ready to brush him off with a vague excuse, only, that isn't fair to either of us. I blurt out the truth instead, "Because I have to make sure I'm strong enough."

"Strong enough for what?"

"To do the independent thing."

"You are without a doubt the most capable and stubborn woman I know." His assertion comes with an aggrieved chuckle. "What's making you second-guess yourself?"

"The whole having separate lives in two states."

"It's the same life together, just with a built-in excuse to travel," he says. "Hell, Napa is practically down the street. This could be amazing for us." There's a plea in his voice now that breaks my heart.

Every bone in my body yearns to yield. To say what I know he wants to hear. That his plan is freaking incredible and basically a dream come true. But doubts bubble to the surface, the stress of the wedding and investigation enhancing my uncertainties. About us and if we can withstand the distance. If *I* can withstand it.

"For now," I manage to whisper, my mouth suddenly parched.

"This has never been about just for now, not for me." It's not only aggravation that I sense, but hurt.

I hurry to add, "Not for me, either."

"Then what are you saying?"

"Look, this is hard to do over the phone." I lick my lips, wilting into the couch. Both cats shoot me reproachful looks, as if they can comprehend all the ways I'm letting them and everyone else down. "It's about the future. If what works for us now will work down the road."

There's silence at the other end of the line. "I know this is a big change. But whatever comes our way, we can handle it. You and me. I believe that."

"I want to, too."

There are voices and chatter on Reid's end of the line. "Hang on." He muffles the receiver so I can't make out the words exchanged. "My buddy just showed up. But—"

"It's okay. Go. Do your thing."

"We're not done yet. Not even close," he states, so clearly and simply I know he'll put off his chef friend for me, risk convincing him to join his new restaurant.

"Look, you don't want to keep your friend waiting and I need sleep. Desperately. I'm not making any sense. Please, let's shelve this."

"Don't think you're off the hook, we're going to finish this later," he says. "I love you."

"Love you, too." I lean back into the cushion with my phone clutched to my chest, longing to disappear inside the weave. My chest aches and my eyes sting, the weight of what was said and left unsaid threatening to suffocate me.

My mom said one of the hard parts of relationships is figuring out how to grow together. But how do you do that when you're used to growing alone?

Vineyards are typically organized by blocks of individual varietals, the chemical makeup of the fruit being easier to track and control. That is, except for port.

Port is predominantly a field blend, a mishmash of grapes grown, harvested, and fermented as one. Perhaps as a nod to its Portuguese origin, which used upwards of fifty types for a single vintage, or perhaps because if it's not broken, don't fix it.

Either way, with so many different flavors, structure becomes a key component, for which there's no metric. Only experience and gut instinct.

While I scraped by with my Pikes Peak Port-Style, that was wine. This is life, and I fear I don't have enough of either.

A persistent knocking wakes me up the next morning.

I'm not sure what's more shocking, that I actually fell asleep or that someone is at my door at this ungodly hour.

I mean, the birds aren't even awake yet, the tree outside my bedroom window lacking their happy chirps.

The knocking grows louder. With this racket, soon my neighbors will be up and complaining.

I kick the covers off my legs, startling Zin in the process, who, once I'm up, sneaks her way into my vacated spot, nuzzling in as if it were her own little nest.

William gives the kitty equivalent of a shrug and hops off the bed, his black tail twitching as he leads the way into the hallway. I follow, tugging a hoodie over my tank and rubbing sleep from my eyes.

William sits on his haunches by the entryway table, his ears twitching. I guess it's a good sign he isn't running for cover; chances are it isn't a murderer then. Still, I take no chances.

I press my eye against the peephole right as a fist connects with the other side of the door.

I jump back, heart hammering, and then let out an exhale, unlocking the dead bolt and swinging the door open for Carolyn.

"I didn't think I'd be your wake-up call," she grumbles, arms over her chest.

She looks me up and down, taking in my pj shorts, overlarge hoodie (Reid's), and disheveled hair. She may not be dressed to the nines, but she at least looks sporty in a pair of yoga pants and airy tank with so many twisty straps I'd need a map to put it on.

We have the same narrow face, her long hair accentuating the shape while my bob softens it. And our eyes are the Cooper eyes, slanted ever so slightly and blue-gray. Hers are dusted in shimmery pink, and mine are, well, completely riddled with bags, but there's no denying the similarities— no hiding from our shared roots.

"Late night," I explain through a yawn.

She furrows her eyebrows. "Yeah, for me, too."

Carolyn doesn't need to know about my tense call with Reid after our already-long night, or how it left me so gutted I lay in bed for hours, replaying it in my mind, debating if I should call him back.

"Coffee?" I ask.

"Love some." She flashes me a smile that's so Carolyn, sarcastic one second and completely genuine the next. As if she doesn't know how to come across.

I wave her inside and stumble into the kitchen, busying myself with the filter, coffee grounds, and water. It's some sort of cruel joke that so much is involved in making coffee when one is entirely uncaffeinated.

Carolyn takes in my eclectic mishmash of furniture and decor. My belongings are a mix of holdovers from my college era and nicer duds I've invested in since, trinkets from around the world giving the place a unique, bohemian vibe.

Carolyn has never been here, our families usually congregating at one of our parents' houses or a third-party location, and I find myself nervously anticipating her reaction.

"Nice place," she says with an approving nod.

"Thanks," I say. I fumble for the on switch on the coffeepot. "It's not the biggest, but rent is manageable." Or rather, barely manageable, which is all you can hope for in Boulder.

"It's just you, though, right?"

"And a cat—well, actually two at the moment."

"Having space of your own is priceless."

I don't even know how to respond to that, so I switch gears. "Hey, what's going on with you and Xavier?"

"What makes you think something's going on?"

My mom and I agreed to keep mum about the wedding crasher, and that includes the many observations sprinkled through his podcast. Hence, I go with the simplest: "You guys seemed friendly by the pool."

"Because we are friendly," she says. "I like Xavier, he's smart and, contrary to many in his position, refreshingly modest. But that doesn't mean we're romantically involved."

I'm tempted to pry more, but bite my tongue. Carolyn owns who she is and I can't fault her for that.

The happy sound of gurgling permeates the air, bitter and earthy aromas making my body sag in relief at the promise of coffee. I prop my elbows on the countertop. "So, what's up? Another family member in dire need of assistance?"

"Not that I know of, but it's still early." She cocks her head to the side, a leery glint in her eye. "I wanted to give you the login for my mom's email. We both think you should have it."

"Emma's okay with that?"

"She'd have caved eventually anyway."

Okay, that would be a no. "That's awfully presumptive." I spare a thought for Emma, whose kind nature is so easily taken advantage of.

Carolyn sits on one of the wicker stools on the other side of the counter. "It isn't really up to her. The sooner we figure out what they have on my mom, the better."

"No argument here."

"Can I borrow your laptop?" She gestures to where it sits, charging at the far end of the counter.

At my nod, Carolyn slides the device in front of her and begins typing, her fingers flying across the keyboard.

I pass her a mug full of coffee and procure a bowl of sugar—kept for Reid, since he prefers his coffee sweeter than I do—and cream. She ignores the accoutrements and drinks it black, her eyes never leaving the screen.

I'm taking my first life-giving sip of coffee when she says, "The password is Emma0111."

I wonder how Carolyn feels knowing her mom's email password relates to her sister. "I bet she uses your name and birthday, too. Alternates."

Carolyn visibly shudders. "God, I hope not. She's a hack waiting to happen."

She turns the screen toward me, already having navigated to the Sent folder.

I don't have to look hard, which is for the best given the caffeine is still hitting my system.

The two most recent emails were sent to Prynne. I filter using her email address and—voilà—a history of their mostly one-way correspondence. Grace sent five total, of which only one received a brief response. The first was from six months ago, with the rest sprinkled throughout spring and summer.

I scour them with a fervor usually reserved for the latest issue of *Wine Enthusiast*, my insides coiling into a knot of ice. What started as a plea to protect her daughter's wants transformed into something very, very different. I don't have to read between the lines to understand the implied threat.

"Have you read these?" I ask Carolyn, taking a steadying sip of coffee.

She nods soberly. "I knew Mom was mad, but I had no idea she'd basically been harassing the wedding bimbo." At my raised eyebrows, she rephrases, "Fine, planner."

"Did your mom say anything?"

"Not much. She was pretty tired last night, went straight to bed after granting me access."

"And you let her get away with that?"

Carolyn tosses her hair over her shoulder. "Until this morning when I confronted her with these. She admitted to sending all but the last two, said she had no idea where they came from."

It's only because this is Carolyn, and she doesn't easily take offense, that I feel comfortable giving voice to my next question. "Do you believe her?"

"She was really upset when she saw them, felt terrible even though they weren't her fault." She gets to her feet and straightens her back resolutely. "In short, yes."

I exhale a tiny puff in response, going for another sip of coffee only to find my mug empty. "Mind if I print these out?" I ask. "Then I can log out of Grace's account."

"You have a printer?" Carolyn scoffs.

"Of course, I'm a business owner."

Sure, printing is old-school, and there's roughly a 30 percent chance my printer has ink and actually operates as requested. But there's something about hard copies that makes it easier to spot key details.

"Knock yourself out, tree killer." Carolyn sets her mug in the sink before taking her leave.

The emails read as follows:

Wed, Jan 19, 5:54 AM

Hi, Prynne,

We haven't had the pleasure of meeting yet, but you're planning my daughter Emma's wedding and I wanted to email you on a delicate matter. Emma

is the quiet one in a loud family and I want to
make sure her voice is heard. I'm sure you deal
with this all the time and trust you will use your
best judgment in making sure her desires are
upheld.

Sincerely,
Grace Bostwick

Prynne's response is short and to the point.

Wed, Jan 19, 3:01 PM

Hi, Grace,

I look forward to meeting you and already love your
daughter! Will do my best to give her the best day of
her life.

Xoxo,
Prynne

Ugh, Prynne is one of those people who sign off with an
"xoxo" even when she doesn't know the person. At all.

The next email from Grace was sent roughly two months
after that, her tone cooling.

Tues, Mar 8, 10:12 AM

Prynne—

Emma's been keeping me posted on her upcoming
nuptials and I have concerns. There isn't one thing
that sounds like her. I'm replying to my prior email
with hopes that you'll please reconsider your plans.

*Especially the cat, which clearly came from Emma's
great-aunt and not her.*

*Best,
Grace*

This one went unanswered, and clearly unheeded.
Which is probably why not even a week later, she sent
another missive.

Mon, Mar 14, 8:43 PM

*Okay, I'm putting my foot down with the chocolate
fountain. Emma and Nash both think it's ridiculous and
said their opinions have been ignored through this
entire experience. I won't hesitate to contact the Better
Business Bureau.*

This email got an auto-reply saying that Prynne would reply as soon as she had time. Which apparently, she didn't.
Ouch.

Although you know what they say about squeaky wheels,
and given the absence of a chocolate fountain on the banquet table, Grace was finally heard—er, read. Maybe thanks
to her next email. Which, as aggravated as she may have
been, definitely crosses a line.

Sat, May 14, 11:33 AM

*Prynne, I've had it!! You can't brush me off like you do
everyone else! Do something to correct the situation or
there will be consequences!!!!*

And the last email, which was sent the day before Emma's wedding.

Fri, Jun 10, 7:22 PM

You'll be sorry!! I warned you!!!!

A shiver snakes down my spine. Okay, so Eli *may* have a point about these implicating Grace. Especially if the authorities think she penned them all, which, let's be honest, why wouldn't they?

But I have my doubts, and it's not just Grace's word for it.

There's something here, some trace of the killer accidentally left behind. I flip through the sheets of paper over and over until I have to leave for Vino Valentine, willing the answer to appear like a 3-D image in a Magic Eye picture. Whatever it is eludes me, leaving my spidey senses tingling.

Chapter Fourteen

Whether spurred by my difficult talk with Reid, my oddball conversation with Carolyn, the shocking content of the emails, or some combination of all these things, I drive myself to Vino Valentine.

That sounds like such a simple statement: I drive myself. But it's a huge victory for me.

Sure, I went five below the speed limit, gripped the steering wheel with white knuckles, and practiced yoga breathing the entire way. None of that changes the fact that I did it.

It imbues me with a foolhardy confidence that makes me feel like I can do anything. Like solve a murder.

Flavors need to be sussed out of a wine. Decanting, aerating, and swirling are all techniques of letting the hallowed beverage breathe so that undertones such as tobacco, leather, or perhaps fresh-cut grass can come forward.

I tackle the emails in a similar fashion. I leave them sprawled beneath the tasting counter, out of sight but not out of mind, and reread them every chance I can in hopes that a clue will make itself known.

Sloan fidgets next to me, reviewing her copious notes on everything fermented grapes, a neat binder full of colorful tabs open before her. We take turns exhaling in frustration, mumbling under our breath, and tackling the few tables that come in. If she wonders what I'm pondering, she doesn't say. Sloan is in her own world, cramming for her exam.

She's slated to leave after closing today for her Master Sommelier exam. It will be held first thing in the morning, by invitation only, at a swanky resort in Aspen. I can practically see the tension radiating out of her.

"You know, you already have everything in there down pat," I say with a gesture toward her binder.

"So you're saying it's what's *not* in here I should be worried about." Sloan twirls a pen between her fingers, another one tucked behind her ear.

"That's not—" I shake my head.

"Just giving you a hard time." Her crimson lips twist into a crooked smile. She's in her customary suit and trainers, which is probably good given the amount of pacing she's doing. "This is the only way I know how to prepare for a test."

"Hey, you do you."

The bell signals the arrival of a large party of women, decked out in a medley of bike gear and trendy exercise attire, their bikes parked haphazardly outside my storefront. They file in, nodding and chattering companionably. They vary in age from midtwenties to early forties and have that glossed look. Sleek, high ponytails, a light application of makeup that achieves that coveted balance of primped and natural.

I plaster a winning smile on my face as I greet them. "Here for a tasting?"

"And then some," one of the younger gals pipes up with a mischievous grin.

A lady in leggings and a tennis top steps forward, clearly the leader. "Yes! We're with the St Julien!" She speaks very quickly and with all exclamation points, bouncing on the balls of her feet. Seriously, she could give Sloan a run for her money in the movement department.

The St Julien is the swankiest hotel in Boulder, attracting locals in want of pampering and luxury travelers, like Reid's family, who stayed there during their ominous visit last fall. While we're on decent terms with his mother now, it still makes my skin crawl thinking of my confrontation with his father in that esteemed establishment.

"We work in events and coordination!" the lady adds.

This last part rings in my ears, pushing all other thoughts aside. Do you know what the St Julien hosts a lot of? Weddings. And do you know who plans those receptions? These ladies.

I straighten, rolling my shoulders back and lifting my chin, even as nerves send a kaleidoscope of butterflies flitting through my stomach. Suddenly, I'm glad I took a few extra minutes getting ready this morning. Because, while you're not supposed to judge a book by its cover, in my line of work, I'm often selling myself as much as my product.

"Parker Valentine," I say, extending my arm for a firm handshake. "I'm the owner and would be more than happy to assist however I can." I guide them to a group of oak-barrel tables near the floor-to-ceiling windows that overlook the

rolling foothills. "Best view in the house, plus you can ma-
neuver chairs or tables however you'd like."

"Thanks!" The leader takes in the twinkling lights adorning the shelves, flickering pillar candles, and vases of fresh
flowers with keen eyes. "We're having a bonding day!"

"Biking and wine tasting sounds like a win to me," I
respond, and mean it. Perhaps I should plan a bonding day
for Sloan and me. Obviously, our activity would involve
something besides wine tasting. Maybe whitewater rafting
or an escape room.

As the party make themselves comfortable, I start passing around tasting menus, but the leader shakes her head.
"We'll each take a taste of the lot!"

"Ooh yes!" another responds through a bout of giggles.
"I'm parched after the ride here."

I collect myself—and the menus. "Coming right up, with
a round of ice waters." *And multiple baskets full of crackers.*

I get busy, eager to impress.

I line sparkling crystal glasses along the countertop and
pour from open bottles stashed beneath, working my way
through varietals from the lightest whites to the heavier
reds, the colors shifting from pale straw to deep plum, finishing with my ruby port, served just below room temperature, the viscosity like syrup and just as sweet.

Fun fact: ports produced anywhere except Portugal can't
legally be called *port*, similar to how only sparkling wines
from Champagne, France, can be dubbed as such, hence
the name for mine: Pikes Peak Port-Style.

"Pop quiz," I say to Sloan.

She side-eyes me. "I'm listening."

"What's the typical alcohol content of port?"

"Eighteen to twenty percent." She doesn't need my confirmation to know she got it right. She casts her gaze to the

group of women, the tapping of her pen causing the liquid in the glasses to ripple. "You're being awfully generous with your pours. Are those chicks royalty or something?"

"Might as well be." I cork the bottle of port and tuck it safely back in its nook, aromas of licorice and blackberries wafting toward me. "They're from the St Julien. They could send heaps of business my way if I don't bungle this."

"Why exactly are you so interested in breaking into the wedding industry?"

"Besides the obvious boost to business?"

"Yeah," she says with a shrug. "I mean, you've got a solid clientele. Why not just ride the wave of your success and coast for a bit?"

Because I don't do coast. The retort is on the tip of my tongue, but I hesitate. Truth is, I'm wired to always be reaching for something, to continue raising the bar. It's something Reid and I have in common—have always understood about each other.

And if I'm being honest, Reid inspires me. Seeing him take this career step has made me consider what I want in my professional life as well as my personal.

Which is why we might just be able to make it work. And by *we* I mean me. Reid has made it abundantly clear he's all in.

Sloan kicks the underside of the tasting bar, bringing me back to the present.

"Because I want to expand," I finally say as I add the tasters of port to the trays. Busying myself by filling cups with ice, my back to Sloan, I continue, "Maybe open another tasting room. Somewhere downtown. Union Station in LoDo would make an excellent location."

"You're right," Sloan says. "That would be a killer location. Good luck."

"You, too," I say with a nod at her stack of notecards.

Sloan helps me deliver the trays and palate cleansers to the cluster of tables and then slips away while I put on my entrepreneur hat.

I point out which varietal is which and the prominent flavors they might notice in each (basically a stroll through a farmers' market), describe my winemaking philosophy (grounded in tradition but with a flair for modern techniques), and share where my grapes are sourced from (Palisade on the Western Slope of the Rockies).

In short, I schmooze.

"Wow!" the leader says when I finish my spiel. "You've given us a lot to think about—and taste!"

I know overwhelmed when I see it. There's a chance, in my excitement, I *may* have come on too strong.

"I'll leave you to it," I say, backing away slowly. "Say the word if you need anything else."

My cheeks flush as I turn away. Why did I share so many details about my winemaking process? Why did I recite my grape-grower Gus's latest wine joke? Why can't I just be cool?

Oh, right. Because when it comes to my passion, my enthusiasm bubbles forth without reservation.

"Yum!" one of the girl hollers to another.

That's when it finally hits me. What's bothering me about the emails.

The exclamation points.

In all of the emails except the last two, Grace's punctuation was subdued and to the point, period.

Would it be enough to convince Eli that Grace didn't write them? Doubtful. But it was worth a shot.

I construct a text directing his attention to the punctuational disparity between the emails, leaving out how I got access to them. I finish with a desperate appeal: *The messages are nothing but another attempt by the murderer to cast shade on the case. Please, at least consider it.*

I don't hear back, not that I expected to.

The table of St Julien personnel is sipping their way through my wine. Their expertise levels vary from the novice who downs an entire sample in one gulp to the expert who sniffs, swirls, and gurgles each sip. The leader falls into the latter category and I find myself studying her.

My gaze must draw her attention because she glances my way with a frown, dumping the remainder of her Pearl Street Pinot into a discard vase. That can't be a good sign.

Maybe because you're so obviously desperate for approval. Jeez. Give her a little space.

With no other patrons, and Tuesday midday being typically slow, that leaves me to my musings.

Who could have sent the emails from Grace's account in the first place? Not in a malicious-existential sense, but in a technical one.

Unfortunately, that list is longer than it should be since Grace needs to majorly up her password strength. But it had to be someone close enough to her to know she has a daughter. And to know that daughter's name and birthday.

Who uses that many exclamation points? People trying to convey severity, excitement, or menace. In framing Grace, is it possible the killer left behind a bit of themselves, a bit of their natural conduct? There's a niggling at the back of my mind like a knotted vine I can't trace. The harder I try to tease it out, the more tangled my thoughts become. I let it go, hoping for illumination if my subconscious is given a chance to mull.

And who had it in for Prynne? She was bossy and cut-throat with vendors in addition to brides, and I sincerely question whether she had the taste and class to pull off the events she advertised. But this is premeditated murder we're talking about, a carefully orchestrated act, not some heat-of-the-moment attack. The time stamps on those emails prove it; if Grace didn't send them, that means whoever did planned everything months in advance.

There's some unknown part of Prynne, some transgression in her past that set everything in motion. I can feel it, sense the shadows lurking in the background.

A chill runs up my spine as I recall the way Chastity watched me when I inquired about her friend, the studied way she dabbed at her eyes and leveraged her emotions as a distraction. There was real grief there, sure, and a plea to not press—for me to let it go—and maybe a touch of guilt. Chastity was the reason Prynne was hired for the job, after all, the instigator for the over-the-top ceremony.

"Did you say something?" Sloan asks.

"What?" I ask. "No. At least I don't think so."

"I thought I heard you mumble something about bouquets. This whole wedding business is really getting to you."

It's not a good sign that I'm talking to myself. In public. At least at home I have Zin as an excuse.

"I need to make a call," I say.

But just as I say that, I'm hailed by The Table.

"Parker!" the leader shouts with a distinguished wave.

I straighten my skirt and blouse and hustle over. Their table is a wreckage of empty stemware, liquid rings left by dewy water glasses, and cracker crumbs. The volume of their chatter has ticked up a notch and their faces are flushed and, if I'm not mistaken, happy.

"How was everything?" I ask hesitantly, my lips twitching against a forced smile.

"Your wines are divine!" the spokesperson responds with the rest of her team nodding along. "Especially the port. I've never tried port before. It's so silky."

"Thank you. I'm flattered," I say, holding a hand over my heart. *Play it cool*, I tell myself, biting my tongue to keep from gushing more.

She narrows her eyes and in them, I recognize a fellow business-minded woman. "Do you offer discounts if bought by the case?"

"Of course," I answer. "I can get you a detailed list of my pricing by unit."

"Excellent! We have so many couples who want to go local with their weddings and I really think this would be a big hit."

My heart soars and I feel elated, buoyant, as if I'm walking on clouds. I come back down long enough to exchange business cards and promise to email her my prices and a menu that afternoon.

"Now, back to bonding!" She claps her hands together and gestures for her group to stand.

This pronouncement is met with trepidation as the ladies haul themselves and their belongings back to their bikes, less enthusiastic about their ride back than they were about the wine they just imbibed.

Buzzed on my unexpected success with the event planners, I dart into the back, leaving a twitchy, yet entirely capable, Sloan in charge of the front.

I lean against the farmhouse sink, letting the cool metal

bite into my lower back, facing the space I transformed into a warehouse. Stainless-steel vats stretch from floor to ceiling, at the ready to be filled with juice at harvest, and on the opposite wall are rows of oak barrels, containing a variety of wines in different stages of fermentation. And through a sealed glass door, kept at ideal humidity and temperature, is my cellar, full of the remainder of my product.

If I continue selling like this, I'm going to have no choice but to expand.

Which is as scary as it is exciting.

That's the thing nobody tells you about dreams. How terrifying it can be living it, everything you've worked for balanced on the point of a corkscrew. But, as I've told Reid multiple times now, sometimes you have to take the plunge and hope for the best. I run a hand through my raven locks, shoving that thought to the back of my mind to ferment a bit longer.

Then I hold my phone to my ear; I'm not sure I've ever been so excited to call my mother.

"Hey, Mom," I start. "I've got a few updates for you." I quickly rehash Carolyn's drop-by this morning and my discovery about the emails, finishing with, "After we hang up, go update your passwords. No family members, no birthdays. Got it?"

"No offense, Parker, but I haven't used your or Liam's names in my passwords for at least a decade. It's always elements for me."

"Pardon?"

"From the periodic table. I work my way through, one column at a time, rotating by month. I'm on the noble gases now."

That is so fitting. "Happy to hear it." I pace by the shelf holding my lab equipment, running my fingers along each precious tool. "Now that I'm convinced of your cyber safety, think you can you get Chastity to Vino Valentine this afternoon?"

She sighs into the receiver. "Must I?"

"To give Eli someone other than Grace to home in on, yes." Eli still hasn't responded to my text and chances are he's busy now digging something else up on Grace. We're good enough friends I know how he operates. "We need to know what Chastity isn't saying about her BFF."

"I'll get her there," my mom grumbles. "By hell or hoax Lululemon sale."

"You're devious," I say through a snort. "And I love it. Okay, I'm going to snap pictures of these emails and send them over. Take a look and let me know if anything stands out to you."

"I'll put my little gray cells to the task," she says, a breathy eagerness in her voice usually reserved for NASA launches.

My lips twitch into an amused grin. At the same time, I'm a little worried about what sort of floodgate I may have inadvertently opened by agreeing to let her help in the first place.

"Don't forget about Chastity," I say. "Getting her here is paramount."

That tempers her excitement. "See you this afternoon."

Chapter Fifteen

Happy hour at Vino Valentine starts at four o'clock and goes until closing at six o'clock. What began as a ploy to draw in the after-work crowd has become one of my favorite times at my winery.

The congregation is an eclectic mix, as it always is, of the professionals I'd hoped to entice, art aficionados lured by nearby galleries, moms in need of adult company, bikers (both of the cycle and motor varieties), and everyone in between.

There are special deals on flights of tasters, plus snack packs purchased from a local grocer with rustic crackers, cheeses, and fruit. Laughter and chatter abound, the mood lighter at the end of the day. The sun hangs low over the Flatirons, giving us front-row seats to a picturesque backdrop, the mountainside cast in shades of coral and gold. Acoustic music playing quietly over the speakers completes the relaxed ambience. Even I can kick back, mingle with my customers, and soak up the cheer like a cabernet does tannins from oak.

At least, that's usually the case.

The bell over the door jingles with a new arrival. A jolt of excitement courses through me when I see who it is: Chastity.

Her peroxide-blond hair is curled to perfection and she's in a fuchsia summer dress with a deep-cut V and skyscraper-high heels. She shifts her clutch from one hand to the other, looking about her uncertainly.

My mom did it. She got her here, and Chastity doesn't appear to be confused by the lack of upscale athleisure wear, so win-win.

I make ready to intercept, debating which question to ask first, but freeze midstep. She's not alone.

More family members and then the entire wedding party traipse in behind her. My uncle, the groomsmen, brides-maids, bride-to-be and her fiancé, all trailed by my parents and a somber Grace.

I should be elated at the chance to show off my goods to extended family. Instead, I fight back a choice swear word. This will make it almost impossible to ask Chastity about Prynne. *Almost* being the operative word; I'm nothing if not determined.

"What a surprise," I say, coming around from behind the tasting bar. "Thank you all for coming. Let me show you to the best seats in the house."

"You mean, the only ones open," Carolyn pipes up, rest-ing her overlarge sunglasses atop her head. Even though it comes out sassy, there's an unmistakable sense of awe at my bustling winery.

"True," I respond. "But they're also my favorite."

As I did with the bonding team from the St Julien, we smoosh a bunch of tables together. Jack, Nash, and Xavier do the heavy lifting while I dash in the back for a couple extra chairs.

My mom follows hot on my heels, looking a little too pleased with herself.

I wait until we're in the back and out of sight of my customers before turning on her. "I meant for Chastity to come solo," I hiss. "How are we supposed to get the truth out of her now?"

My mom furrows her eyebrows, the corner of her mouth twitching. "You didn't say she had to come alone. This was the only way I could convince her. She didn't buy that I wanted to catch up with her."

I rub my temples. "Probably because you've never made her feel accepted."

She seems to shrink, dipping her chin in disappointment and, if I'm not mistaken, embarrassment. She sheepishly fidgets with the strap of her tote, the cotton fraying at the seam, her frizzy silver hair catching the light.

And suddenly, I feel horrible. Worse than horrible. Like the gunk I scrape out of my wine press after harvest.

I exhale my frustration. "It's fine. I didn't mean to snap."

"I think I can make it up to you," she says, blue-gray eyes sparking with intelligence.

"How?"

"I found something."

My ears prick up. "In the emails?"

She nods, rocking back and forth with suppressed energy. "Did you notice anything about the dates?"

"Obviously not," I say, biting back my impatience. "Care to educate me?"

She pushes her glasses farther up her nose. "Well, the

two that weren't written by Grace were sent during wedding events."

"What do you mean?"

"May fourteenth was the bridal shower and June tenth
was the rehearsal dinner."

I blink rapidly as a lightbulb switches on in my brain.
Here, I'd been so consumed with who could've guessed the
password to Grace's email, but what if the infiltrator didn't
even need it? What if they accessed her account through
her mobile device? Let's face it, she probably doesn't lock
her phone, and she would've been too distracted at both
events to notice it missing for a few minutes.

But that's not all.

Whoever sent the emails and set Grace up was at both
parties, which could be only a handful of people, and was
likely a woman, since the bridal shower was strictly No
Boys Allowed.

"This could be the key," I say with a meaningful glance
through the slitted window to the tasting room.

Our crew is half-sitting, half-standing, awaiting the chairs
I'm supposed to be getting. Nash whispers something in Emma's ear and she giggles; Carolyn, Josie, and Xavier strike
up a conversation with hopeful looks toward the bar; Jack
gazes out the window, at ease with his hands in his pockets;
and my dad plays referee for my uncle, Chastity, and Grace.

I hate being wrong, but all signs are pointing to one of
them being a killer.

My mom and I return to the tasting room with renewed
purpose.

Our mission: question the wedding party without arous-
ing suspicion—from them or the rest of my patrons.

We deposit the spare chairs, only to find Sloan has been hijacked by Chastity, who's interrogating my assistant about what cocktails we serve, or rather, don't serve.

"Not even a manhattan?" Chastity asks in disbelief, hip and bottom lip jutting out in equal measure. "What about a blue Hawaiian?"

"Sorry, we only have wine." Sloan adds helpfully, "And sparkling water."

New mission: rescue Sloan.

"I'll be right back to take care of you guys," I announce to the table, looping my arm through Sloan's.

"Remember, you still owe me a large—like, can't see the bottom—glass of wine," Carolyn says, pointing between her eyes and mine.

"Right. Magically refilling glass, coming up." I give a strained chuckle as I lead Sloan back to the tasting bar.

She trips on her way behind the counter, almost sending a tray of empty glasses crashing to the floor. I lurch forward and right her with one hand while snagging the tray with the other.

"Thanks for the assist," Sloan says. "Your family's, uh . . ."

"I know." I pat her on the shoulder.

"Don't get me wrong, they're great, just *a lot*."

"No, really," I say with an exaggerated nod. "I get it. Just be glad Aunt Harriet decided not to show up with her cat."

Sloan's eyes widen in horror. "She brought a cat to a wedding?"

"Believe it or not, he wasn't the least well-behaved guest." I place empty stemware into the dishwasher and put the tray on top of the stack by the sink. Then I turn back to Sloan. "Can you handle our regulars? If so, I'll get the Brady Bunch."

"You've got yourself a deal," Sloan says. "No take-backs."

I sigh. "Alas, there are no take-backs with family."

I return to the table, where everyone has made themselves comfortable. Emma and Nash are nestled in the middle, the glue holding everyone together. Around one of the adjacent oak barrels are the parents, with the other being a glorified kids' table. Only, the adolescent banishment is far easier to swallow now, because: wine.

I clap to get everyone's attention. "Who wants a drink?"

Every arm goes in the air.

All the better for questioning. The alcohol will encourage tongues to wag.

"How about we work our way through my tasting menu?" I suggest.

This is met with general assent, albeit a pouty "If that's really all you have" from Chastity.

Jack waves me over. I lean down so I can hear him over the commotion.

"Do you have coffee?" he asks. His blond hair is swept neatly to the side and he's clean-shaven, in khakis and a button-up shirt, more put together than I've seen him yet. "I've got to stay sharp—and more importantly, awake."

"Big plans later?"

He gives a nonchalant shrug, resting his forearms on the tabletop. "If you call a red-eye to London 'big.'"

"Back to the grind?"

"No rest for the wicked." His lips twitch into a side-smirk. "And I finally caught up on sleep—not sure how my dad did this for so many years." There's a sad edge to his tone in addition to bewilderment.

The hair at the nape of my neck prickles. I sense eyes on me before I notice Josie's penetrating stare. From the way her brow is drawn, she appears puzzled—and maybe a touch worried. It takes her a moment to notice I've caught her ogling and when she does, she looks away quickly, nostrils flaring.

What was that about? She can't be weirded out about an innocent conversation between me and Jack, can she? I mean, Josie detests Jack. Can't stand to be in the same room as him, couldn't even bring herself to be escorted by him down the aisle. She ditched him halfway to the altar, but only after digging her fingernails into his forearm.

Jack clears his throat and I refocus on his quest for caffeine. "I don't have coffee, but the Laughing Rooster next door does and it's the best in town."

Jack pushes his chair back with a screech against the hardwood. He heads for the door, tossing a quick "thanks" over his shoulder.

My mom accompanies me to the tasting bar. She knows her way around here, having helped out when I've been between assistants or needed a weekend getaway. We're a well-oiled machine. She arranges stemware while I wield a wine bottle like a baton in a parade, efficiently adding a taster to each glass, plus an extra pour in Carolyn's.

"Okay, battle stations," I say to my mom as we hoist the laden trays.

I start with Carolyn, setting her glass in front of her with a wink.

"You've always been my favorite cousin," she says.

"Well, my only competition is Liam." *And wait till he hears about this little gathering; he'll be both relieved and bummed to have missed it.*

I continue, placing glasses around the table, meeting up with my mom on the other side.

"We're starting with the Mount Sanitas White," I explain. "A crisp blend that reminds me of my favorite hiking trail. You'll detect notes of citrus, peaches, and honey-suckle."

I don't even mind that no one does a formal tasting. In fact, it's a common misconception in the industry. Vintners don't care how our wine is enjoyed; it's more important that it *is* enjoyed.

Everyone gushes appropriately as they discuss flavors they taste and aromas they detect, which vary from the accurate to outlandish. Well, all except for Jack, who lifts a to-go mug from Laughing Rooster in my direction in a mock toast.

Even Chastity musters up a "It's sweeter than I thought it would be," which I'll take to mean she's appeased. At least until she discovers why she's really here.

"Keep 'em coming," Carolyn says, waving her empty glass in the air.

"You got it."

The next few minutes are spent catering to my family. Having had my fair share of customers, from the easily content to the demanding, I can safely say they sway more toward the latter. There's always a question or request, although with my mom's help, we ease into a rhythm. The diminishing of glasses slows and everyone is lulled into a sense of relaxation and safety. It could almost pass for a normal happy hour.

Carolyn regales the table with an exploit from her office. "So then I told him, if he continued working on tasks that were out of scope of the project plan, he could take his attitude to the Upside Down."

Xavier guffaws and Michael utters a "Thatta girl."

Emma interjects, wisps of her honeyed hair falling into her face, "That's not very nice."

"Don't worry, the Upside Down is what we call HR."

From her pursed lips and the subtle shake of her head, Emma isn't convinced.

While she's able to distract herself with her handsome, good-natured fiancé, the simmering tension remains. It's like a canary in a coal mine, a song that warns of greater trouble, which ripens into reality as I make the rounds with a bottle of my Campy Cab. That's when the proverbial grape must hits the fan.

My uncle starts it with a not-so-subtle dig at my mom.

"Glad you aren't busy with work this visit," Michael says to my mom as I'm midpour, deep ruby liquid splashing into his crystal bowl.

Close in age, but opposite in everything else, it's no surprise my mom and uncle rarely see eye to eye. It got worse when my aunt Laura passed away, the youngest of the three siblings being the tether holding them together. Now, they usually settle for forced commingling, loving each other for the sake of their shared DNA.

"Actually, I was scheduled to go in, but I took a personal day," my mom answers evenly.

"Really?" I ask, casting her a quizzical glance. "I didn't know that."

Michael lifts his hand in the air to make a point, although he looks equally prepared to swing a golf club in his emerald-green polo. "Because you've come to expect otherwise."

"That's enough, Michael." A warning flashes in my mom's eyes.

"It's the truth, though," he grumbles. "You've never made family a priority. Not sure what's different this time."

My dad opens his mouth to respond, but I beat him to it.

"That's not fair." I swoop to my mom's defense, which surprises me as much as it does her.

Because I've often felt the same way as Michael, having gotten used to taking the backseat to my mom's and dad's professions, only to realize there are no backseats or front seats. There's just a lengthy row of haphazardly organized chairs and a family of imperfect people trying to do the best they can. In short, it was on me, too.

I continue, "My mom has always put family first."

Michael barks out a laugh. "Yeah, like when she accidentally ruined my prized baseball cards with her science kit, forgot to pick me up after soccer practice, or conveniently had an important internship the semester I was stuck home with mono." He fiddles with the stem of his wineglass, a mean smirk on his face. "And no one ever says otherwise. They just let you be brilliant, never mind who gets stomped on in the process."

The rest of the party is a study in avoidance. Grace rolls her eyes skyward and mumbles something under her breath that sounds suspiciously like *Not again*. Carolyn and Emma pretend to be absorbed by something outside the window, the rest of the wedding party following their lead.

"Hey, this is my business and I would appreciate it if you didn't make a scene," I say with enough severity to be heeded. "Especially when we have more important things to worry about."

"Of course, you're taking her side," Michael says, twisting to face me full on. "You don't know any better."

I raise my eyebrows and unclamp my jaw. "You wanna know what I do know? That I can choose who to serve and who not to serve, so please mind your manners." *Before the rest of my customers are scared away by your petty drama.*

Already neighboring tables are observing our confrontation with undisguised curiosity.

A talking-to from his niece makes Michael squirm in his seat, and apparently convinces him to keep his mouth shut.

"Great. Who's ready for the next round?" I don't even wait for a response before I rage-walk to the tasting bar.

I blindly grab the bottle of Snowy Day Syrah from underneath and brace myself to return, rolling my neck in either direction. The time has come for answers; no more Ms. Nice Parker.

I don't realize I have a shadow until my mom lightly touches my elbow. "Thank you."

"Don't mention it." I try to wave her off, but she stops me.

There's a steadiness in her gaze that conveys the meaning behind her words. "Michael has always had a problem with me. It's rooted in a childhood where he unjustly felt neglected as a middle child. I appreciate what you said."

"It's what we do, right? We have each other's backs." I shrug, planting my hands on my hips. "And hey, I've seen worse. Remember the wine-tossing incident on opening day? Which was quickly overshadowed by a dead body."

She gives me a small smile. "At least there's no bloodshed."

"Not yet. There are still two wines left to taste and, as Michael just proved, everyone is primed to let their true feelings fly."

With that, we head back, an awkward vibe still emanating from the space.

I pour samples of my Snowy Day Syrah into ready glasses, jammy aromas of berries and a punch of cloves and pepper tickling my nose. "You'll notice velvety blackberries, mocha, and even vanilla on the palate, which makes the perfect companion for mulled wine, or in the summer, sangria." I direct their attention to the armoire, where sachets are displayed for sale.

When I get to Grace, I spot her phone lying on the table and with that, I have my in. "How do you like your Android? I've always been an iPhone gal myself, but was considering switching."

"It's a phone. With the miracle of the internet, apps, GPS, all way more than I need. Young people don't realize how good they have it."

I nod as if this were the first time I've heard such a notion and segue to what I'm really curious about. "Do you lock your phone?"

She grows sheepish, massaging her wrist with her opposite hand. "I know I should, but I don't have time to fumble with a passcode. Besides, who would want to break into my phone?"

"Someone trying to place blame for murder."

Grace jerks, knocking her glass of wine over. Purple liquid dribbles across the table and onto the floor.

"Is this about the emails?" Emma asks, scrambling to help sop up the mess with napkins.

"Yes." I lend a towel and together we mop until there's nothing but a faint lavender sheen to the oak and a sticky residue on the floor. I'll clean more thoroughly later. For now, I refocus on what's important. "I read them, and the last two, the ones the detective is hinging his case on, aren't real. Someone got to your mom's phone and sent them from her account." I stop, not ready to divulge the *when* part of the equation.

I peer at the faces surrounding me, gauging reactions. Eyes widen and jaws slacken as astonishment mounts. In everyone except for Josie, who resolutely stares at a knot in the oak.

"Wait, you read them?" Emma challenges. Her cheeks are rosy and her voice rises to a screechy pitch. "How? When was this decided and why didn't I know about it?"

I look to Carolyn for help. She rolls her eyes as if to say *weakling* and explains, "I gave her access. Mom and I talked last night and decided it was for the best."

"Really, dear," Grace interjects in an attempt to soothe her daughter. "If it clears up this misunderstanding, why not?"

"Why not? WHY NOT?!" Emma gets to her feet in a jumble of limbs and chairs. Nash reaches for her but she jerks out of reach. "Because maybe I would have had something to say. I HAVE THINGS TO SAY!"

Emma shakes with the intensity of decades of repressed emotions. We wisely let her continue.

"Did I want a big fancy wedding? No. Did I want to wear a rib-crushing dress that made me look like a cream puff? No. Did I want a cat to walk down the aisle ahead of me? Also, noooo." She draws out that last word, chest heaving. "No one ever thinks I might have some ideas, too."

My entire winery is watching this scene unfold, but like carbon dioxide trapped in a bottle of wine, there's nowhere for her torrent to go but out.

"We know—" Michael starts.

"Don't even," Emma interrupts. "You sided with Chastity every step of the way, convinced me to go along because it would be better for the family. Ha." A maniacal bark of laughter escapes her.

She rounds on Carolyn, lips trembling. She wipes at her eyes. "It's not about the stupid emails. It's about the fact that you guys made a decision without me. You don't even think I have a voice."

Carolyn leans back as if she's been slapped. "I had no idea."

"Yes, you did," Emma says. "You went behind my back and did this, assuming I'd just go along with it. Well, guess what, I'm sick of going along with everything. Nice, compliant Emma has left the building."

I'm tempted to give her a round of applause. After everything she's put up with, it's good to see her taking charge.

Emma huffs and seems to come to a decision. "In fact, I'm actually leaving the building. I've had enough." She scrambles to unhook her purse from the back of her chair and makes for the door.

The bell over the door chimes and Emma is gone.

Chapter Sixteen

We all look from one to the other, stunned into companion-able silence while the rest of my winery erupts into a fervor of whispers.

"Shouldn't someone, I dunno, go after her?" I finally ask, shifting in my flats.

Nash shakes his head. "Trust me, Emma needs space to process. I'll check on her in a little bit." His eyes drift toward the door and then back to mine. "She'd want me to make sure everyone gets back okay."

"Where do you think she's going?" Jack asks.

"Back to the motel?" Carolyn suggests. "Emma may have blown a gasket, but she's still Emma. She wouldn't do anything rash."

Jack gets to his feet, cradling his cup of coffee. "If that's the case, maybe she'll give me a ride. I've gotta get to DIA."

DIA is the Denver International Airport, a major travel hub that welcomes passengers with the infamous bucking bronco statue that's notorious for falling on—and killing—its creator. With glowing orange eyes and a stormy disposition, I've always found it to be a disconcerting, yet strangely vigilant, sentry.

"Is this really the time to beg Emma for a favor?" Josie asks, tossing her napkin on the table, her face twisted in disgust. "Selfish ass."

"Now, kids," I say. "The entertainment for the evening has ended."

Jack ignores me and snaps back at Josie, "Some of us actually have jobs. I've gotta jet either way. I'll catch an Uber if I have to."

He exchanges customary dude handshakes with Xavier and Nash. "Keep me posted if you two lovebirds decide to get hitched."

Without missing a beat, Xavier responds, gesturing between him and Nash, "Pretty sure we're going to keep our relationship professional."

Nash snorts and responds more seriously, "I will, man. Safe travels."

Jack strolls out of Vino Valentine, every inch the suave international man of mystery he claims he isn't. I watch as he hails Emma. She slows her Prius and gestures for Jack to hop in, barely pausing long enough for him to do so before peeling out of the parking lot.

"I should've seen this coming," Grace murmurs with a forlorn look at Emma's empty chair.

"No, I should've been a better listener," Michael says. He takes Grace's hand in a show of solidarity and then turns to my mom. "And I shouldn't have jumped all over you earlier."

"Water under the bridge," my mom says. "I should have done more over the years to make my priorities clear."

"Okay, this is getting too Hallmark for me," Carolyn says. "Parker, what else are we tasting?"

"I think it's time to call it a night," my dad interjects in a decisive tone. "We've all had a lot of excitement, and I have a move to make." He waves his phone in the air, Scrabble-bots illuminating the screen.

My stomach plummets. *Not yet*, I want to shout, *it's too soon!*

Josie, Xavier, and Nash don't hesitate in getting to their feet, eager to be rid of my family. Can't say I blame them.

Desperate, I flap around them like a distressed chicken, waving them back into their chairs. "It's not even six yet. And you haven't tried my port! No good tasting is complete without port." Which is a complete lie. While dessert wines round off a tasting in a satisfying way, a syrupy sweetness that settles the taste buds after an exciting flavor adventure, it's most definitely not a requirement.

My mom picks up on my hint. "Parker's right."

"Now I know why you defended your mom," Michael grunts. "You're of the same stock."

"Michael," my mom starts.

He raises his hands in surrender. "I meant that as a compliment. Give a guy some credit."

"Why don't you get the last wine, dear, while we settle the bill," Grace says, always the voice of reason.

"Mom, will you get the check? Don't forget to apply the special family discount." I grip my beaded necklace, feigning searching faces at the table in indecision. "And Chastity, why don't you help me in the back?"

She freezes like a deer in headlights. In fact, her expression isn't fair to deer. Her mascara-rimmed eyes open wide in alarm and she stammers a response, "M-me?" She runs her palms down the skirt of her dress. "But—I . . ." She trails off, unable to vocalize an excuse.

She glances toward my uncle, but Michael, for once, doesn't immediately rush to her aid.

Her agitation solidifies my resolve. Chastity wouldn't be so nervous to be alone with me if she didn't have something to hide—something she was worried I would dig up.

"I could use your opinion." I flash Chastity my most innocuous smile. "I'm working on a new label design and you clearly have good taste." I keep my face blank so as not to give away the utter falsehood of this statement.

"Oh, sure, I guess," she says, appealing again to my uncle, who merely nods encouragingly.

Hesitantly, Chastity gets to her feet and follows me to the back of my winery like a grape being led to the press.

Sun cascading through slitted windows ricochets off stainless steel, dousing the space in blinding light and elongated shadows. The chatter from out front dulls into the hum of appliances and the clicking of Chastity's heels against the concrete flooring.

"This way," I say cheerily. "It's in my cellar."

The smaller room I lead Chastity into is lined with racks of wine bottles lying on their sides, organized much like my tasting menu. It's chillier in here, a crisp fifty-five degrees Fahrenheit, the temperature ideal for aging, maintained by a sealed door.

I stroll to the far corner, running my fingertips over the smooth glass bottles.

Suspicion flits in Chastity's eyes, but she continues behind me, her lips in a thin line. "Really, I'm not sure I can help. I don't know anything about the wine industry."

"Pish posh, you know more than you think." *Did I really just say "pish posh" like I'm Mary Poppins or something?* "Did you recommend Prynne for Emma's wedding?" I subtly loop back around my cellar, strategically placing myself in the doorway to block Chastity in.

"I helped spread the word about Blush whenever I could." She shrugs, looking about for the imaginary label designs. "What exactly did you need my advice on?"

I lean nonchalantly against the doorframe, legs crossed, and decide to cut to the chase. "When I talked with you the night of Emma's wedding, I got the impression there was something you weren't saying about Prynne."

"That's why you asked me back here?" Chastity demands. "Unbelievable. Michael warned me about you lot."

My eyebrows shoot up into my bangs. As if *we* are the dramatic ones of the clan.

She starts stomping toward the exit but I throw an arm out to stop her. If there's a body feature I'm especially proud of, it's my arms, strong and toned from climbing and the labor involved in winemaking. With a steady gaze, I dare her to try me. "What is it about Prynne? Did she do something, make someone upset?"

All my far-fetched notions come back to me, people she could have upset and the ones she definitely did. The caterer, Grace, and, whether she admits it or not, Josie. And that's just a single wedding. Who knows how many Prynne offended in her misguided attempts to deliver matrimonial bliss?

"That's none of your business," Chastity says through gritted teeth. "I refuse to speak ill of the dead."

"So, you're saying there is ill to speak of?"

"I didn't—I just—" Chastity crosses her arms over her chest, accentuating her ample cleavage, and bows her head like a battering ram. "I'm not doing this."

I hold my ground. "It could be important."

She swipes at her nose, a loose strand of blond hair falling in her face. "Let me through."

"Don't you get it, whatever you know about Prynne could be the key to figuring out who killed her," I implore, my voice rising a notch. "Don't you want justice for your best friend?"

She freezes. Her eyes flit briefly to mine and what I see is a crack in her facade. She's listening.

I continue, "I would, if it were me." Not that Sage would ever be in this situation, but if worse comes to worst, you'd better believe I'd go to the very gates of hell to avenge her. And she'd do the same for me; heck, it'd give her the opportunity to wear her Wonder Woman cape and be the sort of crusader she relishes in fiction.

Chastity catches her lower lip in her teeth, ready to break. All she needs is one more nudge.

"Whoever murdered Prynne could go after someone else. Unless they're stopped."

When Chastity speaks, her voice is barely above a whisper. "Before Prynne was a, uh, wedding planner, she had another job." Her throat bobs as she swallows and I lean in to better be able to hear. "She was one of those people who helps direct planes."

"An air traffic controller?"

"Yeah, that's it." Chastity nods, tugging on the skirt of her dress. "She loved it, watching the planes, seeing families off on adventures, being a part of a team—a part of something special. Travel sparks happiness in people, sparks memories, I think she's always wanted to be involved in something that could do that."

I fit this puzzle piece in with what I recall of Prynne. She certainly worked hard to create something special, something perfect, but it was always her vision, not that of others. The brides and grooms who were happiest were those whose wants aligned with hers.

But why all the secrecy? What's so bad about a career change?

I let my arm fall to my side, mystified. "Why did she quit?"

"There was an accident." Chastity fidgets. Tears glisten in her eyes and cling to her eyelashes. "She made me promise not to say anything, was embarrassed she told me in the first place. Margaritas were always her downfall." She gives me a sad smile.

"We all have a weakness." I give her shoulder a reassuring squeeze. "Go on, what kind of accident?"

"Prynne went to work sick one day, doped up on decongestants and cough syrup. She didn't even realize she was light-headed, she fell asleep on the job."

My mouth goes dry and I silently will Chastity to speak faster.

"Someone died. A pilot."

Dread seeps into my bloodstream like molten lava. "Were there passengers?"

"No, thank God," she says. "It was a ghost flight for maintenance. Empty except for the pilot and copilot. The copilot survived, but the pilot . . ." She shakes her head slowly.

"How long ago did this happen?"

"Ten years ago, maybe," Chastity says. "There was a

formal inquiry and deposition with the Federal Aviation Board—or whatever it's called—but they never found anything. Prynne quit and took the truth with her, worked odd jobs and took courses on hospitality and event management until she had enough to start Blush. She never looked back."

"Until a rowdy night of margaritas," I mutter, rubbing my chin.

I mean, there are warnings on those medications not to operate heavy machinery while taking that stuff. What made Prynne think she could guide a plane, nay *multiple* planes, to safety while under the influence? The answer pops into my head instantly: She didn't think she could take a day off. For whatever reason, we tend to feel more indispensable than we actually are. And perhaps she went in that day for a pick-me-up after feeling poorly, to borrow joy from the job she loved.

My mind reels through what I've been told. This pivotal part of Prynne's history provides the most tangible motive yet—that someone could want revenge for her boneheaded blunder.

I cycle through who was in attendance at the wedding who could somehow be related to this former version of Prynne. Realization hits me all at once, a truth that rattles my gut and wrenches my heart. It's as if my insides are being sifted through a crusher de-stemmer.

Jack.

He followed in his father's footsteps and became a pilot, after losing his dad in a plane crash as an adolescent. He'd told me as much. And the timing fits; ten years ago, Jack would've been a teenager.

Doubt trickles in. Because Jack seems so even-keeled,

maybe a touch misogynistic, but for the most part all right. Sure, Josie hates his guts, but Nash vouched for him.

But it's too much of a coincidence.

Which goes to show how you can think you know someone and yet not know them at all. And how wrong impressions can be—or how easily manipulated.

At some point, Jack must have learned about Prynne. Possibly dug into the accident himself or recognized her from the deposition. Try as Prynne might to hide her dirty little secret, it would've been public record that she'd been investigated in relation to the crash. How far of a stretch would it be for a grieving young man to seek an explanation for the loss of a parent? To convince himself someone was to blame?

Either way, Jack did it. He knocked Prynne over the head with a rock, planted an obscene amount of evidence, and, to throw the authorities off his track, framed Grace.

Only, how did he pull it off?

Even the most meticulous planner would've struggled to keep the ducks of his masterminded scheme in a row. While Jack fits, there's a fuzziness around the edges I don't understand, like a flavor on my tongue I can't quite place. And it nags at me.

Chastity shifts and I realize I'm still blocking her in, standing so still I might as well be a bottle perched in the surrounding wine racks.

"Do you think that's why Prynne was killed?" Chastity asks with a pitiable sniffle, face blotchy and eyes rimmed with red.

"I think you already know the answer to that."

"Don't tell Emma, please," Chastity says. "She already thinks so little of me."

"Ohmygod, Emma!" I slap a hand against my forehead,

a jolt of fear inciting me to move. I back out of the small space and pivot, breaking into a jog as I make for the door to the tasting room. Expletives pour out of my mouth faster than bubbles from a shaken bottle of cava.

Why didn't I see it sooner? Why didn't I insist someone go after Emma? Why didn't I wear better running shoes?

And then my mind supplies another question, one that's equally upsetting: *What if Jack gets away?* He was on his way to DIA, ready to fly off into the sunset.

I'm going so fast, I slide into the edge of the tasting bar with a yelp. Vino Valentine has mostly emptied since I was in the back with Chastity. Sloan is in the middle of closing tasks—extinguishing candles, cleaning and stacking baskets, and loading the dishwasher—while my mom collects credit cards from the Table of Doom.

"Psst, Mom," I say.

She doesn't register, not until I throw a palate-cleansing cracker at her. It bounces off her hair and onto the floor. But it works. She rubs the back of her head as she turns in my direction.

Hers isn't the only attention I grab. A miffed Josie emerges from the restroom, catching our strange interchange, her too-close-together eyes narrowing.

My mom hustles over and I speak in a hurried whisper. "I have to go. Emma could be in trouble. Stay here, okay?"

"What sort of trouble?"

"Jack . . ." I shake my head, fumbling for my purse beneath the counter. "I'll explain later."

"Let me come with you. It could be dangerous."

"It'll tip him off if we all rush over there, and it'll take too much time. I've already taken too long." How else can I convey this isn't the time for a mother-daughter bickering match? "Call the police for me, make sure they get a mes-sage to Eli to get to the Longview Lodge ASAP."

I watch the argument leave her, watch her set her chin and steady herself. "You can count on me."

"Thanks, Mom," I say, giving her a swift hug. "Love you." I have this thing, maybe because of how suddenly my aunt was taken from this world, but, upon parting, I like to tell the people I love that I love them. Just in case I don't get the chance to do so again.

She gives me a squeeze back and then lets go. "I love you, too."

I turn and run straight into Sloan. "Where are you off to?" she accuses, eyebrows furrowed.

"Just have to pop out for a moment," I answer vaguely, my tone weird and clipped as I inch closer toward the door. Knowing my mom can handle things here, I add, "Hey, why don't you head out early? Make sure you're able to hit the road and get to your snazzy resort in time for some beauty rest. And good luck on your test tomorrow, not that you need it. You're going to crush it."

"Don't jinx me," Sloan says, shaking out her hands.

"You've got this. Call me after." I pat her shoulder, as much in support as for leverage. "Gotta dash."

In the back alley, I hop into Reid's jeep, the combination of urgency and anxiety freezing me in place. I take a deep breath and remember what my dad said: *There's a differ-ence between feeling helpless and being helpless.*

I'm not helpless. And I have somewhere to be.

With steady hands, I start the ignition. I steel myself as I back out, images of Jack flashing through my mind. The twist of his lips takes on a malicious quality, his worldly vibe becomes what I suspect it's been all along: detachment, and his supposed witticisms are exposed as being just plain mean.

The drive passes in a blur. I bypass rush hour by navigating alternate routes. I traverse Pearl Street and take a lesser-known avenue that runs parallel to Boulder Creek, then cut through campus, college students milling about, on their way to dinner on the Hill or night classes.

It's not until I pull into the parking lot of the motel that it dawns on me. I drove here. All the way. Without having a panic attack.

All it took was someone I love to be in a potentially life-threatening situation. Which obviously isn't a reliable way to distract myself behind the wheel, but at least I have one win under my belt.

I don't take so much as a millisecond to celebrate this feat, though. Because Emma's Prius is parked in the space across from me.

I sprint inside the motel, heart pounding louder than my flats against the asphalt.

Chapter
Seventeen

Emma isn't in her room.

In the dingy hallway of this godforsaken motel, I force myself not to succumb to my mounting dread. My limbs are heavy with lactic acid, and adrenaline spikes my system, making me twitchy.

Logic. When in doubt, use logic. Sometimes that's all you have left, and occasionally, it can be enough.

I put myself in Emma's shoes.

She's (finally) erupted at her family and stormed off to seethe in private. But as Carolyn pointed out, she's still Emma. Even in her frenzied state, she agreed to drive Jack back to the hotel. She's kind to her very core, the sort of person who would also schlep him all the way to the airport.

So, I hightail it to Jack's room.

I knock on the door, fidgeting with the heel of my flats. Sure enough, Emma answers. "Parker—wait, what?"

Emotions dance across her face. Surprise, amusement, and then, as if reminding herself she's supposed to be angry, consternation.

I peer around Emma and into the room, where Jack is zipping up his suitcase. He's a study in contradictions. Blond hair swept to the side in an attempt at neatness but for a few strands intentionally mussed at the front. His posture one of duty, yet an eagerness in his swift motions. Carefree visage but with keen eyes that miss nothing.

Time stretches in the seconds our gazes lock. Babies are born, grapes ferment into wine, and Jack understands that I know what he did.

I curse my poor acting chops, my blatant features that arrange themselves into a snapshot of my thoughts.

Jack is a tornado of action. He drops his luggage back on the quilted bed and moves toward Emma, snagging a letter opener from the desk and seizing her from behind. In a moment, he has the blade held to Emma's throat.

"What the—" Emma starts, pulling at Jack's arm, but it holds fast around her neck, his other arm tightening around her waist.

Emma might as well be a gnat for all Jack notices. His attention is laser-focused on me. "Take a step inside, nice and easy, and let the door fall shut."

The last thing I want is to be trapped in a room with a murderer. Especially not here, in this cramped room with its drab furniture and musty scent of mothballs. Cut off from anyone who might be able to hear a shout for help. But Jack presses the blade deeper into Emma's throat, causing her to cry out in pain.

"Now," Jack growls, gesturing with his head.

I do as he says.

My eyes dart between Jack and Emma. I try to communicate different sentiments to each: to Jack, that I'm harmless and following his directions, and to Emma, to remain calm and that we'll be okay. It's no easy task.

The door clicks shut behind me, echoing with the finality of a death sentence.

Don't think that way, I tell myself, *you've been in worse binds than this.*

Silently, I take stock. The closet door to my left is open with a luggage rack folded beneath plastic hangers. The windows on the far side of the room are shut and locked, although the blinds are open to a view of the parking lot. An unplugged coffeepot, stained ceramic mug, and empty water glass sit on the dresser.

As for my person, my car keys and pepper spray are tucked in my purse, both of which would come in handy if my bag weren't dangling uselessly at my side.

"What's going on?" Emma asks, not grasping the severity of the situation—nor the danger she's in. "Hello, it's *me*, Emma. Stop messing around." She gives his arm another useless tug.

Jack dips his chin, his breath blowing wisps of her hair. "I'm sorry you got dragged into this, Emma."

My mouth opens of its own accord and I snap, "She was always in this, though, wasn't she, Jack?"

"In what?" Emma struggles against his hold, wriggling this way and that. "What the hell is happening right now?"

"You owe it to her to explain," I urge.

Because here's the thing: Jack likes Emma. Everyone likes Emma. Which means he won't harm her unless coerced. Not to mention, there must be a small part of him that wants to confess what he did—and why. So he can take Prynne down in reputation, too.

I continue, "It was her wedding day, Emma deserves to

understand. And I know—I know what Prynne did. I'm sorry." Deep down, my heart gives a tiny pang for Jack. Very deep and very tiny, mind you. He did kill someone.

Jack's face scrunches sourly and for a second, I think he might start bawling. Then his baby blues harden into steel. "Prynne killed my dad."

It's such a simple statement, but it sucks oxygen out of the room, like the sparging of wine before the cork seals.

Emma freezes, even though I want to tell her to keep fighting. This is her chance, while Jack is distracted. But she's too stunned and the opportunity vanishes.

"When did you realize it was her?" My hands are still raised in front of me and I shift my feet cautiously, as if testing the bounds of a rope.

"At the groomsmen's tux fitting. I recognized her in an instant, could barely hold in my shock." The ghost of a smile flits across his lips. "I almost called her out then and there, told her who I was and how completely she wrecked my life." He pauses, his smile turning maniacal. "But then I had another idea."

"Murder her. At your friend's wedding."

"Give her a taste of what she deserved."

Ah, justice, that sweet yet taunting ideal that motivates as easily as it derails. How far have I gone—how many investigations encroached on—in the name of it? For the better, mostly, unlike Jack. Yet, it baffles me that the same motivation can be the impetus for vastly different actions.

"It seemed too perfect," Jack says. "I could take my time, orchestrate how to get rid of Prynne and get away scot-free. In fact, I'll be flying over the Atlantic in roughly"—he has the audacity to check his wristwatch—"two hours, never to return."

The blood drains from Emma's face and I fear it's from

the tight hold Jack has on her, but then she bares her teeth and doubles down on her efforts to break free. "How could you?"

"How could I *not*?" Jack chokes out a laugh that makes tears prick at the corners of his eyes. "Prynne acted like she was queen of her own fantasy universe, showed no remorse for anything."

"Like you're showing remorse now?" Seriously, why can I not keep my trap shut? I bite my tongue to dam the deluge.

It doesn't matter; Jack doesn't even hear me, his gaze growing distant. "Do you know the worst part?"

I shake my head and Emma does the briefest movement she's allowed.

"Prynne didn't even recognize me." He pauses, stricken, letting this sink in. "I waited outside her hearing years ago, overheard her explain away her accident that cost someone their life—a family their father. She saw me in the hallway, saw the result of her mistake. And walked right past me without saying a word." He crinkles his nose, readjusting his grip on my cousin. "My scheme solidified while she prattled on about cuff links and the benefits of tails."

"Nash trusted you." While Emma's voice is full of anguish, her eyes are clear and focused intently on me. She mouths something silently and I blink in confusion.

Keep him talking.

I blink again, twice in understanding. I have no idea what Emma has planned, but it's more than I have, which is nada.

I lick my lips. "Your jet lag, the hangover you were nursing?"

"A convenient excuse to be left alone."

It amazes me there are people who can lie as easily as they breathe when I can't even fib to a cat. "Let me get this straight," I say. "You corner Prynne in the service entrance, knock her out with a rock you hid earlier, and plant the evidence."

"In a nutshell," he acquiesces, wobbling his head back and forth.

"The hair, the petal, the cologne, the planted emails?"

"Diversions, and clever ones, if I do say so myself."

"How did you do it all?" I ask. "The emails . . . you weren't even at the bridal shower. How'd you get ahold of Grace's phone that day?"

"Now, what would be the fun of telling you everything?"

I don't have time to wonder at what he isn't saying, about the proverbial space between the nut and the shell and the bits I could be missing. Because Emma makes her move.

She elbows Jack in the gut. Hard. He drops his weapon and Emma kicks it across the room. "That's for Prynne." She lurches forward, twists out of reach, and takes Jack by surprise with a knee to his groin. "That's for my mom." She shoves him back onto the bed, where he slams into his suit-case. "And that's for me." Her voice rises with each state-ment and she huffs in satisfaction.

With one hand on his stomach, Jack props himself up, surveying something over our shoulders. His eyes twinkle maliciously. "Very good, but you missed one thing."

"What?" I ask. I turn slowly, a pit opening in my gut and a tingling sensation radiating outward.

A new voice answers: "Jack didn't do this alone." Josie stands in the open doorway, pocketing a hotel key, a smug expression on her face.

"But you two hate each other," I blurt out stupidly.

My brain can't connect the Josie who was at my winery with the Josie standing before me. She's in the same canary-yellow dress, hair pulled into a side ponytail, and overdone makeup that makes her appear clownish. It's in the way she holds herself, her straightened posture and the sway of her hips.

"It's called acting," Josie says.

"On one side, doll," Jack shoots back. "Let's be honest."

"Would you shut up, Jack?" Josie stomps her foot, nostrils flaring. "If you haven't noticed, I'm saving your ass."

Emma pipes up. "So, you mean to tell me, I've spent the last six months keeping you two separated, only to have you go behind my back?" Her tone veers from disbelief to anger. "Un-freaking-believable."

Remorse washes over Josie's face, exposing her heartbreak and despair, as fresh as ever. She recovers a moment later, her callous mask sliding back into place.

Other details come back to me, more puzzle pieces falling into place. The wedding crasher Kyle Garcia/Earnest Merriwether saying he saw a bridesmaid and groomsman canoodling. My assumption was wrong, as assumptions often are. It wasn't Carolyn and Xavier that Kyle/Earnest saw, it was Jack and Josie.

Josie, whose wedding Prynne helped plan until her fiancé dumped her before their rehearsal dinner, citing that planning a wedding together made him realize how unhappy they'd be married. Gotta admit, seems like the guy—Bob, I think it was—made the right call.

"You blamed Prynne for what happened between you and Bob, didn't you?" I ask.

Josie sashays closer to me, making me press against the wall, throat bobbing. "At first, I liked that Prynne took my side. She insisted I have everything I want for my special day. She made me forget it was supposed to be *our* special day." There's a rawness to her speech, an irrevocable hurt.

"She goaded me—us—into the most expensive venue, caterer, decor. Eventually, the pressure got to Bob."

She invades my space bubble, getting up in my grill, so close I can see pimples shining through a thick layer of foundation. Must be all the chocolate. "Where else was I supposed to place blame?"

"Um, yourself, maybe?" I try.

Josie spits, her saliva landing on the carpet dangerously close to my shoe. "And you." She rounds on Emma, her face contorting. "How dare you ask me to be in your wedding after what I've been through?"

Kudos to Emma, who merely crosses her arms over her chest. "I didn't want you to feel left out," she argues. "And I dunno, I thought it might help you move on."

"Just like how you encouraged me to get back in the dating saddle and set me up with him!" Josie screeches, finger extended toward Jack.

"He's not that bad," Emma starts, and then winces, changing course as she recalls the last few minutes. "Or I didn't know how bad he was. Whatever. You're my oldest friend, I wanted you to be happy."

Tears trickle down Josie's cheeks and she wipes them away with the back of one hand. "Happy? Pfft. There's no such thing as happily ever after. Not for people like us." She gestures between her and Jack.

I find it curious she lumps herself in with Jack, and even more curious that he lets her.

As for Jack, he appears completely at ease on the bed, arms resting behind his head, back propped against his suitcase. His gaze drifts skyward toward the window, and, from the lilt to his mouth, I daresay he's entertained.

If his confession weren't enough, his behavior belies his guilt. Which snaps something else into place.

Josie's heartbreak has grown into a festering wound that warps her sense of reality. Jack knew about her fragile state from their blind date and, later, when he needed an accomplice, took advantage of it.

"Did Jack tell you why he never called you back for a second date?" I ask, stirring the pot. If I can pit Josie against Jack, perhaps she'll see reason. Emma is her childhood friend, after all.

"Like I care," Josie retorts, but from the way she looks at me, she very much does.

Her breakup shook her confidence, planted the seed of self-doubt, giving life to a fear we all wrestle with at some point: that we might end up alone.

"He said you blubbered about your ex through the entire meal." I drive the wedge deeper. "Somewhere in there, you let it slip you knew the woman planning your friend's wedding. Which was why Jack eventually recruited you. He knew he could convince you—that he could use you."

Josie sits with the harshness of that truth. Chest heaving, her eyes flit to Jack.

"The emails. They were you." I can picture Carolyn flashing her phone at me, mocking the sheer number of emojis and, more important, exclamation points Josie dropped in their group Slack.

That's what was nagging me about the emails; I'd seen similar messages from someone in the wedding party.

Josie doesn't even acknowledge me. She seems to be doing some fast thinking, her bottom lip caught in her upper teeth.

"The flower petal, the tulle, the hair." I can imagine how it transpired. After she faked her meltdown and Carolyn told her to pull herself together, Josie snuck away. Her mascara had even still been smudged during the procession, the result of a hurried touch-up after busying herself elsewhere. "And they were your footprints in the service hallway, staged with shoes larger than your feet. You did Jack's dirty work."

No response again. But none is needed.

I turn to Jack. "The rest was you. You're the one who stole Xavier's cologne while he was fumbling around with his tie. You sprayed it in the hallway after the deed was done. You're the one who killed Prynne."

Jack pushes himself to his feet and slow-claps. "You really do have it all figured out, don't you?"

An alarm sounds in my body, shooting through my fingertips like grape tendrils through a trellis. I sidestep, knocking my foot against the wood of the dresser, until I reach Emma. I swing my arm outward in front of her, protectively, effectively sandwiched between two enemies.

Growing up at the gateway to the Rocky Mountains, I'm no stranger to predators. Coyote, bears, and mountain lions were a mainstay we learned to guard ourselves against. Coyotes and bears are, for the most part, harmless, more afraid of us than we are of them. But not mountain lions. They're wily, and harder to manipulate. The most imperative thing is not to break eye contact.

I keep my eyes locked on Jack, the would-be mountain lion of the pair.

"Pity I can't stay to see how this all plays out." He pats his back pocket to check for his wallet and gives a merry wave. "I've got a plane to catch. Good luck with the pigs, Jos, it's been real."

Jack backs up toward the window and I can see his plan laid out clear as chardonnay. The motel is ground level. All he has to do is hop out the window and vamoose. And with his connections around the world, once he's slipped through our fingers, we—Eli—will never catch up with him.

Not on my watch.

Sensing the time is now or never, I reach into my purse for my trusty pepper spray.

If there's any advice I could give to women, it's this: always carry pepper spray. Mine has come in handy more than I care to admit. From making me feel safer walking solo at night to actual dispensing, it's been a lifesaver. And this is a new canister.

I twist the nozzle, careful to aim it away from Emma and me, and lift my arm.

That's when I'm tackled from my other side.

The wind is knocked out of me as I land on the king-sized bed. My back smarts; the mattress may as well be a rock for how firm it is. I take a deep gulp of air and try to get up, but Josie straddles me, locking my wrists in place.

Guess I didn't convince her to come back to the light.

"Take me with you or I'll let her up and help them stop you," Josie shouts at Jack, making a desperate play for her own escape. "I swear to God, I mean it."

Jack's jaw works back and forth as he hisses an exhale. Finally, he snaps, "Fine. But we have to hurry."

"So, hurry," Josie returns.

Grumbling to himself, Jack turns back to the lock on top of the window.

It almost seems like punishment enough for these two to be stuck together in an eternal sparring match. Almost. But Prynne, even though she was far from perfect, deserves more. Emma, for her derailed wedding, deserves more.

And Josie made a fatal mistake: she underestimated me.

She doesn't know about the barrel rolling, case carrying, and harvest punch downs involved in winemaking. Tasks that left me aching and sore the first year but in peak physical condition now.

The TL;DR version: I'm tougher than I look.

My worries from the last few days bubble to the surface—that I'm not strong enough, not independent enough, lacking in some way. And they all fall away.

I wrench both arms to the side, sending Josie toppling off the bed.

The only problem is, my pepper spray goes with her.

I scramble to my feet and assess.

There's no new invaluable tool or miracle solution. In fact, I'm down my go-to defense. At least I'm not entirely without allies.

Emma squats beside Josie and, before her bridesmaid can reorient herself, wraps one arm under her neck, securing her elbow just beneath Josie's chin, and the other around her torso. I haven't a clue what sort of hold this is, but it works. No matter how hard Josie strains, she's good and stuck.

"It's how we restrain large animals at our clinic," Emma explains, slightly out of breath.

Apparently, Emma's tougher than she looks, too.

"Nice," I say, turning back to Jack.

He takes in this turn of events with an impressed nod, seemingly relieved to be rid of his partner in crime and wholly unconcerned. He reapplies himself to the rusted window lock, causing the entire mechanism to pop loose from the frame.

Thank goodness for shoddy fixtures. The Longest Day Lodge strikes again, only this particular shortcoming works in my favor.

While Jack swears and switches to brute force to open the window, his arms and fingers shaking from exertion, something in the parking lot catches my attention. My heart leaps into my throat in a weird combination of hope and horror.

My mom is in the parking lot, loitering near her Nissan Leaf, which is parked adjacent to Reid's jeep.

She studies the outside of the motel, the frantic look of a mother searching for her child plain on her face. She tugs at her tote, which keeps slipping down her arm, her blouse billowing in the wind. Her silhouette is captured by the setting sun, the mountains emblazoned with an orange light while the rest of the land is granted a reprieve from the intense rays, if not the heat.

My mom and I have never been on the same wavelength. It's like, if I'm broadcasting Taylor Swift, she's listening to NPR or *maybe* Fleetwood Mac. Even so, in that moment, I narrow my eyes and send whatever vibes I can into the universe.

Come on, come on, come on.

It's as if everything around me fades into the background. Emma, Josie, and even Jack. I home in on my mom, who pivots slowly and locks her eyes on mine.

Holy Viognier, it worked.

Her lips turn downward, her eyebrows draw closer together, the lines of her forehead forming a V, and her hair practically cackles with electricity. She gets an expression I faintly recognize from missed curfews and bombed tests. Only, the subject of her displeasure is Jack instead of me or, as was more often the case, Liam.

She riffles through her bag while marching purposefully toward us, her strides surprisingly fast and long.

"Oh no," I mumble.

"What are you yammering about now?" Jack asks.

"Nothing." *And everything.*

We've all heard the saying *Too many cooks in the kitchen*,

but what about *Too many sleuths in an investigation*? If my mom joins the fray, that's one more person whose safety I have to account for. There's nothing for it, though, no feasible way for me to warn her off. Not if I want to stop Jack, who's finally managed to nudge the window open.

I make a decision. I run forward to slam the window shut, or maybe just throw myself at Jack. Anything to give the police and Eli more time to get here. To put an end to this without anyone I love getting hurt.

Jack sees me coming in the reflection and throws me backward with the momentum of his shoulder. I connect with the corner of a table and rub at my smarting side.

And that's it. He's going to escape. He opens the window the rest of the way and punches through the screen.

I push myself off the table and make for him again, but he kicks out at me in warning before throwing one leg over the sill.

That's when my mom appears on the other side of the window.

"Not my daughter, you—you—microbial cell of a human." Only my mom could whip out such a sciency insult at a moment like this. She sprays Jack full on in the face with pepper spray.

Jack doubles over, tumbling outside and onto the cracked and crumbling cement with a grunt.

My mom towers over him, an indomitable figure in a leopard-print tunic who makes it clear she is not to be messed with. Her own canister of pepper spray pointed directly at his person, her eyes reddening from proximity to the tear-inducing chemicals.

I should add, the reason I always carry pepper spray is because my mom taught me to.

Patrol cars round the bend and tear into the parking lot, sirens blaring and lights flashing.

Relief crashes through me as adrenaline dissipates. I slouch against the wall, suddenly unsteady. "Thanks, Mom," I say, at a loss for words.

"Of course, Parker," my mom answers, as if it were the only course of action.

I never imagined my mother would be my knight in shining armor. Gazing at her now, in all her off-kilter, low-key glory, I can honestly say, I have no idea why not.

Chapter
Eighteen

"Took you long enough" I grumble to Eli.

Jack and Josie are officially in custody. Jack didn't have any fight—or flight—left in him when the authorities took over for my mom. And Josie had even less left, apparently trying to garner pity by dissolving into tears, which, spoiler alert, didn't work.

I took no small amount of pleasure watching them get loaded into the back of the same patrol car, as unhappy about the prospect of riding together as being apprehended. Their bickering could be heard until the driving officer twisted in his seat and barked at them to shut it. They really do deserve each other.

Now we're in the lobby of the Longest Day Lodge, savoring the air-conditioning, weak as it is.

Having already finished with me, paramedics check over Emma, with my mother being next in line.

Besides a few minor bumps and bruises, I should live to sniff, swirl, and sip another day.

Emma, on the other hand, seems lost in her own world, physically okay, but mentally distraught. I can't imagine learning a friend was capable of aiding and abetting a murderer. Because while Josie wasn't the one who ultimately took Prynne's life, she did plenty to make it possible—and make sure Jack would get away with it. If it hadn't been for yours truly.

Emma has Nash, though, who will need support of his own. But what is family if not the people you lean on in times of strife?

"Parker," Eli starts, his warm brown eyes meeting mine. "I owe you an apology. For not taking your concerns seriously."

Eli is dapper in a navy suit with pristine collared shirt underneath. As for me, well, I'm worse for the wear, my skirt and blouse a stretched-out, rumpled mess, but I'm still standing, and that's what counts.

We've stationed ourselves near the reception desk, a smattering of rubbernecking guests lingering in the periphery. I want to tell them they're better off not knowing what happened here. Better off not knowing what nightmares have occurred under this roof.

If this leaks to the news, renovation or not, the Longview Lodge will be thrust into the limelight. But maybe they could recover yet; just look at what *The Shining* did for The Stanley Hotel in Estes Park.

"Haven't you learned by now that I'm always right?" I feign a dramatic eye roll.

Eli snorts. It's good to see him smile, to be on the same side again. "I find that highly suspect, but in this instance, you were right." He scratches the back of his head in a sheepish way, his perfectly slicked dark hair going askew. "I should've realized this case was a mess from the start."

"Eh, you had to do what you thought was right. Even if it led you to an arthritic middle school teacher who would sooner remarry my uncle than harm a living creature. I mean, really, how could you have suspected Grace?"

He grimaces, but then shrugs. "We had to do our due diligence. We released her when we realized she didn't fit the profile."

I can hardly bite back my grin; Eli is almost as fun to rib as Liam. "Hours later."

"Okay, enough. Point taken," he says. "I owe you one."

"You owe my mother one, and she's not likely to forget it." I cast a glance at her across the lobby. "In fact, I think you've got a potential recruit on your hands." She preens as an officer approaches to get her statement, ignoring the paramedic measuring her vitals.

"Don't tell me there's two of you," Eli says, aghast.

There's a tinge of pride in my voice as I respond, "Yeah. And prepare yourself, she's even more stubborn than I am."

"I find that hard to believe."

"You've been warned," I say with a click of my tongue.

Through the sluggish sliding glass doors that comprise the main entrance, I watch the rest of my family and the remainder of the wedding party disembark from two vehicles. My dad leads the way, followed by my uncle and Chastity, Grace and Carolyn, and Nash and Xavier. Honestly, I'm surprised it took them this long to get here, but now that they are, they're eager for a reunion.

Chaos will descend momentarily.

I shift my attention back to Eli. "See you at climbing Thursday?"

"You bet," Eli says. "Take care of yourself, Parker."

"You, too," I respond, shooing him away with my hands as my family closes in. "Now run! Run while you can!"

He chortles as he hurriedly jogs away, heeding my advice.

The scene that follows is disgustingly full of adoration. If Carolyn thought we resembled a Hallmark movie before, we're basically a Disney Channel special now. You'd never know we were at one another's throats an hour ago. I suppose that's how it goes with family. You drive one another bonkers and in return you get steadfast support. Seems like a pretty good deal, at least now that the real culprits have been extracted from the mix.

After Eli and his band of officers vamoose, hugs abound, more prevalent than obscure produce references at a wine tasting. And if there's a nucleus, it's Emma.

She wraps her arms around everyone in turn, her mom, dad, sister, my parents, Nash, Xavier, and even Chastity. It doesn't escape my notice that there's still reservation in Emma's movements, a question in her eyes. She's not the only one; Chastity is subdued, clearly wrestling with her own demons and torturous what-ifs.

What if she'd never pushed Emma to hire her friend to plan her wedding? What if she'd spoken up sooner about Prynne's history? Questions that would haunt her until she accepts that sometimes fate has a will of its own.

After what they deem a sufficient reunion, Carolyn and Xavier retire to a corner in conversation. While they're not canoodling, per se, it wasn't completely outlandish for me to think there's *something* going on there. I just don't know what.

I watch them with narrowed eyes, wishing I could read

lips. Xavier shifts awkwardly, which is basically his MO, as Carolyn extends a hand for him to shake.

I don't have time to puzzle over their mystery agreement. Because without preamble, Nash lifts Emma off the floor and twirls her around in a sweeping embrace. Her laughter is like the clinking of glasses, a joyous sound of pure delight that cuts through the remaining tension. Her smile mirrors that of her fiancé, as if they exist in their own private bubble.

It makes me long for Reid. My heart clenches and my fingers ache to run through his hair, dig into the soft, worn cotton of his shirt. What I wouldn't give to breathe in his minty, herbaceous scent, to rest my head in the crook of his shoulder, the nook I've come to think of as my own.

I check my phone for texts from Reid. There aren't any, although I hardly expected there to be with the way our conversation ended last night. The ball is decidedly in my court.

I type out an olive branch of a message. *Turns out it was Jack, in the service hallway, with a rock.*

Three dots appear followed closely by Reid's response. *That's some game of Clue, Parks.*

Me: *Josie was in on it, too.*

Reid: *Guess they didn't hate each other as much as you thought.*

Me: *Oh, they absolutely did. They just found common ground.* There's no sign of further communication on his end, no ellipses or magnifying glass that signals he's searching for just the right GIF. So, I add, *Speaking of common ground, I miss you.*

Reid replies immediately: *I miss you, too. We didn't get to finish our conversation.*

I chew on the inside of my cheek until a hint of copper registers on my tongue. The conversation where I admitted to doubting myself—us. Where I admitted I was thinking about the future, which doesn't necessarily entail a veil and cummerbund, but has the potential to.

I remember the surge of confidence I felt when I took on Josie. How my worries evaporated when faced with something bigger. It's not that they disappeared entirely, more like that negative voice in my mind quieted. And has remained quiet.

How could it not? Look at what I've accomplished in the last few days. And Reid has never once made me feel alone.

We'll finish it. I start and stop typing as I try to sum up my feelings, imagining my own dots appearing and disappearing on his screen. *Together. Just as we'll continue.*

Emma and Nash waltz up to my side, Nash holding my cousin's hand so tight, I wonder if he'll ever let go.

I shoot one last text to Reid. *Only, not now. Family stuff <3* Then I tuck my phone in my pocket and focus on the happy couple.

"Thanks for everything, Parker," Emma says.

"Hey, thank *you*," I amend. "If you hadn't been there to handle Josie . . ." I trail off with a *tut*, unable to vocalize the possibilities.

"If I hadn't been so absorbed in my wedding, I would've realized she was still hung up from hers. Then I got mad and left you all and was essentially helping Jack escape. He would've, too, if you hadn't come after me." She shivers as if chilled, despite it being roughly four thousand degrees inside this stuffy lobby.

Nash jumps into our self-blame game. "We all missed something." He fiddles with a hemp bracelet around the wrist of the hand attached to Emma. "If I hadn't been such a dismal judge of character, none of this would have happened."

"At least we got them in the end," I say. "I'm just sorry you guys didn't get to have your wedding."

Emma and Nash exchange a meaningful glance before my cousin asks, "Hey, what are some good hiking trails around here?"

"In Boulder?"

"Yeah," Nash draws out the word.

"There's Chautauqua, hiking to the first and second Flatiron is fun with great views." I sift through my vault of Boulder intel, continuing to rattle off, "Then there's Sanitas, which is a personal favorite of mine, that's what my white blend is named after. Bear Peak is solid, too, although that one's a little tougher and a farther drive to the trailhead." I can practically smell the refreshing pine and dirt of the trails, feel the whoosh of fresh air enter my lungs. "Let me know when you guys are going and I'd be happy to play guide."

"Uh, that's okay, we've got it," Emma says hurriedly. "We'd better, you know, circulate."

She tugs on Nash's arm and together they make their way to where Xavier and Carolyn are still chatting. Xavier relaxes at the appearance of his business partner, more at ease with Nash than the rest of the world, and tells him something which, oddly, inspires Nash to shake Carolyn's hand and Emma to beam at her older sister. *Interesting* . . .

I'm ready to join them and get to the bottom of this new development when my mom materializes at my side. "Well, Nancy Drew, you did it." Her eyes are red and watery from the pepper spray, as I'm sure mine are.

"All thanks to you, Miss Marple." I give her shoulder a nudge. "Your chemistry know-how certainly came in handy."

"Not as handy as your people skills," she says. "How'd you get Chastity to talk?"

"I reminded her of what was at stake," I start. Truth is, when you work behind a bar, you get to know what makes people tick, how to get them to open up. "I think she wanted to tell someone. Prynne's secret was eating away at her almost as much as her friend's death."

"I'll remember that for next time."

At my sharp look she adds, "What do you think about a mother-daughter private eye agency? We could call it Valentine Vindication." She waves her hand in an arc to illustrate and I swear I can't tell if she's joking.

"Lest we forget, I already have a business, which reminds me . . ." I make a show of glancing around, panic rising. "Who exactly is at my store?"

My dad strolls up and passes me my shop keychain with a tiny wine bottle attached. "After you left, your mom was in such a state, I urged her to go after you. I locked up Vino Valentine and followed with the circus."

I give him a one-armed hug. "Thanks, Dad."

"It was the only way I was going to get any peace."

"You sure about that?" I ask. Because something tells me neither of us have heard the last about my mom's new flair for crime solving.

Chapter
Nineteen

The next day, I receive a phone call from the St Julien event planner, who books me—or rather, my wine—for not only one event in the next month, but two. Which will put Vino Valentine firmly back in the green zone, and just in time to start thinking about harvest.

In between stammering thank-yous, jotting down pertinent details, and doing a happy dance, my phone buzzes with a text from Emma.

Emma: *Last minute get together at Chautauqua tonight, I'd love it if you could be there.*

Me: *Count me in. Can I bring anything?*

Just yourself, she responds. Then, not even a second later, she adds, *And wine!*

Which is how I find myself, after closing shop, hauling a cooler stocked with bottles of wine from Reid's jeep. Sloan has the other handle, having tagged along as a way to channel her excess energy after her Master Sommelier exam. Which she recently returned from—and passed with flying colors.

"Can you believe they included a Chablis?" She rehashes her sweet success, still in pressed slacks and a formal blouse with her hair neatly tied back, the only nod to her funky style being colorful trainers, which, on principle, she refused to part with. "What a softball."

"It's only a softball because of your impressive education and extensive research. You would've been fine if they'd included something as far-fetched as a Falillry."

She freezes and my arm is tugged backward, the cooler acting like a rubber band between us.

"What varietal is that?" Sloan asks.

"A figment of my imagination." I grin at her cheekily. "Too soon?"

She exhales a deep breath. "Don't scare me like that."

"Come on, you already passed, you can relax," I laud, although I know she'll do no such thing. Sloan coasts as much as I do, which is to say, not at all. "Let's get you a glass of wine and cheers to your success." I aim us toward a space between two picnic tables, but Sloan uncharacter-istically trails behind, her motions slow and uncertain as her grip falters.

"Listen, Parker, I—" She swallows. "Since I passed my test, I have something I want to talk with you about."

"Ah." Suddenly, it dawns on me what she's going to say. I set my end of the cooler on the ground and give her my full attention, hands on my hips. "Can't say I'm surprised."

Sloan's eyes dart to mine, searching for disappointment or anger, seemingly relieved by what she sees instead: sup-port. "You're not?"

"I knew this was temporary." I muster a weak smile. I'm

going to miss Sloan, her company and crazy-efficient work ethic. "So, what's next?"

Sloan plays with the end of her ponytail. "I got an offer out in California, at a French restaurant in Yountville."

I raise my eyebrows, impressed. "Napa will be lucky to have you."

"I'll get you a table if you come visit, and treat you to a glass of the best wine, at least outside of Colorado."

"I'm gonna hold you to that." With multiple people I care for out west, looks like a trip is in my future.

We continue picking our way across the park and to the open tables beneath a considerable oak tree. We set our libations and paper cups against the trunk—enough for twenty, even though at the moment there are just the two of us.

An expansive field of neatly trimmed grass sprawls out across the hillside, bordered by more leafy trees, a dining hall, and auditorium. Rising above us are the Flatirons, steadfast and majestic. Parked along the dirt parking lot are an assortment of food trucks. They gather here weekly for what's been dubbed Hungry Hungry Hump Day, filling the thin mountain air with scents of earthy spices, grilled delicacies, spun sugar, and waffle cones.

A light breeze eases the brunt of the heat, along with providing entertainment. A kite in the shape of an octopus flies high in the eggshell-blue sky, a parent and young child holding the attached string, and an ultimate Frisbee game is in full swing, the disc coasting on gusts.

All told, it's one of those picturesque nights that make me love my little sliver of the world.

The lazy gait of my brother and Sage's bobbing strawberry-blond head catch my attention. There's a third figure with them, shorter and with something slung over his back. I wave at them and they amble over. It's only as they get closer I recognize the third wheel: Jimmy Mickelson.

"What's this about?" Liam asks when he's close enough.

I shrug from my perch on a bench. "Emma just said a gathering, not much more."

"Sounds like you got the same invite we did." He nods at Jimmy. "Figured since it was a party and all, I'd invite a friend."

Jimmy unshoulders his guitar case and greets me with a swift kiss on either cheek, doing the same with Sloan. My assistant swoons, more than a little awestruck.

Jimmy absorbs his surroundings with smooth nonchalance. "No party is complete without music," Jimmy says, patting his instrument.

Soon, the rest of the family and guests I recognize from the wedding join us (no crasher, I'm relieved to report). Everyone is equally perplexed, both by the summons and the rock star in their midst. That is, until Emma and Nash make their grand entrance, not from the bus stop or parking lot, but from the trailhead.

They exude a contagious joy, flushed from hiking—and, it seems, from something else.

"We're married," Emma squees, flashing her ring finger, adorned with a silver band that has a delicate diamond setting that suits her to a T.

"We exchanged vows beneath the arch between the first and second Flatiron," Nash elaborates, tucking Emma close to his side, his own left hand sporting a handsome chrome ring.

You see, there's this law in Colorado that says you can marry yourselves. Be the officiant, the judge, the everything. It seems Emma and Nash finally took the reins of their nuptials and have done just that, with a spectacular view of Boulder and the foothills rolling out beneath them, the world literally at their feet.

Now we all get the pleasure of celebrating with them. And I mean ALL of us. Even Harriet came down from Estes, with Clyde trotting at her heels in an adorable kitty harness.

I give my former charge a pat on the head. "You seem happier here than in that stuffy ballroom, buddy."

"That makes two of us," Emma says, holding the leashes of her beloved Labradors, Darcy and Apollo, who dutifully flank her, tails wagging and tongues lolling.

I give my cousin a tight squeeze. "Congratulations!" And to Nash a clap on the shoulder. "Welcome to the family. So happy for you both."

"Thanks!" Emma bounces on the balls of her feet. "We finally decided what mattered most was, you know, getting married, and through all this thought, why wait? And Apollo and Darcy got to be there with us." She scratches the ears of the dog with the more block-shaped head, whom I know to be Darcy.

"Makes sense to me." And it did. This feels right, more right than any of their prior plans.

She and Nash flutter between loved ones, eventually leading the way to the food trucks, where they come away with vegetarian street-style tacos that look too good to pass up. And I was right. With grilled chipotle sweet potatoes, spicy salsas, thinly sliced radish, and an avocado-cilantro vinaigrette, all wrapped in a warm corn tortilla, they're the pinnacle of perfection.

While I momentarily mourned the lack of cake, which should be against wedding law, there is gelato. An entire truck full of flavors. Berries, because 'tis the season, but also classics like stracciatella, pistachio, and dark chocolate rich as sin. I end up going basic, vanilla flecked with vanilla beans, that I top with a splash of my Pikes Peak Port-Style. The creaminess of the gelato paired with the silky port and its flavors of blackberry and honey is so satisfying, soon I forget all about cake.

"Now that is a brilliant idea," Carolyn says, approaching me with her own cup of gelato—raspberry, judging by the vivid red. "Can I get in on that?"

"What's family for?" I pour a splash of port over her ice cream. "Hey, what's going on with you and Xavier and Nash?"

"Didn't you hear? I'm their newest recruit," Carolyn says. "I'm joining their company as a project manager."

"Wow, that's . . ." I trail off, stupefied.

"I know, no one saw it coming," Carolyn says, pushing her sunglasses up on her head. "I've been wanting to make a career change for a while and this seemed like a good opportunity. I had to convince Xav, though. They're still a start-up and don't let just anyone on their payroll."

That explains all the side conversations and her trying to win him over. "Congratulations."

"Cheers." Carolyn clinks her bowl with mine and digs into her gelato.

The sun slowly dips beneath the mountain peaks, casting a hazy blue and orange filter over the evening. Jimmy proffers his guitar and serenades us with acoustic versions of his hit songs, a crowd gathering around us to listen. I can already tell this get-together will be legend, one of those shindigs our family will be talking about for decades to come.

Liam and Sage plop down in the grass beside me.

"I see that look on your face, you know," my brother says.

"What look?"

"That wistful one that says you're deep in your head."

"Excuse you," I retort. "I'm thoroughly enjoying the moment." I pluck at a dandelion that's gone to seed and twirl it between my fingers.

Truth be told, I was thinking about Reid. How I wish he could be here to see this, but also how it's strangely okay that he isn't. I don't mind being alone, don't even mind the prying questions from Harriet anymore. Going to events solo means I get to decide when I want to go back for seconds or jump into an impromptu soccer game with my best friend or camp out and stargaze.

Besides, this will give me a helluva story to relay later, and Reid will tell me about his night and we'll connect in our own way. Because we love and care about each other and in the end, that's all that matters.

I make a wish and blow the dandelion seeds, watching them catch flight on the wind and float away.

Sage nudges me with the toe of her sandal, her gaze caught on something behind me. "Did you make a wish?"

"Of course."

She crinkles her nose at me. "Good, cuz I think it's about to come true." She tugs Liam to his feet by his elbow. "Come on, I need more gelato, stat."

I watch them walk away together, arms wrapped around each other, a happiness settling over my shoulders like a warm blanket. That's when I hear footsteps behind me.

I turn to find Reid. Here. In the flesh.

All six feet, some inches of him, tanned and lean. Sandy hair with caramel undertones, green eyes that flash with impulsivity, that bemused lilt in his smile that resembles a mischievous smirk, and the dimples. God, how I missed those dimples. And everything attached to them.

I'm so stunned by his appearance, I sit, frozen, and drink him in, my mouth hanging open in the epitome of eloquence.

"How—what are you doing here?" I finally bring myself to ask.

Reid offers me his hand. I take it, the warm calluses as familiar to me as my own fingertips.

"Let's go for a walk," he says.

Reid leads me to the trailhead and, without saying a word, we steadily start climbing. The full moon casts a pale glow on the trail, dusting the grassy field in silver. Gravel crunches beneath our shoes and my calves whimper at the steepness. We don't go far, though, settling on a bench that over-looks the park, the lights of Boulder twinkling in the background.

I nestle into the nook, the curve of Reid's shoulder that's just the right size for me. His cotton T-shirt is soft and smells of his laundry detergent and mint, even if there are faint foreign scents beneath—hotel soap and the lining of his suitcase.

"How is it that you're here?" I prompt.

"I caught an earlier flight," he says with a shrug. He drapes his arm around me and rubs tiny circles into my up-per arm. The entirety of his focus is directed at me. "It's not that far."

"A little over two hours," I say. "But your investors, your new restaurant."

"It'll still happen. As long as you're okay with it."

"You can't put that on me," I say, holding a palm to my chest. "It has to be your decision."

Reid musses the back of his hair. "The thing is, I've made

enough decisions on my own. I don't want anything that might drive a wedge between us, and from what I sensed, this might."

"Look at you, waxing about commitment." My eyebrows rise into my bangs as I blink in wonder.

When I first met Reid, he was a perpetual bachelor, unaccustomed to dates that lasted into the next day, let alone week. I remember my hesitancy when we embarked on a relationship, how I put up extra guards around my heart, not knowing how far sheer chemistry could take us. But at some point the tables turned and Reid became the steady one, the one with his eyes set on our future.

"When you find your person—your pairing, as you call it—you do whatever you can to hang on to them." His thumb stops rubbing circles and he shifts to face me, his knee grazing mine. "The restaurant in California would be great, a fun professional challenge, and for what it's worth, I don't think it will only work for right now." He implores me with his eyes, and it's only now that I notice the bags underneath, the worry in them. "We can make this work for whatever our future holds. Whatever adventure life throws at us."

I grab his hands. It's my turn to massage, to soothe, and let him know how much I care. "I think you might be right."

"What?" Reid asks, sitting up in surprise.

I rephrase more confidently. "You are right."

"But what about your freak-out on the phone?"

"I'm sorry about that," I say with a grimace. "I was dealing with stuff the wedding kicked up, and I can't guarantee it won't happen again. In fact, there will inevitably be more freak-outs. But with or without those, all I want is you."

His entire body heaves in relief. "Are you sure? It's a lot of travel."

"I love travel!" I declare, wondering if I might become

the type of person to talk in exclamation points. "That means more delicious cuisine in my freezer."

He laughs, shaking his head. "I swear, you're only with me for my food."

"Obviously," I say, pressing a kiss on top of his hand so he knows I'm kidding. "Next time, there'd better be truffles."

"You can count on it."

"Besides, you've kind of inspired me." I wriggle in my seat, nervous to share my shiny new pipe dream for Vino Valentine. "I've been toying with the idea of opening a second tasting room, maybe downtown Denver, near Union Station."

"I can see that," Reid says thoughtfully. "It would suit you. And Vino Valentine."

"Thanks," I say softly, buoyed by his support.

"And I can help you navigate the land of leases, I've had a crash course."

"Did you get the place? Secure the funds?"

"The place is mine, if I want it. All I need to do is sign on a few dotted lines." He gives a mystified snort. "My friend even agreed to come work with me, which means weekend getaways will be way easier."

"I know just the place," I say, thinking of Sloan. "Take the property. Sign the forms. Let's do this."

"In a minute." Reid's gaze falls to the ground, at how our feet have somehow gravitated toward each other and tangled in a comfortable mess. "There's something else."

"What?"

"Well, it's about all those frozen meals. See, two fridges and freezers are an awful lot to keep stocked. Not to mention, poor William will get whiplash moving back and forth."

My breath catches in my throat and my heart hammers in a hopeful rhythm. "Oh?"

"Maybe when I'm here, your place could be mine, too?" There's an uncertainty, a hesitancy I've come to learn means Reid is putting himself on the line—his heart on the line.

I don't let him hang there alone for long.

"I'd love that."

"Are you sure?" he asks. "I don't want you to feel pressured. This is something I've been thinking about for a while."

The way he gazes at me is all the reassurance I need. The thrum of my pulse and butterflies in my stomach sing their agreement.

"I'm sure," I say. "No need to put William through that. And Zin will be thrilled."

"More food for her to sneak."

"She and I both," I say.

With Reid by my side, the stars twinkling overhead, and the city sparkling in the distance, I don't think life can get any sweeter. Then the sound of Jimmy Mickelson's soulful lyrics and melodic guitar harmony reach us, complementing the steady chirping of crickets, proving me wrong, once again.

Reid tilts my chin up and brings his lips to mine. They're soft, yet sure and solid. The spark that's always been there courses between us as bright as ever. We take a minute, relishing in the sheer pleasure of our reunion, our mouths nipping and grazing while our hands make their way into each other's hair. I nuzzle my cheek against the divine scruff along his chin, holding him close.

"Hey, we should get back down there," Reid says with a wave at the park.

"That's right, the tacos are to die for. Seriously, they'll pass the Reid Test for sure." Flavor genius that Reid is, it's tough to earn his respect when it comes to food.

"That, but also, what's a guy gotta do to get an introduction to your family?"

And that dripping sound you hear? That would be me, melting into a puddle of mushy goo.

"Oh, you think you're ready?" I answer, my voice rough with emotion. "Harriet's been on me all weekend about my mysterious beau. Pretty sure she thinks I made you up."

"Let's go prove her wrong then, shall we?" Reid throws me a rogue wink and we make our way back down the mountain to the family and friends waiting below.

Chapter Twenty

Two months later

I swipe my finger along the countertop, coming away with a layer of dust. I shake it off and continue pacing around the space.

It's not much to look at. Yet. But with a few tasteful changes, it could be.

Add classy storefront signage with the brick siding and a few oak-barrel tables along windows that overlook the fountain outside Union Station, and a major revamp of the bar with a good scrubbing and floating shelves for stemware. Plus a few carefully chosen photographs (begged from Liam) on the walls, strands of twinkle lights around the perimeter, pillar candles galore, and this will make a fine new tasting room for Vino Valentine.

It's in lower downtown Denver, across the street from Emma and Nash's apartment, whom I have to thank for knowing about this venue.

Not only does it boast a dynamite location, being near enough to the train station and business district to attract the happy hour and commuter crowds, it's also LEED certified. Which got my juices flowing for a new sustainable wine to add to my menu. But I'm getting ahead of myself.

"So?" I ask, one eyebrow cocked as I spin my tablet around in a slow circle.

"It's perfect," Reid answers on the other end of our Face-Time session. He's hard at work in San Francisco, overseeing construction and meeting local farmers to feature on his menu, both of us on our way to becoming restaurant and vintner moguls.

"'Perfect' is a bit of a stretch," I concede. "But it has potential."

"What I mean is, it's perfect for you." I can hear the smirk playing on his lips before turning the screen around to face me. "I can see how amazing it's going to be." His green eyes twinkle and his hands are clasped, propping up his strong jaw.

"That means a lot coming from you."

Seriously, as strange as it is for this independent gal to admit, Reid's opinion matters to me. Maybe more so than my mom's and Sage's, who did an initial walk-through with me. Of course, they were both impressed and gushed their approval. Even my mom, who, not that long ago, was adamantly opposed to my vocation. Not that she has any room to talk with all the true crime podcasts she's bingeing, and I've seen the cold case reports she intentionally leaves open on her laptop when I'm over for dinner. To which, I continue to feign ignorance.

"I could say the same, Parks. How're things at home?"

Reid moved in the week after our heart-to-heart, at least with what belongings wouldn't be making their way to California. To be honest, it doesn't feel much different than it did before, although my—our—apartment is fit to bursting when we're all lounging in it. Two cats take up more space than I thought possible, especially when they're both in accordion mode, spread across the floor like the tripping hazards I secretly think they're trying to be.

"Same as ever. My dad is ready to watch Zin and William. I've warned all three of them, repeatedly, on the dangers of overindulging on kitty treats."

"How'd that go over?" Reid asks, bemused.

"About as good as you can imagine. I saw the new jumbo bag of Greenies my dad tried to hide in his jacket pocket." I shake my head, picturing the fun they'll have while I'm gone. "Speaking of: tomorrow."

Reid lowers his voice, giving it a gravelly undertone that sends shivers up my spine. "Tomorrow."

"I'll see you at the airport?"

"I'll be outside baggage claim holding up one of those embarrassing signs." He stretches his arms out, a goofy grin in place.

"What will it say?"

"Truffles, Esq., of course. Which I will have on my person." He procures a plate from offscreen, multicolored spheres of perfection, from cream to pink to espresso, topped with nuts, caramel, and cocoa powder. I can practically smell the chocolate through our connection.

Honestly, this guy knows the way to my heart. "Can't wait. For all of it. To see you and how things are coming along at Sporks"—the somewhat cheeky name for Reid's second restaurant—"and Sloan is adamant we go for dinner."

"I've got a driver lined up for us." He links his hands behind his head and leans back in his chair. "This will be a weekend to remember."

"Until tomorrow. Love you."

"Love you, too."

The unexpected crops up in winemaking as well as life. Overzealous yeast, must that dries up, not to mention the subjectivity of flavor. But sometimes that's when I appreciate being a vintner the most. In thinking of the last few weeks—the chaos and upheaval—I wonder if it's because of the unexpected bits rather than in spite of them that I believe happily ever afters really do exist.

Recipes and Wine Pairings

Roasted Red Pepper, Goat Cheese, and Balsamic Bruschetta

(Serves 4 to 6)

1 cup jarred roasted red peppers, medium-diced

1 tablespoon capers

2 teaspoons balsamic vinegar

1 teaspoon olive oil (plus extra for drizzling)

¼ cup fresh basil, chopped

Salt and pepper (to taste)

Good rustic bread, sliced ½ inch thick

1 garlic clove, peeled

1 4-ounce package of goat cheese

Preheat oven to 425 degrees F.

Mix roasted red peppers, capers, balsamic vinegar, olive oil, basil, and salt and pepper in a bowl and set aside.

Place bread on a sheet pan and drizzle with olive oil. Bake for 10 minutes, turning halfway, until golden brown and perfectly toasted. While bread is still hot, rub one side with whole garlic clove.

To assemble, add a generous helping of goat cheese to each slice of bread and top with a spoonful of pepper mixture.

Suggested wine pairing: a medium-bodied Chianti with hints of dried fruit, smoke, and herbs.

Grilled Chipotle Sweet Potato Tacos

(Serves 4)

3 sweet potatoes, peeled and sliced into 2-inch wedges
5 canned chipotle peppers in adobo
2 garlic cloves, peeled
1 tablespoon canola oil
Blue-corn tortillas
1 avocado, sliced
5 radishes, thinly sliced
¼ cup cilantro leaves
1 lime, sliced into wedges

Boil sweet potato wedges in pot of water for 12 to 15 minutes or until just fork-tender. Drain and set aside to dry and cool.

In food processor, add chipotle peppers, garlic, and canola oil and blend until smooth.

Preheat grill to medium heat.

Once cool enough to handle, brush both sides of sweet potato wedges with chipotle-garlic mixture. Grill 2 to 3 minutes per side.

Warm tortillas on dry skillet over medium heat for about 30 seconds per side.

To assemble, add desired amount of sweet potatoes, avocado, radishes, and cilantro leaves to a tortilla. Top with a squeeze of fresh lime juice from one of the wedges, and enjoy!

Suggested wine pairing: a crisp Verdejo with flavors of lime, grapefruit, and fennel.

Blackberry, Port, and Gelato Sundae

(Serves 4)

1 6-ounce package of fresh blackberries, sliced in half
1 teaspoon sugar
Pint of favorite vanilla gelato
4 shots of port*

In bowl, toss blackberries and sugar to macerate for 30 minutes.

To serve, add scoop of gelato to bowl and top with spoonful of blackberries and one shot of port.

I recommend a tawny port with undertones of berries, licorice, and honey.

Acknowledgments

When my editor first floated the premise of a wedding for Parker's next adventure, I worried I wouldn't be able to do it justice. My husband and I got married in a courthouse and had a party the next day with friends and family to celebrate—not exactly traditional. In fact, we planned our honeymoon *first*, not even knowing that was what it would become. But after ruminating, I realized maybe this could work. Maybe I did have something to say.

I've attended formal affairs that were the whole nine yards, intimate ceremonies where the bride and groom married themselves (an actual law in Colorado), and everything in between. I think what matters most is the love between the couple, the family they're merging and creating together, and that they do what's right for them.

Thank you to my brilliant editor, Miranda Hill, for that initial brainstorming session, where we bounced ideas off of each other—giving life to an adorably mischievous feline ring bearer—and for all your invaluable insights thereafter.

I couldn't have asked for a better home for my series than Berkley. Thank you to my entire team—Mary Baker, Elisha Katz, Randie Lipkin, and Liz Gluck.

Thank you to my agent, Pamela Harty, for your wisdom and support. I'm so grateful to have you and The Knight Agency on my side.

Massive shout-outs to Samantha Dion Baker for another gorgeous cover and Brooke Hoover for giving voice to Parker in the audiobooks.

This book is rightly dedicated to my family, which stretches across the country and even overseas to the small country of Slovenia. Thanks to each and every one of you for making me the person I am today.

Thank you to my parents, who have always encouraged me to follow my dreams and remain a constant source of inspiration.

Thank you to my husband, John, whom I met in much the same way that Emma met Nash. Who knew a brief stairwell encounter would alter the course of our lives in such an awesome way? Thank you to my daughter, Sophie, who continues to amaze me as she grows into an incredibly kind, silly, and curious human. I love you both more than you know.

And last but certainly not least, thank you, readers. Without you, this book would never have come to fruition. Cheers!